TIK-TOK

CANDACE ROBINSON & AMBER R. DUELL

Midnight Tide
PUBLISHING

For Lauren

CHAPTER ONE

TIK-TOK

TWENTY-THREE YEARS AGO

$S$and was a pain in the ass.

Literally.

That was what Tik-Tok got for letting the sea witch, Celyna, ride him, buck-naked, on the beach all afternoon. Decades upon decades of yearly trysts and still, he hadn't learned his lesson. Against a tree or in her glass house were the only reasonable options on the island of Isa Poso. There wasn't anything *but* sand here—save for trees, sea life, and an occasional patch of salt grass. It didn't matter if they kept their clothes mostly on because the gritty particles snuck into every crevice.

Celyna was worth the irritating chaff between his ass cheeks though. Her light blue skin, the iridescent scales scattered up and down her arms, how her dark green hair floated around her head as if she were underwater, the fluid way her body shifted over his. His cock twitched despite the fact that he had just come inside her minutes ago. She fucked gracefully, each movement as smooth as if she were swimming. Honestly, he'd be willing to

1

make the trip to Isa Poso twice a year instead of once if she were willing to use her second-sight that often.

The silver waves of the Nonestic Ocean gently rocked the sea witch where she floated, sprawled on its surface. As Tik-Tok treaded water beside her, the middle finger of his left hand grazed over her abdomen. Up and down, leaving goosebumps in its wake, teasing. Tracing her hips, gliding along the curve of her breast, circling her hard nipples. If he were the sort of male to settle for one female, he might be tempted to ask for more, but he wasn't. And neither was she.

Thank the sea gods. There was nothing worse than a clingy female.

Celyna's dark, orb-like eyes turned languidly to his red ones, just as his fingertips met the curls between her legs. "You should head back to your ship before it gets dark."

Tik-Tok took in the setting sun and let his hand drift lower. "Aren't you forgetting something?"

"Am I?" She ground against his palm. "Perhaps I need another reminder."

Tik-Tok growled playfully as he grabbed her hips and pulled her toward him. Her second-sight worked only during an orgasm and he'd given her multiple. "I would love nothing more than to bury myself in you a third time today, but"—he paused to stroke his tongue up the length of her sex, tasting her sweet flavor— "as you pointed out, it will be dark soon."

With a dissatisfied grunt, Celyna lowered her legs into the sea. "You must bargain with an unknown queen for two things," the witch said as if she were suddenly bored with his presence. "First, the ring I gave you."

"My ring?" He held his right arm up—the low rays of sunlight gleamed on the golden surface, the joints clearly mechanical—and stared at the silver band. The ring was always cold where it circled his digit, his metal hand having no body heat to transfer, but he'd grown accustomed to the sensation. Celyna had given him the trinket the year before with the instruction to keep it close—a useless task that left him restless all year. At first, he'd assumed the reason would make itself known as the months stretched on, but it had only served to calm the clash of different powers inside himself. It also had the power to transfer magic between fae, but there was no way in hell he was doing that. Tik-Tok's gaze darted to the other rings he wore, all gold, some with gems and some plain. "Which?"

Celyna rolled her eyes. "You know which, pirate."

He grunted. There was a bigger picture to keep in mind—a portal to find. To open. To explore. Among ... other, more important things. "And the second thing?"

"When you retrieve the ring from the unknown queen, you must exchange it for possession of a female who has yet to be born."

"Come again," he blurted, jerking back. There were a lot of calculating things Tik-Tok didn't mind doing, but *possessing* a female? No. He didn't want a slave, nor did he want anyone on board his ship who wasn't part of the crew.

"Do you want your portal or not?" she asked, impatient.

Of course he wanted his portal. He'd spent far too long and sacrificed too much to let the quest fail.

When Tik-Tok said nothing, she continued, "You will collect your ring from the queen at the same time you collect a female with silver hair and brown eyes. She will be well-known to the queen. Bargain for both things at once or the queen will not let the female go."

His nostrils flared. "And what am I supposed to do with her?"

The witch smirked. "She's the only one who can open the portal—but not until she's ready."

She can open the portal? His pulse raced. *Finally.* Everything was about to pay off. All he had to do was find an unknown queen. How hard could that be? While he was stuck doing the deranged Wizard's bidding—another one of Celyna's tasks—he'd sailed the entire world. The fae he must bargain with was bound to show up eventually—they always did if Celyna saw them in her visions.

Celyna slid forward and pressed her lips to his. His fingers tangled in her hair, holding her close, extending the kiss a few moments longer. As they broke apart, he nipped playfully at her bottom lip.

She nipped back and used one finger to push his body away from hers. "I'll see you next year." Then she sank beneath the silvery waves, her form disappearing from view.

Tik-Tok let out a warm, victorious laugh as he swam back to shore for his clothes. The portal was within reach.

Find the queen.

Acquire the female.

Fulfill his life's work.

A devious grin spread across his face.

CHAPTER TWO

NORTH

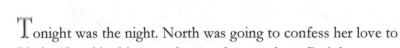

Tonight was the night. North was going to confess her love to Birch. Then kiss him anywhere and everywhere. Be it her room, his room, the grass, the water, wherever he wanted.

Birch.

She'd been in love with him for as long as she could remember. His short blond curls, his dark orange eyes, his muscular body, his skills with a bow… But it wasn't just how he looked. He was gentle, kind, strong, and valiant. He was *everything*.

Birch was there when her father—Tin—was too strict, when her mother—Thelia—was too demanding. He'd brought her wildflowers when she'd felt lonely, sad, or just because. There were nights when Father and Mother were sleeping so deeply that she would sneak out of her room to watch him get in extra practice with his bow. Then, after, her body was always so wound up with wanting his kisses, his hands stroking her bare flesh, him inside her, that she would seek release from her own fingers. For years, she'd known he would only see her as a youngling, but she wasn't anymore. North was twenty now. She wasn't as shapely and alluring as her mother or grandmother, but she hoped he was able to see *her.*

In personality, North wanted to be more like her grandmother—Reva. Bold. Daring. But she wasn't as powerful as Reva or Thelia. She was without magic, while everyone else in her family could bring the Land of Oz to its knees if they chose.

Thelia could tear the world apart, Tin was able to open portals and wield an axe better than anyone, Reva created storms, and Crow—her grandfather—had magic that allowed him to shift into a bird. While she had nothing…

Outside her window, the night had already swallowed the world—it was time. Birch would be where he always was when they visited her grandparents in the North: behind the palace, practicing his archery near the stables. North had already told her family she was tired and would retire for the night, while Thelia and Reva played a game of cards, with Crow occasionally joining in, as her father watched. Tin and Crow rarely spoke to each other unless they had to, but they tolerated one another in the same room. An improvement from her youth when they'd constantly instigated arguments.

North wiggled into a simple yellow dress with pearl buttons lining the front. She ran her hands through her silver wavy hair.

Quietly, she tied the corner of her sheet to the bed post, then knotted a few more together before carrying them to the window. She pushed up the glass and let the sheets spill over the side. Giving it a sharp tug to make sure the fabric was sturdy enough, North grabbed onto the cloth and shimmied down the side of the palace. Green vines speckled with blue and white flowers covered the Northern palace walls. A cold wind blew fiercely, disheveling her hair as tiny snowflakes swirled around her. The cold didn't affect her though, not as it would a human's sensitive flesh.

Once her feet hit the ground, North craned her neck to search the garden. Trees with ivory blossoms and pale azure leaves enveloped the area—icicles caught the moonlight where they hung across the curved branches. Snowdrop flowers cloaked almost every inch of the landscape at the palace, aside from the winding paths leading to the entrances. Stars painted the sky around a sliver of moon, giving off a bright yellowish radiance.

In the distance, faeries sang a slow, melodic song. A blue glow flickered from small snow bugs as they danced above the faeries. North inched to the side of the palace and peered around to the back where two guards chatted with one another.

"Gods," she muttered under her breath, knowing if the guards found her, they would report her to her grandparents right away.

North hesitated, deciding to go the longer route, but then a faerie with iridescent wings hovered above her, seeming to notice her predicament. Holding her breath, North motioned her head at the guards. The faerie gave her a beaming smile and darted forward, spewing an elaborate question. As soon as the guards' attention fell on the faerie and her inquiry, North hurried past them on light feet to a cluster of trees, then straight for her grandmother's stables.

She trekked across the hard ground, wearing her warmest boots, and skirted around the icy trunks. In the distance, she caught a glimpse of soft light spilling over the field.

North sidled up to the dark building, its obsidian bricks glistening from the glow. The light coming from the field turned out to be dozens of lit candles, forming a circle, with two lanterns in its center. The flames highlighted Birch's golden hair, the deer-like antlers at his forehead, his tight tunic and pants. Was this for her? Did he somehow know she was coming to confess to him how she felt?

"Birch?" North called, taking a few steps forward.

He whirled around, his eyes wide. "North?" he said. "You shouldn't be out here."

Shouldn't be out here? Her stomach sank as realization struck her. "This isn't for me..." She should have known—he'd never treated her as more than a sister.

"For you? It's for Gemma." He paused, moving toward her. "I'm planning to ask her to marry me tonight."

Her cousin. Not North. Her *cousin*.

She hadn't even known that he and Gemma were more than friends. Hurt bubbled inside North, laced with anger. She turned, sprinting back toward the palace. But she wasn't fast enough. Birch gripped her elbow, halting her. Her back struck his chest, and she couldn't stop the butterflies from storming through her, even though he was going to propose to her cousin. North had always looked up to Gemma, and she could see why he would want to marry her, but that didn't make it any better.

"What are you doing?" Birch asked, the first to pull away. Otherwise, she would have stayed pressed up against him for all eternity.

North looked around for her cousin, but she wasn't there yet. Gemma probably knew about her infatuation. Both Reva and Thelia could tell, but North had always denied it.

"You're asking her to marry you?" North whispered.

Birch bit his lip. "Yes."

"Why?" She could have said anything else, but apparently, she was one to relish in humiliation.

"Why does anyone marry?" His tone came out low, steady. "Because they love one another."

"You can't." Why couldn't she just stop talking? Why did she have to appear more like the child he saw in her, instead of the grown female she was?

His face softened as he studied her. "North..."

"I love you," she rushed the words out. "I always have." Her heart couldn't hold it in any longer, and if it did, it would break. More than it already was.

Birch placed his hands on her shoulders, and she hoped this was the moment. The one where he realized they were meant to be. His throat bobbed as he watched her, not seeming at all surprised at what she'd just confessed. "You don't," he finally said, his voice gentle.

"I do." She felt the tears pricking at her eyes, wishing he could slip directly into her heart, her mind, and see how much she did, because maybe then, he would love her too.

"North, I can't."

She winced. "You're only saying that because of my father."

Birch released a sigh, not taking his hands from her shoulders. "I would sacrifice my life for you, you know that. You're like a sister to me, and I love you, but I don't feel the way you want me to." He paused and gnawed on his lip. "Please go home before Tin finds you out here."

North inhaled sharply, her gaze darting everywhere but Birch's face. Something in her broke … shattered. "I understand," she forced out the words, even though she didn't mean them. "I'll go."

Turning out of his grasp, she started for the palace. North ducked behind a tree and glanced back as Birch slowly spun to go, as if he'd been debating whether to escort her home himself. She continued to watch while he walked back to his candles. And she knew that he would worship Gemma's body right in the circle of flames after he proposed to her and she said yes. Taking a deep swallow, she wiped the hot tears from her cheeks.

North peered at the castle, her chest as hollow as the collection of her grandmother's vases inside. She couldn't go back right now, simply to sit in her room alone, crying herself to sleep.

Instead, she would do something *daring*. She'd been saving herself for Birch, for when the time was right. But it would never happen now.

Blowing out a breath, she hurried to the front of the castle, across the bridge, to the part of the woods where fae went every night to have a good time, to not have to think, or worry.

Faeries filled the air with laughter while dust from circling sprites lit up the night. The wind continued to bite her skin, but she barely felt it as she slipped past icy trees and snow-covered bushes to join the revelry.

Fae skidded across the frozen lake, some half-dressed despite the cold evening. Along the bank, couples chatted, drank, and danced. Others were naked, mounted atop one another, their hips rolling. She lifted her chin, trying not to seem inexperienced, as she crept closer.

A fae with bark covering most of his body glanced up as she passed and held out a vial full of emerald dust. North nodded—her usual set of rules didn't apply tonight. He sprinkled some glittering flecks onto her wrist and she licked it clean, letting the high wash over her. Grabbing the full mug of mead at his side, North drank half of it before strolling off. The world seemed to brighten.

She needed to find someone, *anyone*, who would serve her purpose. A fae stepping off of the ice caught her attention. He was already shirtless, his red hair spilling down over his shoulders. Beautiful was the only way to describe him. He wouldn't be forever hers, and she didn't need him to be. Whatever happened next would only be to keep the ache from her heart for tonight. Before anyone else could claim him, North sauntered to the male and grabbed him by the wrist.

"Come on," North said, not meeting his eyes. She would be brave while the dark of the night helped to conceal her nervousness.

The male arched an eyebrow as he studied her. "Which tree?"

With a false grin, she brought him to the nearest trunk. The drug pulsing through her made her too high to care if anyone watched—she only wanted to feel better.

"Open your mouth," he said, pressing a finger to her lower lip.

North listened as he pulled out his own vial of emerald dust from his pants, sprinkling some on her tongue before coating his own with gold from a different pouch. He licked his tongue against hers, mingling the dust, and warmth spread through her, so much so that she forgot everything. It didn't take much time to learn how to match the movements of his lips. Then, as she discovered what to do, their kisses became frantic, desperate, as the dust soared within her. She loosened the tie at his pants, pushing her hand inside and squeezing his length. It felt different than she'd imagined—smooth and soft, yet hard.

And even though she didn't want to think about Birch, his face still haunted her as the male hiked up her dress, then lifted her so her legs wrapped around his narrow waist. North wanted to pretend Birch loved her, that she had her own magic, that she was good enough—even compared to her family. But she couldn't. Shame spread through her.

"Stop!" she shouted, desperate.

The male froze, releasing her as though she'd burned him.

"I can't." Avoiding looking at him, she adjusted her dress.

"I thought... North..." His voice came out gentle.

Of course he knew who she was. Everyone here did. How could they not? She was the granddaughter and daughter of the Land of Oz's leaders. Not only that, but she was like a daughter to the Queen of Oz. Three powerful females. And she was nothing.

"It's fine. It's not your fault. It's mine." North turned to leave and swayed unsteadily as the woods spun around her.

The dizziness remained until she reached the castle walls, thankfully avoiding any guards, and approached her window. Only when she looked up to climb the tied sheets back to her room, did she realize they were gone.

Gods.

"You snuck out," a voice growled behind her.

Closing her eyes, she sighed and turned around, trying not to wince. "Father, I—"

"You said you were *tired.*" Tin's silver irises burned brighter than the stars as he glared at her. "You lied."

"Father..."

"You really thought Birch wouldn't tell me what happened?" Her father's gaze remained hard.

11

"He had no right," North murmured. She supposed Birch didn't stay to propose if he'd already tattled to her father. A desperate part of her liked that he had.

"He cares about you."

"Like a sister, I know." North didn't want to think about it anymore.

Tin's shoulders relaxed. But then they tightened again as she stumbled, no longer able to maintain the charade of sobriety. He caught her by the arms and took a whiff—his entire face became stony.

Her tongue felt heavy. "Father...."

"You're never leaving my sight again."

Chapter Three

Tik-Tok

There were times when Tik-Tok thought the sea witch was fucking with him. Mostly in the last few years. *It isn't time,* Celyna had told him last year. And the year before that. And the one before that. Every single one of his yearly trips to the seer had met with the same three words for over two decades now.

It isn't time.

Like hell it wasn't.

Tik-Tok had done everything Celyna had told him to do for *decades*. Every year, she'd given him a new task that was meant to bring him closer to his dream. He'd tracked down a magical compass, held a mutiny against his old captain, severed his own arm, and helped that cunt of a mortal wizard—*who had held his compass hostage.*

Running the Wizard's errands was easily one of the darkest parts of his history. Willingly helping keep the Land of Oz under the mortal's oppressive rule, giving up even a sliver of control over his choices, made him want to murder someone. And those monstrous addicts guarding Oz in Orkland. *Damn.* It was enough to make even the most hardened of fae squirm.

13

But then, as Celyna had promised, he'd reacquired his compass. Followed immediately by making the fated deal with an unknown queen—for a female with silver hair and brown eyes. Ozma and Jack had been unexpected but a relief. Not only had they wanted the Wizard dead—something Celyna hadn't mentioned—but they'd been desperate enough to take his ring and promise him a female with little convincing.

All of that just to hear the sea witch tell him *it wasn't time?*

No. To hell with that. He wanted to open the damn portal to another world just like the witch had promised. Celyna didn't personally care about the portal—as long as she got a good fuck in—so the lack of forward motion didn't bother her. Tik-Tok could wait another fifty years for all she cared. That fact had somewhat soured their yearly tryst.

Palming his magic compass, Tik-Tok flicked the golden top open. "Starboard, ten clicks."

"Aye, Captain," Rizmaela, his first mate, said from where she stood behind the ship's wheel.

He'd picked up the cynical female dwarf a few years back after watching her take out three males singlehandedly when they wouldn't leave her alone at a tavern. The three dwarfs started by asking to buy her a mead which she refused, so naturally they thought she would agree to join them for a foursome instead. *Idiots.* He'd never seen a dwarf pull a dagger from their boot faster than Rizmaela had.

When she merely removed an ear from each instead of killing them, Tik-Tok knew he needed her on his crew. He'd lost numerous males and females to their egos already, so he valued someone who knew the meaning of restraint. Rizmaela rose through the ranks faster than anyone else on board. Most of the crew were brownies—not cutthroats—but he'd also recruited others. Two elves, Respen and Dax, who were both irreplaceable to his sanity out at sea. Cyrx, a goblin he'd met playing cards, and, perhaps most surprisingly, a siren named Echo.

Now all he needed was the sea witch's next set of

14

instructions. A bone-deep tingle told him he would get his wish this time. It was as if fate were reassuring him. Coaxing him to hope. He wasn't sure if the sensation was trustworthy, but he wanted it to be.

Tik-Tok propped the elbow of his gold, mechanical arm on a rain barrel, letting the sea breeze whip his black hair around his face. "I have a good feeling about today," he said more to himself than to Rizmaela.

"I hope you're right," she said in her usual gravelly voice.

He grinned at her. "Am I ever wrong?"

"Is any male?" she joked.

Tik-Tok barked a laugh and checked his compass again. Right or wrong, he did what he wanted, when he wanted, and his crew knew it. If they didn't like it, they were free to leave whenever they docked. Or, if they were particularly defiant, *before* they docked.

"Port, two clicks."

"Aye, Captain."

The final leg of the journey took half a day, and the closer *The Temptress* sailed to Isa Poso, the more restless Tik-Tok became. His fingers rapped against the rain barrel, and he felt the prick of what would've been a splinter poke at one of his gold fingertips.

"Land!" a brownie, Kaliko, shouted from the crow's nest.

Tik-Tok's heart slammed into his ribs. The tingling sensation that gave him hope now bubbled and foamed inside him. Slipping the compass into the pocket of his dark pants, he strode toward his quarters.

"Prepare to drop anchor," he commanded Rizmaela over his shoulder.

The dwarf was already shouting orders to the crew when he kicked shut the door to his room. He shrugged a deep blue jacket with gold buttons on over his loose white tunic, changed out his good boots for his old, and tugged on a pair of gloves. Finally, strapping one of his swords to his hip, he returned to find the

15

crew tying down the black sails of *The Temptress*.

"Will you be long?" his first mate asked, rubbing her gnarled hands down her leather pants.

He shrugged, watching the brownies prepare the smaller boat he would use to row to the island's shore. "As long as it takes."

Sometimes Celyna made him wait, sometimes she met him on the beach and quickly ushered him away. Either way, they always ended up fucking—even if it was a quick tumble on the sand—so she would have the vision he needed.

"Let the crew relax while I'm gone, but stay aware. No ale for anyone," he said in a stern voice. The last thing he needed was to return with a clear purpose only to have a ship full of useless drunkards. "We'll be departing as soon as I return."

Rizmaela jerked her chin in understanding and he strode toward the rowboat. "Ready?" he asked, climbing in. With a final tug on a knot, the brownies nodded. "Lower away."

As they slowly eased the boat down onto the shimmering silver water below, Tik-Tok took in the island. The aquamarine sand reflected the sun like a mirror. From far away, the island looked like a floating blast of light, but close up, the sand shimmered beautifully. Tall trees with smooth, white trunks grew a variety of exotic fruit while, farther on the island, the trees barely stood taller than Tik-Tok. Their leaves were crystalline blues and greens, in contrast to the pink salt grass that sprouted in patches all over the sandy beach.

Once the boat landed safely, the pirate untied the ropes holding it to *The Temptress* and gathered the oars. He eagerly sped through the quiet waves. Celyna would have a task for him today—she had to. Enough had been sacrificed for his goal—friendships, limbs, sanity—that waiting any longer would send him over the edge. And that wasn't taking his crew into consideration. He'd promised them a portal and their patience would only last so long. Unfortunately, he couldn't man a pirate ship on his own.

The boat scuffed against sand a few yards from shore. Tik-Tok hopped out, water splashing up his legs and seeping into his old boots. Dragging the boat the rest of the way, he toed a few bright red crustaceans from his path and followed the familiar stone walkway to the sea witch's home. The island was small, the witch the only permanent resident, and even she spent most of her time in the water. He skipped over the stepping stones while ignoring the cries of sea birds circling above. His gaze was fully focused on the glass building ahead.

Nestled into a thick patch of the smaller trees, Celyna had built her home in the only somewhat livable place on the island. Purple flowers flowed down the roof and hung from the eaves like curtains. Coral grew in a small pond nearby, surrounded by a collection of sea glass in all shapes and sizes.

"My favorite pirate has returned," a female said from the side of the home. "I expected you yesterday."

Tik-Tok stalked forward, rounding the corner of the glass house, to find the sea witch using her magic to carefully weave water into a basket. Her familiar dark green hair drifted around her head and her two fin-like ears peeked out on both sides. As she worked, her scales sparkled over her blue skin and, finally, she raised her black, orb-like eyes to meet his.

He cleared his throat, struck by her beauty as he was every time he visited. Their meetings were a simple transaction. He thoroughly enjoyed fucking her until she forgot her own name—the other fae he had made scream with pleasure throughout the years were nothing in comparison. But that was all he and Celyna were to each other. *A great fuck.* "The sea is unpredictable."

The witch smiled, revealing each slightly pointed tooth.

"You seem talkative today," Tik-Tok mused. Sometimes she greeted him with endless tales, other times, no more than *it isn't time.* "Do you have my next task?"

The witch watched him thoughtfully. "Will you not seduce me first?"

Tik-Tok crossed his arms. Would he give her an orgasm so

she would have a vision of his mystery female? Yes. Many. Was he feeling particularly *giving* at the moment? Not at all. "I've fucked you for the last twenty-two years without reward."

"It isn't *payment* for what I see," she growled.

Tik-Tok shrugged. *No.* It wasn't payment—they both genuinely enjoyed the pleasure, no strings attached, but the weariness of waiting had put his libido on ice. "Is it time yet?"

The sea witch stood, her seaweed skirt bouncing with the sudden movement. She sauntered forward, took Tik-Tok's chin in one hand, and kissed him harshly on the lips.

Surrendering to the taste of her—both salty and sweet—Tik-Tok nearly forgot his question. It wasn't until she nipped his bottom lip, drawing a drop of blood, that he pulled away. "Feisty witch," he growled.

Lifting Celyna, he pressed her up against the glass of her home and slid her upward until her legs rested over his shoulders. She was bare beneath her skirt, giving him unimpaired access to her slit. He shot her a knowing smirk at how wet she was. "Seems like you missed me."

"I missed your body," she crooned, grabbing his hair and bringing his face to her sex.

His tongue flicked her bundle of nerves and he grinned at her gasp. But, as much fun as Celyna was, he was too impatient today. His tongue ran down her opening, plunging inside, swirling as she ground against him. A groan slipped from his throat at the taste of her and his cock begged for attention, but his mind refused to release him to the pleasure.

Portal, portal, portal.

Increasing his pace just like Celyna liked it, he tore an orgasm from her in no time. Her legs spasmed on the sides of his head, her back arched. It felt as if she would pull every hair from his head as he licked her clean, but he didn't mind. He knew, as the fluttering continued, she was seeing exactly what he needed her to. Finally, her grip on him loosened and he carefully set her on her feet. She reached for his pants with a dazed expression.

18

Tik-Tok brushed her hands away and stepped back from her. "What did you see?"

With a sigh, the witch bent and lifted her new basket. "Visit the queen and force her to make good on your agreement."

"Queen Ozma?" His pulse hammered in his ears. "The female is finally mine?"

"That *was* the deal you struck, wasn't it?" She cast a look to his gloved hand. "Don't forget your ring was part of the bargain."

Tik-Tok rubbed his chest, his heartbeat painfully fast. *It's time. She's mine. The* portal *is mine.* "Yes, that was the deal."

"Then go to the Emerald City and claim your prize."

It was hard to catch his breath, his focus zeroing in on the end goal. How many more tasks would come after this one? How many more *years?* He shook his head. *It doesn't matter.* His next task was ready.

And, just as he'd sensed the witch would have good news, he felt a tether to the unknown female. A link tying their destinies together. Gentle vibrations of an undeniable bond locked into place, warming his chest, beckoning him nearer.

"I'm expected by the merfolk," the witch said, interrupting his thoughts. "Next time, come earlier and we can finish what we started."

He grinned, his libido suddenly in overdrive. If he wasn't in such a hurry to get to the Emerald City, she would completely miss her meeting with the merfolk. "Promises, promises," he told her, winking.

But, before the year was up, he hoped there would be no need to visit again. Because he would sail the Nonestic Ocean and find his portal long before that.

CHAPTER FOUR

NORTH

"If I could, I would tie you to the chair and make sure you stayed here where it's safe, but your mother wouldn't allow it," Tin said, his silver eyes boring into North as he leaned his head against the door of her room. "You're lucky I'm not going to tell her that you snuck out of your grandmother's palace. Tomorrow we leave to celebrate Brielle, so please try to behave." This would be her first time meeting Ozma and Jack's daughter since she'd been born a month ago.

North hated disappointing her father, but she wasn't a child anymore. She wasn't the youngling who constantly followed him around and hefted his axe as if it were her own. While she still wanted to make him proud, she was also finding herself, becoming an individual.

"I'm sorry, Father. But you don't understand what it's like to not be enough or to make mistakes." Her head drooped as she clasped her hands together in her lap.

Tin took heavy-footed steps to her bed and knelt in front of her. Under the orange orbs' illumination from the ceiling, his iron scar seemed to glow. As usual, his hair was pulled back in a knot.

"You think I haven't made mistakes? I've told you the stories. You know I've felt the same." His voice came out gruff, yet soft, as he lifted her chin. "North, magic doesn't always come right away, and if it never happens, then it doesn't. There's more to life than power."

By her age, if she was going to have it, she should have already.

"Are you still angry?" she asked.

Tin rolled his gaze to the ceiling and let out a long sigh. "Fuck yes, I'm angry, but I love you. Even when you act without thinking. Oz isn't perfect, and there are dangerous fae out there." He pressed a light kiss to her forehead and stood. Adjusting his axe on his hip, he turned to leave, then peered over his shoulder. "There are guards below your window now too. I know you're not a youngling anymore, but it's for your safety. Strangers are traveling through the area to reach the capital, and you know I trust no one."

North smiled. "No one but Mother."

"And you." He shot her a hard stare like she should have known better. "Goodnight."

"Goodnight."

North fell back onto the mattress, letting her body bounce as she stared up at the ceiling, watching the light orbs gently sway. Tugging back her hands, she pretended to throw axes over and over at the center of each invisible target, hitting its mark. This, every night, was the only way she could get herself to fall asleep. She was decent enough with an axe, but that was only because she'd wanted so much to be like her father. Even so, she missed the marks when she hurled one. However, she could twirl an axe and slice someone down if they were close enough.

Shutting her eyes, still throwing pretend axes, North tried to stop feeling sorry for herself. To pretend as though she'd never gone to see Birch or had her first kiss, and more, with a male she didn't love. At least she would get to see Ozma, Jack, and Brielle soon.

North pulled dress after dress after dress from her traveling trunk. Each one ended up on the floor of her bedroom in the Emerald City Palace. Loose, poofy, tight, awful, awful, awful—nothing ever fit right. A knock came at her door, making her drop the fabric.

"Come in," she called, not bothering to look up when the door creaked open.

"You're not dressed?" Thelia gasped.

North whirled around to find her mother, perfect as ever. Thelia's chestnut hair fell to her shoulders and a silver dress covered in sparkling jewels concealed her body, the cloth of the arms flaring out at the ends. She bet her mother had been dressed for hours, tapping her fingers together while waiting for the event to start. Her gaze dropped to Thelia's swollen belly. North would have a sibling soon, and this child might possibly have magic. She hoped her sibling would, so he or she wouldn't have to feel the way North did. North already had a softness for the child—she'd always wanted a sibling. But it had taken her parents a long while to conceive again, and they'd thought it would never happen. Then twenty years later it had.

"I don't have anything good enough to wear." North blew out a hard breath, pushing the silver locks away from her face. Even after everything that had happened with Birch, she wanted to appear beautiful for him. Not like a child.

"Let me help you then," Thelia said, pity forming in her brown eyes. In that expression, North knew something was wrong.

"What is it?" North asked, picking up the dresses from the floor.

"Birch is engaged to Gemma."

"I heard he was going to propose." And she supposed he

had.

"Are you all right?" Her mother pressed her lips together, and North could tell she was worried about her.

North took a deep swallow, tears brimming at her eyes, and she shook her head. She hated that she needed someone, but right then, she really needed her mother. North dropped the dresses and threw her arms around Thelia, holding her tight. "I thought... I thought..."

"I know. I've always known," Thelia said softly, stroking North's hair. "And if I'd known Birch had fallen in love, I would have warned you."

Love... North's heart felt as if it had just spilled out of her chest and dropped to the floor with a sickening plop. She lifted her head and peered up at her mother, determined. "Can you at least help me look as though I'm worthy?"

"You're the worthiest female in all of Oz." Thelia smiled and turned North around. "Let me start with your hair." With practiced motions, she began to braid her daughter's hair.

North kept quiet as Thelia styled the top half of her hair into a full crown, pressing flowers into sections from the vases on her nightstand. The rest of her locks hung just past her shoulders. Thelia took a silk dress of deep purple, handed it to North to put on, then said she would be right back.

After North finished slipping on the purple silk, Thelia returned with a few things to accentuate it. A sheer copper skirt to layer the bottom half of the dress, then a soft chestnut leather piece that covered her shoulders and arms, leaving a gap of bare skin above the tight bodice of her gown.

"There." Thelia grinned, taking a step back. "Beautiful as always."

North turned to peer at herself in the oval mirror hanging on the emerald wall. Within the glass, she still appeared childlike, due to her height, heart-shaped face, and doe eyes. All she could focus on were her flaws and how, if anything, she was possibly cute. But beautiful...? "It's perfect," she lied to her mother.

Thelia clapped her hands and drew North into a hug. "I love you."

"I love you, too, Mother." North wished she could be like Thelia, but she knew she would never live up to it. And her mother's heart was so brilliant that she would love North with all her flaws and misgivings anyway.

"We have a celebration to attend." Thelia waved North to follow her out of the room, then walked beside her down the emerald hall. North's heart pumped with elation at finally getting to see Brielle for the first time. Ozma and Jack hadn't arrived at the palace yet—they'd been at their secret cottage for the last month.

As she descended the steps, her hand touching the cool glistening marble of the banister—she wished that she were still high from the emerald powder. She didn't think she could handle seeing Birch with his betrothed this evening.

Music floated through the air, fiddles and flutes, swift and gorgeous. Laughter accompanied the welcoming sounds. With each step, the noise grew until she reached the bottom of the stairs, her gaze falling on a crowd of various fae filling the ballroom. Even in a space cluttered with bodies, she spotted Birch's tall frame and blond hair across the room right away.

North stood on her tiptoes to see if anyone was beside him—her cousin—but she couldn't tell.

"Get closure," Thelia whispered, knowing, and patted her shoulder. "I'll see you in a while."

Closure. Perhaps that was what she needed. He was still her friend, even though she would war with herself about wanting more.

North nodded and skirted around bodies dressed in fine spider silk gowns, decorative head coverings, shoes of the finest leather. Chandeliers of silver and green hung from the ceilings, and along the walls were paintings of the various territories of Oz. She followed the high archway of the ceiling until she came upon Birch. Thankfully, he was alone, guarding the area, a sword

24

at his hip and his bow across his chest. His hooves were bare, and he wore a light gray tunic and tan pants.

He met North's stare, cocked his head at her and smiled, his eyes dancing playfully—even though he knew what she'd confessed to him. How she'd looked a fool.

"Does this mean you're not ignoring me for all eternity?" he asked, holding out his hand to her.

"Perhaps." North placed her palm against his and he pulled her beside him. The fact that he didn't act different toward her made her heart sing.

"If this is ignoring, then I'll take it."

She smiled, wishing she could stay touching him for the entire night, but he was in love with someone else. *Bah.*

"So you'll still be my guard, right?" she asked as she watched fae placing honied desserts into one another's mouths, gulping down wine, kissing.

"To serve you is my first duty." He bent his knees so she and he were eye to eye. "Always."

And that would have to be good enough.

"May I borrow her for a bit?" a voice called behind her, drawing her attention away from Birch.

Reva.

Her grandmother was dressed in the darkest of blacks, a tight gown with a train trailing along the floor, heeled boots, and the swells of the tops of her breasts for all to see. She looked wickedly perfect, like a dark enchantress. If North had worn that, her father would have chopped off the head of anyone who so much as looked in her direction.

"Love doesn't always happen the way we want it to, does it?" Reva murmured, draping an arm around North's shoulders. Of course someone had told her grandmother, and she was sure it had been Thelia.

"It did for you," North mumbled. Shame washed over her for saying that because she knew the story of how long Reva and Crow had been separated from one another before reuniting.

25

Twenty-one years, and both Reva and Crow had not been themselves for eleven of them. They hadn't reunited with Thelia until that time either, when North's mother had discovered who she truly was and had conjured Reva and Ozma from a dark place with her magic.

"You don't even want to know how many males I went through to find Crow." Reva laughed. "You're young, and there will be more. Enjoy the pleasure. Have fun. Live."

"Easy to say when Tin's not your father." She had a feeling that Tin would have had a hard time accepting Birch, and he'd known him for years.

"Tin is just protective, that's all."

Something landed on North's shoulder and talons scratched lightly through the fabric of her dress, causing her to jump. Her eyes fell to black feathers and a sharp beak. "Grandfather." North grinned.

Crow let out a low caw before leaping from her and transforming in front of them in a cloud of smoke. A few obsidian feathers trailed to the stone floor.

"Haven't started trouble yet, have you?" He chuckled, lifting a beaked mask and pushing it to the top of his head, revealing the light scar over the bridge of his nose. His hair was entwined with feathers, and he wore a deep blue tunic paired with dark pants.

Before she could give a snarky response, a horn blew, its sound long and loud right outside the closed entrance. The entirety of the room silenced, everyone spinning to face the opening doors. North stood on her tiptoes again, so she could catch a glimpse of Ozma, Jack, and the baby when they entered. But someone's melon of a head blocked her view.

"Need me to lift you on my shoulders like I used to?" Crow chuckled.

North rolled her eyes but almost took the offer.

Still chuckling, Crow grabbed her by the elbow and tugged her to the side for a better view. "Look here."

26

She peered through a space between a gray-haired pixie—Whispa—and a dryad, to see two fae guards enter the room in uniforms of blue and emerald. Behind them followed a female with long blonde waves cascading to her waist and an orange-haired male with freckles. Ozma and Jack. In Jack's arms was a child swaddled in a light blue blanket. Gold crowns with blue and green jewels sat atop their heads. Ozma was draped in an emerald silk gown with a sapphire cloak, the silver slippers shining on her feet, and her wings hidden for now. Over her eye rested a patch that matched her cloak. Jack smiled brightly in his knee-high boots, leather pants, and silken tunic while Ozma greeted each fae as they passed. They walked down the ornate velvety carpet to their glistening gold thrones awaiting them at the far wall.

The fae of Oz hadn't known who Ozma was until she defeated the Wizard and regained the slippers. Then the world discovered that Queen Lurline and King Pastoria had been cursed to forget they'd conceived a child.

Beside the thrones, the guards stood tall as Ozma and Jack took their seats, beaming as they peered down at their child.

Reva nudged North forward, knowing she wanted to see the baby as much as anyone, even though Reva, because of her close friendship with Ozma, had the right to greet the child first. North knew she couldn't argue, so she made her way forward until she stopped in front of Ozma.

The Queen of Oz's dazzling blue eye scanned her over, and something like pride shone brightly on her face. "You look just like your mother and father," Ozma chirped, motioning her forward. The queen rested her gaze on her child in Jack's arms. "Brielle has been waiting to meet you."

"Hello, Jack," North said, wanting to hug him, but his hands were too full. "Hello, Brielle."

"We have a few gifts for you." Jack grinned. "I'll grab them from our room after the celebration."

Jack always had the best gifts. Beautiful writing quills,

adventure books, seeds for unique flowers.

"May I?" North asked, reaching a hand forward, antsy to hold the baby.

Jack nodded, holding Brielle forward. North pressed a hand to the child's soft cheek, hoping she would have as much strength, magic, and gentleness as Ozma. That she would be just as giving and caring as Jack.

As she was about to pick up Brielle, the doors burst open with a bang. North straightened, leaving Brielle with Jack, and whirled around, focusing on a male entering the hall. His hair was obsidian and sleek, his red irises blazing. Gold studs lined his pointed ears. He sauntered toward them as if this were his palace and he was a king. Thick-soled boots clunked against the floor, and the jingle of the metal adorning both his cobalt coat and the ruby sash around his waist echoed through the now-silent room. His hand hung too close to the golden sword dangling at his hip.

Two of Ozma's guards rushed forward. The male twirled his hand in the air, and a gray hue flooded across their bodies, casting them into stone. "Anyone else care to become a permanent fixture?"

"Everyone stop!" Ozma shouted.

No one else rushed forward, but the other guards, including Birch, were poised for Ozma's next command.

"Tik-Tok," Ozma said, her voice hesitant when he came to a stop before them. "Change them back."

Tik-Tok. North recognized the name immediately—he was the pirate from Ozma and Jack's past who had helped them break through the barrier around the Wizards home.

"All in due time. You know how it goes." He winked at Jack where he sat, frozen with fear, on his throne. "I've come to collect the female"—he held out his hand—"and my ring. A bargain is a bargain."

What bargain?

"You're not taking the child," North gritted out, narrowing

her eyes. She lunged forward and shoved the male's firm chest. She may not have magic, but she would create the best barrier she could between him and the infant. With his next breath, he would probably turn her to stone too.

But Ozma wasn't even looking at the baby. She was looking at North.

"My apologies," Tik-Tok cooed, studying North up and down with a smirk. "It seems I've come to collect *you*, darling."

CHAPTER FIVE

TIK-TOK

Chaos erupted in the ballroom. It all seemed to happen in a single heartbeat—one teeny promise to take the female that he was owed from Ozma, and everyone lost their shit. The rest of the guards surged forward, nobles fled, and a loud *caw* echoed off the walls. Tik-Tok narrowly avoided a bolt of green lightning followed by a blast of gray magic. His enchanted arm protected him against magic which was helpful in a room of so many powerful fae, but that didn't make getting blasted by it fun.

Not that he was worried—his enchanted arm wasn't all he had at his disposal. His own magic was just as strong as theirs.

Silver flashed in his peripheral and he pivoted. It was too late to completely avoid the silver-haired male from cracking him with an axe so, instead, Tik-Tok flung out his power with a flick of the wrist, turning every remaining fae to stone.

Everyone except for Ozma, Jack, their child, and *her*.

Though, judging by the murderous look on the young female's face, he wondered if that wasn't a mistake. *No.* It was more fun this way. He would get to see how she reacted under duress before dragging her in front of the entire crew. She was a captive, after all.

Tik-Tok slowly swept his displaced black hair behind his shoulders and stood straight again. He looked over the axe with an appreciative nod as he edged around the now-stone male. *That was close.* The fae would be worth fighting if Tik-Tok wasn't in the middle of something much more important.

"A friend of yours?" he purred to the wide-eyed female. A gentle tug came at his center as he met her stare.

"Her father," Jack replied through gritted teeth. "Tin."

His brows rose. Tin was infamous—an assassin like no other—until his curse was broken by Thelia. And he was about to kidnap their daughter. Smart? Probably not. But Tik-Tok never claimed to be the wisest of fae. He needed the female. End of story.

"He'll kill you for this," Ozma warned. "And I won't stop him either."

"*Mmm.*" Tik-Tok stepped closer to the thrones. "He will definitely *want* to, but we had a deal. So, if he comes after me for taking her, he'll need to come after you for giving her away. I highly recommend spinning whatever tale necessary to keep him … subdued until I've finished with her. *If* I finish with her."

"No," Ozma and Jack said in unison.

"Suit yourselves." His red eyes slid back to the silver-haired female. "What's your name, darling?"

"None of your business," she spat.

Despite her bravery, it was impossible not to notice how violently her hands shook. Yet she didn't move to attack him or to defend herself. He couldn't decide if that was disappointing. "*None* for short, then? It's rather a mouthful otherwise."

She opened her mouth to reply, but Ozma reached back to grab her hand. "North," the queen said quickly. "Her name is North, but she's not the fae we bargained for."

"Isn't she?" He scanned North up and down, feeling the tug again. Silver hair that looked softer than a cloud, deep brown eyes, and known to the queen—exactly what the sea witch had told him. It wasn't her rosy lips, curvy waist, or creamy skin that made his cock twitch. It had been the way she'd risked being turned to stone to shove at his chest. She was a dainty thing, but his attraction to her wouldn't tempt him to change his plan. He would take her and she would open the portal. Nothing more.

Well, maybe... He couldn't deny a good seduction. If she found him half as attractive as he found her, having her naked flesh against his could become inevitable.

"Please," Ozma said with an edge of desperation. "She's the daughter of Tin and Thelia, the granddaughter of Crow and Reva. They have the allegiance of all four territories so, if I let you take her, they'll use all of Oz to take her back. Our deal was before she was born, and if I would have known—"

Tik-Tok snorted. If they wanted to chase him down with their armies, let them try. They would need to pass through at least one other country on their way out of Oz, which wouldn't sit well with the rulers there, then find an entire fleet of ships to reach him. *Good fucking luck.*

"North has no power," Ozma continued. "There are other females who meet your requirements."

"She meets my requirements well enough," he said with false nonchalance. North was the one—he could smell the magic in her, even if they believed she was without it. The pull he felt toward her was undeniable. Fate had linked them, he was sure of it. "I won't harm her, if that's your concern. I may be a pirate, but I'm an honorable male."

"Honorable, my ass." Jack stood, clutching their baby to his chest. "Ozma, we can't..."

"You don't have a choice." Tik-Tok was suddenly in front of Ozma, seething. "We made a binding deal for the unborn female in order for you to defeat the Wizard. If you break it, who knows what will happen." His eyes slid toward Jack and their child in a silent threat. The consequences of breaking a vow were unknown until it was too late, but it was nearly always worse than keeping one's word. Body parts could fall off, loved ones often

32

met an untimely end, or, of course, your own death. Afflictions were common consequences and the sort that made one *wish* for death. "You have an infant to think about now. Denying me isn't worth the risk."

Ozma gasped, her gaze darting to Jack and the baby. Tik-Tok could practically see her thinking as she drew her bottom lip between her teeth. The indecision and guilt. Her inability to say the word *yes* even though it was the only real option.

"I'll go," North said, her voice wavering.

Tik-Tok's breath caught. He hadn't misheard, had he? She was willing? Then why the fuck was he still standing there, arguing?

"North, no." The Queen's voice was hard and unyielding. "You're not going anywhere."

She forced a small smile and squeezed Ozma's hand. "If anything happens to you, Jack, or Brielle, I would never forgive myself."

"If anything happens to *you*, I would never forgive myself either."

North eyed Tik-Tok so hard that he felt it in his core. *What a bold little North Star.* He liked her already.

"He said I'll be safe," she reasoned and scanned the room of stone fae with uncertainty. "His word will have to do."

"I said *I* wouldn't harm you. Same goes for the crew, but no promises on being safe." He was riling the female, but he couldn't help himself. With a smirk, he added, "It *is* a pirate ship, after all."

"Do you want me to come with you or not?" she hissed, then looked back to the queen, her gaze softening. "Let me do this for you, Ozma. I'm not angry with you—you've been like a second mother to me. The deal you made was to save all of Oz from the Wizard so this isn't such a steep price. Besides, you couldn't have known the bargain was about me. And I'll find a way back home."

Ozma nodded once.

33

His smirk grew. *She was his. The portal was* mine. "That's all settled then."

"We haven't settled anything," Ozma growled.

"Blossom," Jack whispered. "As much as I hate this, there's nothing we can do right now. You agreed to the bargain."

"I don't know how long we'll be gone," Tik-Tok said, meeting North's gaze. There wasn't a single tear in her eyes as she straightened, and that ... intrigued him. The sea witch had told him he needed the female, and now he had her. Besides, she would get used to life on *The Temptress*, and nothing she did would thwart his life's work. "If you want to gather any of your belongings, do it now. Be quick."

"Don't hurt them," North pleaded.

Tik-Tok glanced between North and the rulers of Oz. "Why would I hurt them?" When her eyes flicked to the sword at his hip, he had to bite back a laugh. If he wanted the queen and king dead, he wouldn't achieve it with a blade—not when they'd both grown so well into their powers. "I wouldn't waste time arguing about you if I had plans to murder them."

North hesitated before bolting around Jack's throne, putting as much space between them as possible, and fled the room. He wasn't concerned about her fleeing—not when she had already agreed to join him. Had argued in favor of it.

"Now"—Tik-Tok held his palm out toward Ozma—"my ring, please."

She clenched her jaw, leveling a steely glare at him, and reluctantly held her hand out, fingers shaking with rage. The gold ring he'd placed on her finger was untarnished with time. It had allowed her to share Jack's power when she'd had none of her own and was the only reason she'd been able to kill the Wizard. Without Tik-Tok, she and Jack would've been eaten by those vile fruit-addicted creatures, or met their doom at Oz's hand. He'd practically given Ozma her crown—temporarily borrowing one of her subjects wasn't much to ask in return.

Tik-Tok gripped the ring and pulled, but it didn't budge.

34

"You have to willingly surrender it, Your Royal-ness."

Ozma closed her eyes and took a few deep breaths, seeming to calm herself, then nodded.

Tik-Tok pulled again, and the ring slid from her finger. Having it in his possession after all these years was more relieving than he expected. It kept his different powers from getting too jumbled inside him, making them easier to wield separately.

He took three steps back and removed the glove covering his gold hand. When the ring was seated on his digit, the color shifted back to the original silver metal. He flexed his fingers, admiring its return, before replacing his glove.

Behind him, the doors banged open and a huffing, puffing North stumbled back into the ballroom with a small, handheld luggage case. "I'm back," she said as if they hadn't noticed. "Can I … say goodbye?"

Tik-Tok looked over to where Tin was frozen, axe in the air, snarl on his face. Behind him was Reva with her hands outstretched, lightning balled against her palms, a crow frozen midair, and a female, hands twisted as if calling upon a large storm of magic.

No way in hell was he releasing them from their stone prisons. Once he was far enough away from the palace, this particular magic would fade on its own and then they would be Ozma's problem.

"Sorry, my star, but I'm not interested in fighting my way out of here. You can have five minutes with the queen and king to pass along any messages." He nodded to Ozma and Jack. "I'll release a handful of guards now to help you move the others. When we're far enough away, the spell will break, and you won't want their magic hitting the wrong target when it does."

Ozma ignored him, pouncing on North with the tightest hug.

Jack nodded. His face was grim as he took in the room of statues. "Release Whispa now as well," he ordered, pointing to an elderly pixie. "She's harmless and can take our child to safety while we deal with…" He glanced around the room.

Tik-Tok waved a hand at the pixie without a word, releasing her. A shriek fell from her lips, but he was already weaving his way around the others to carefully select which guards seemed the least skilled.

Better to play it safe.

The royals spoke in hushed whispers, the pixie replying through crackling sobs, as he made his selections. He worked slower than he would've liked, to give North a few moments longer. Not that he cared, really, but if she was willing to cooperate, it could make opening the portal easier. So he would play nice until she gave him a reason not to.

"Time to go," he called from the ballroom doors when he'd finished his assessment.

Ozma clung tighter to North as she started to step back. Whispa stood behind them, crying silently while gently rocking the baby. North finally moved away from the queen and buried her face in Jack's chest before stumbling her way over to Tik-Tok.

He held a hand out to North, but she brushed past him without taking it. *Insolent!* He pressed his lips together to hide a smile. As long as she didn't take her attitude too far, he was *really* going to enjoy this.

Slowly, Tik-Tok backed out of the room, taking the knobs of both double doors in his hands. He half expected one of the royals to lash out at the last minute, to demand North stay.

Instead, feathery wings burst violently from Ozma's back, blue light, otherworldly, and shimmering. She whirled on him, her voice coming out low and deadly, the first time he'd seen her truly angry. "Don't think this ends here."

Tik-Tok would've been disappointed if there were no repercussions. As long as he got his portal opened first, he welcomed Ozma's revenge attempt.

With a flourishing bow, he took the final step from the room and closed the ballroom doors. A small, effortless burst of magic

36

tingled from his fingertips as he released the chosen guards from his spell. Almost instantly, Jack's order to stand down came. North clung to her luggage with her lips pursed, a deep line between her brows. But even while scowling, he saw her eyes growing glassy.

"Shall we?" he asked.

Her only answer was to pierce him with a stare.

He chuckled. *Oh, this* will *be fun.* "After you, then."

Chapter Six

North

Everyone North loved had been turned to stone. The only goodbye to her family would be through Ozma and Jack. Her father, mother, grandfather, grandmother, Birch...

North hadn't known Ozma had struck a deal with the pirate. Ozma had bartered a female from the future in order for Tik-Tok to help her save Oz, but hadn't known who it would be. Hadn't known because North hadn't been born yet. North didn't know how to feel—her life had been given away before it even started. But it was what it was.

Before she'd left, Ozma had told her that Tik-Tok's magic would wear off when they got far enough away, but she wouldn't know for certain.

North walked out of the palace and through its protective barrier. A lot of good the magic did to keep nefarious fae out since Tik-Tok had found a way to slip past it. How *had* he done it?

Her steps came to a halt and her eyes widened as she noticed guard after guard had been turned to statues. That was how...

She took a deep swallow and picked up her pace again. It was already darkening, and the streets stood empty. All fae living in the Emerald City seemed to be within the palace walls or celebrating Queen Ozma and King Jack's child inside their own homes.

The sound of booted feet echoed beside her, but she avoided looking at the male. Wouldn't let him see her tears. She'd tried to hold onto the anger she felt earlier in the palace, tried to be strong like her family would have been, but as soon as she'd left the ballroom, realization that she was alone struck, and hot tears slid down her cheeks.

A red cloth slipped in front of her face, as crimson as Tik-Tok's irises. She ripped the fabric out of his hands, threw it on the ground, then stomped on it for good measure. Taking her sleeve to her cheeks, she wiped away the wetness instead.

"Was that really necessary, my star?" Tik-Tok asked as if she had offended him by throwing his gods-forsaken cloth on the ground. *Good.*

"Leave me alone." North kept staring ahead, avoiding his face as she tightened her grip on her luggage. She wondered how Ozma and Jack had been able to tolerate him when they were trying to save Oz.

"You can have some time alone once we're on my ship, but not until then."

They were still in the Emerald City, only a short distance past the palace walls. Traveling to the sea was no easy feat. How would they even cross the sand barriers surrounding the Land of Oz? But if Tik-Tok could turn whomever he wished to stone inside the palace, then she supposed the rogue could get them across. However, it would still take days to reach the sea. Days and *days...*

Hope filled her chest.

Days.

It would take days.

Her father would come for her regardless of who told him not to, who told him to wait. Then there was her grandfather—

39

Crow could easily fly and spot them from above, then send word to the others. Someone would reach them before they got to the sea.

"Come out," Tik-Tok cooed.

Who was he talking to? Or *what?* North inhaled slowly, peering around as the sunlight dimmed.

Above them, an elf wearing a deep green tunic hovered in a large tree. He leapt from the branch, landing directly in front of them. Light brown eyes met hers and blue hair brushed his shoulders.

North took a deep swallow, glancing back in the direction leading to the palace.

"Ah"—Tik-Tok tilted his head—"you thought your loved ones would catch up and rescue you, didn't you? They won't today."

North clenched her jaw. "I hate you."

He grinned, baring all his teeth, appearing like a wild fae beast. "Hmm. I don't hate you, though." He snapped his gloved fingers at the elf, and the other male pressed a hand to each of their shoulders, digging his fingers in.

"I'm Respen," the elf said. "Just remain relaxed."

Before North could wiggle from the elf's grasp, her head spun, her feet touching nothing. A strong gust of wind smacked her face and the whole world was a blur. Her scream stayed silent, way down in the pit of her stomach, trying to claw its way out. She closed her eyes until the spinning stopped and her body no longer felt like it was swaying.

North gasped, her heart pounding wildly. They were no longer in the Emerald City, but on a hard surface, slightly rocking. A ship. Below her boots was a long and wide deck, and curving pristine rails lined the edge of the ship. Tall poles that met at a sharp point held triangular sails and netted ropes—all a dark charcoal shade.

"I'm going to join Dax and Cyrx." Respen said, releasing their shoulders. She watched as he walked to the opposite side of the ship, his blue hair swaying, where he joined another elf and goblin. The elf was tall and slender with dark brown skin, long blond hair, and blue eyes. Deep scars ran across the goblin's orange flesh, his muscles bulging against his tunic, and large teeth poked out of his mouth.

North frowned as she met Tik-Tok's smirk. "You could have at least given me a heads up."

"And risk you trying to run?" He shrugged. "I don't think so."

"I agreed to come, didn't I?" she bit back, her silver tendrils blowing around her face.

"You did, but that doesn't mean you won't try to flee. Or murder me. I wouldn't try either of those things, for the record, because I have an alternate plan if it happens."

North stumbled a few steps to the rail as the ship rocked, and glanced at the last light of day catching the silver swells of the sea, just before night touched down on the water. Except for a few orb-lit areas of the ship, the stars, and the moon, they were surrounded by darkness. She felt Tik-Tok sidle up beside her, closer than she would have liked.

"We're here," she finally said when he remained silent, "so what is it you want me to do? Because I don't have any magic."

He turned to face her, studying her, his eyes roaming her features, his nostrils slightly flared. She stared at him, growing annoyed at whatever it was he was doing. But for the first time, she took in his face. She knew his hair color, his eye color. But this close, those red eyes were like blood, his long, flowing hair the darkest of blacks. Gold studs lined his pointed ears. There wasn't a single blemish or scar she could see. His face was wickedly beautiful. And she hated that too.

"I smell it. The magic deep, deep down inside you. It's there, waiting to burst free. It will come soon, and I'll be waiting." His gaze shifted away from her. "Rizmaela, show our guest to her quarters downstairs." He focused back on North. "I'll meet you there shortly." With that, he shoved from the rail and sauntered

41

to the front of the ship where Respen stood with the two other crew members.

Tik-Tok smelled *her* magic? He was mistaken.

A dwarf with matted copper hair, murky brown eyes, and a bulbous nose hobbled to her. She wore a worn tunic, loose trousers, and scuffed boots, her stocky height coming to about North's shoulder. *This must be Rizmaela.*

"Come on, then," Rizmaela grumbled, taking North's luggage. "The captain didn't tell me he'd be returning with a prostitute today."

North's eyes widened, and she drew in a sharp breath. "I'm not here for that!"

Rizmaela grunted. "Any other female would appreciate being taken by the captain."

What other female? A hobgoblin? "And I suppose that's how you got here?" North fired back.

"I'm here because I earned my place." Rizmaela struck her chest. "After my husband was murdered, I left my home. Chose this."

North didn't say anything else, wouldn't have known what to say to that anyway. She wondered how the dwarf's husband had been murdered. Even if North had wanted to plan an escape, the ship was somewhere in the middle of the sea, land nowhere in sight.

A pole hung across the deck and North ducked under it, then stepped around a few barrels as she followed the dwarf to one of the doors. Rizmaela pulled it open and motioned North down a ladder that appeared sturdy enough.

Gripping the rails, North headed to the bottom and waited. Rizmaela tossed down her luggage, narrowly missing North's head, and it landed with a *thunk*. The dwarf slammed the door shut again.

North rolled her eyes and picked up her case. She took in the small room with a single bed covered in satin sheets and fur blankets. Orbs from the ceiling gave off pale-yellow light. But

42

there was nothing else.

It was a prison.

North let out a sigh but didn't shed any more tears as she rested her luggage beside the bed and sank onto the mattress. At least Ozma, Jack, and Brielle were safe. She truly hoped everyone would be freed from the spell that had made them stone. Tik-Tok had said as much. But could she trust Tik-Tok's word? Ozma seemed to trust him on that matter, so North had to believe her family would be released from his magic.

This wasn't Ozma's fault, even though North knew she would blame herself. North thought back to the story she'd heard as a child about how Ozma and Jack helped save the Land of Oz and Tik-Tok's part in it. Ozma hadn't completely trusted Tik-Tok back then, but he'd done his part in assisting her. Even as a child, North had wished for the multiple abilities he held. Had wanted to go on a ship and sail the sea. Well, here she was...

Her family wouldn't be the only ones looking for her. Birch would be too. She still wished things were different between them. But, as her friend and her guard, he would risk his own happiness, his life, to bring her home. North knew she couldn't get out of this situation on her own, but she couldn't have anyone get hurt because of it.

Since she couldn't flee and wouldn't possibly be rescued for some time, perhaps there was another way... What would her grandmother do if she was North? She would seduce, then kill the pirate. Tik-Tok hadn't hurt her, and North had agreed to come, so killing him felt wrong. Besides, she'd never murdered anyone. But maybe North could try to tempt him, the way Reva would have. And once he felt something for her, when she wasn't a stranger, then there was a higher possibility she would get home this century.

North may not have much experience with physical touch, but she'd imagined every way that she had wanted Birch against her. Then there had been the other night by the tree... She could at least kiss ... and grasp a male's length... North sighed at the

43

last part because she wouldn't know what to do after that, but she could try. Tik-Tok was hard to read, yet perhaps she stood a chance. At least he hadn't looked at her like a sister, the way Birch did.

The door flung open without a knock, and North jerked her chin up to watch as Tik-Tok slid gracefully down the ladder. He grinned as he turned to face her.

"How about you knock next time? I could have been naked," North said, annoyed by the way he came in like he owned the place. Even though she supposed he did.

"I would have closed my eyes." His grin grew wider. "Maybe."

She narrowed her gaze.

"Relax, I knew you wouldn't be changing." He ran the tip of his gloved finger along the empty wall as he inched closer to her.

"What power do you think I have?" North asked, trying to figure out the right opportunity to put her plan in motion.

"Portal magic."

North had already tried to open portals while accompanying her father in the South. She could never do it. "I don't have that."

"Not portals on land, but the sea."

"No one can open portals here," North said.

Tik-Tok looked her over thoughtfully. "No one in Oz, perhaps, except you. Hence, why I've waited so long."

Why was he so worried about opening portals in the sea anyway? She lowered her brows, trying to focus, to see if she could feel any movement of magic within the water. If she did, then maybe she could open a portal, be finished, and then he would send her home. But there wasn't a single stirring of power. Nothing. "I *don't* have magic."

"Rest tonight and I'll help you try another time." He shrugged and turned on the heels of his boots to leave.

"Wait!" she shouted, desperate. "Come sit."

Tik-Tok slowly spun to face her, his brow arched. He didn't leave, though—he took a step forward and sat beside her. Too close. Each time she'd been near him, he'd been too close. Like he didn't understand proximity.

This was perfect though, because if she'd tried to kiss him standing, it would have been awkward with him being over a head taller than her.

With lazy motions, Tik-Tok leaned back, his elbows pressing into the fur blankets. A sandalwood scent enveloped her. "What is it you want?" His words rolled off his tongue like knives wrapped in silk.

She remembered the motions of the drunken kiss the other night, the way she'd instinctually moved her lips, her tongue. North's gaze drifted from his scarlet eyes to his lips, and it wouldn't be the worst mouth she could have kissed. Plump and shapely. A pretty mouth on a dangerously pretty face.

"This," she finally said, placing a hand to his warm cheek before pressing her mouth to his. There wasn't any hesitation or startle from him as his lips moved against hers. He parted her lips with his tongue, then swiped it along her teeth, the roof of her mouth, softly flicking it against her own tongue like he had done this a million times. He probably had. His lips caressed and took and gave. This was nothing like the kiss the other night, not a drunken dance but something she couldn't describe. And his hands weren't even touching her...

Tik-Tok drew his lips from hers and pressed them to her throat, then inhaled. "You most certainly do have magic in there."

Then he stood, peering down at her with a smirk. "I seduce, my star—I am not *seduced*. But, this once, I'm willing to make an exception. Shall we continue? I can keep you up all night, writhing in pleasure, or you can stop playing games that you know nothing about."

Bastard... Her fists tightened as she tried to wipe the kiss from her lips. "I hate you."

"I seem to have that effect on fae. But North, it doesn't stop me from getting what I want. Try making progress with your

45

magic." And with that, he headed up the ladder.

The door gently shut, not like when Rizmaela had slammed it. Even though the click of a lock never came, she was still a prisoner.

North would find another opportunity to make this work.

CHAPTER SEVEN

TIK-TOK

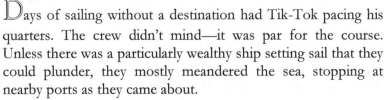

Days of sailing without a destination had Tik-Tok pacing his quarters. The crew didn't mind—it was par for the course. Unless there was a particularly wealthy ship setting sail that they could plunder, they mostly meandered the sea, stopping at nearby ports as they came about.

But now he had North.

North who was going to open the portal for him. North who had tried to seduce him. Her kiss had caught him by surprise, but not more so than the fact that he had *liked* it. Soft lips that tasted like berries drew him in and, despite how innocent she seemed, made him want more. He still wanted another taste—to slip his tongue between her lips and devour her flavor.

But the little star hadn't once left her room since she'd boarded *The Temptress* nearly a week ago, and she'd barely eaten the meals Kaliko had brought down to her. Tik-Tok had left the door unlocked for her because, although she was a captive, there was nowhere to run. But he was growing tired of waiting. She had a job to do, and it was necessary for her to find her magic.

Of course, it didn't matter how willing she was to open the

47

portal if Tik-Tok couldn't *find* it. He knew it needed to be opened in the northeastern part of the Nonestic Ocean thanks to his compass, but that was still a massive area to work with. They had already sailed across it countless times in an attempt to see or feel *something* that would give him the exact location, but to no avail.

"You're going to wear a hole in that rug," Respen said as he magically appeared in the cabin with a tray of salted meat and ale. The elf's blue hair slipped over his shoulder when he bent to set the meal down on the desk.

"Thanks for knocking," Tik-Tok grumbled. *I let my frustration show for one minute, and someone just* had *to walk in.*

Respen glanced over his shoulder at the door leading to the deck. "Sorry, Captain. The door wasn't open and I didn't want to spill anything with the sea as rough as it is today."

He grunted and continued to pace. Would sailing the entire northeastern sea again, this time with North present, change anything? Perhaps being in proximity to the portal's location could rouse her magic. Because it *was* there. The scent of it lingered in his mind, calling to something inside him. It was almost like she wasn't even *trying* to awaken it, holed up in her room as she was.

Respen hesitated at his desk. "Something bothering you, Captain?"

"No," he snapped, continuing to pace. How could he admit that he had no idea what to do with North now that he had her? Not when she willfully refused to acknowledge she had magic. They'd been waiting for her for more than twenty years. "Why are you bringing me food? Where's Kaliko?"

"He's preparing tea for your female and then had some inventory to check so I offered to help."

Tik-Tok spun on his heel, eyes narrowed. "*Tea?* This isn't a damn teahouse, Respen. Why is Cook lighting the fire when the sea is rough?" All it would take was a single ember to fall and the whole ship would go up in flames.

Respen blinked. "I … don't know, Captain. Kaliko told Cook to make sure North was comfortable. Since it's extra chilly today, I suppose he wanted—"

"We have a closet full of fucking blankets below deck." He pinched the bridge of his nose. "And I have a fool on board who would rather burn down my ship!"

Tik-Tok stormed past Respen and thundered down into the bowels of the ship where Cook was bustling about. The brownie was young—but old enough to know better—with a jagged scar running across her neck after a failed murder attempt before she'd joined him.

"Are you trying to kill us?" He slammed his palms down on the heavy table, the legs nailed down.

She whirled around with a yelp. "Captain! I don't understand?"

He scanned the kitchen, lips pursed at the lack of a fire. There wasn't even the hint of smoke in the air—just a warm herbal scent. "How did you heat the water?"

"I asked Dax," she replied with wide, horror-filled eyes.

Tik-Tok felt the anger rush out of him, then roar back to life. Only, now he was angry with himself. He didn't want to take his frustrations out on his crew—they didn't deserve it. If it were anyone else but the found-family on board this ship, he wouldn't have given two shits about who deserved what.

"Right." Tik-Tok smoothed his hair back. The elemental elf, Dax, couldn't create a spark, as his skill lay more solidly with air, but he had enough talent to heat water without fire. He slid the steaming teacup across the table. "Is this ready?"

The brownie nodded.

"I'll take it to her," he said in a gruff voice.

And she better have made some fucking progress with her magic.

By the time Tik-Tok reached North's room, half of the warm tea had sloshed out of the cup. It was still more than he ever would've given her, when water was better for hydration. Maybe Celyna truly *was* fucking with him—sending him after a female

49

without the ability to access her power. He gave two quick raps on the door to announce himself to North before pushing it open and climbing down the ladder.

"What's that?" North asked, scowling up at him from the center of her bed. "Come to poison me now that you've realized I'm telling the truth about my lack of magic?"

Tik-Tok gave her a strained grin. *Get yourself together.* It wasn't like him to lash out like this, but he was *so* frustratingly close. His heart kicked as a memory threatened to surface, but it was quickly locked away again. He had everything he needed—so what was the problem? The sea witch might be seeing him sooner than expected.

"Oh, my star. If I wanted to poison you, I would simply pour it down your throat. Not hide it in tea." He set the cup down on the bottom rung of the ladder and flopped down beside her on the bed. "See, this"—he motioned between them—"only works if we're honest with each other."

North inched closer to the end of the bed, putting space between them. "I will *honestly* kill you one day."

He licked his lips and smirked. "I look forward to the attempt. What shall you do? Kiss me again, then bring a blade to my throat?"

Her nostrils flared as she studied him.

"Well?" He turned to his side, propping his head up on one hand. "Or … will you use magic to kill me?"

"I told you—" she said slowly.

Tik-Tok lifted a piece of her soft silver hair and let it slip slowly through his fingers, meeting her brown eyes. The eyes he'd dreamed about for years. Eyes that belonged to the female who would open the portal so he could get what he desired most. He leaned in, his nose almost brushing hers as he took her chin between his fingers, and inhaled that magical scent. "Your magic carries hints of the sea and sweet, tangy fruit." He released her. "With subtle notes of mint. Unlike your body, which smells of vanilla."

Deny it again, he silently dared her as he inched back to give her space. *Tell me you have no magic.*

"How can you smell it?" she asked in a careful voice. "And if it's true, then why can't I use it?"

Damned if he wouldn't find out. There was something in her tone that sounded as if she *wanted* the magic, that she really thought she didn't have it, and judging by her desperate expression, he believed her. Perhaps she needed a trigger to tap into the power. Something to break the locks off whatever held it back. He stared at her, taking in her perfect features, her alluring scent. *Yes,* he decided. She simply needed help. And that was what he would do to occupy his time until they found the portal. All his frustration could be funneled into something useful.

"I want you to try something." He pulled the golden compass from his pocket. Oz had held it hostage to ensure his allegiance, but it had been unnecessary. Celyna had told him to help the Wizard, and Tik-Tok wouldn't have walked away until it served his purpose. Which was what had brought him to Ozma, and Jack, who had retrieved the compass for him. Then North. "Take this."

"What is it?" she asked, lifting it by the edges with two fingers.

"A compass." He reached out when she settled it in her palm and flicked the top open. Curling black letters—N, S, E, W— marked the face with a spinning gold needle pinned to the center. It was spelled to show him which direction he needed to travel to find what he wanted most, but no matter how often he'd looked at it since North's arrival, the needle never settled. Something about her portal magic must've been messing with it. "It's supposed to point to what I desire most."

She stared at the open compass. "What is it you want?"

"All in good time." There was no point scaring her with the truth of his desire just yet. He peeled the glove from his gold hand and heard her sharp intake of breath. Flexing his fingers, he held it higher for her to better see it. He had a love-hate relationship with the appendage—getting it had required him to cut off his own arm, but it constantly protected him from the magic of others. "Like it?"

She scanned the arm, lingering on the pinned joints. If it weren't for the small pins and the fact that it was gold, it would've looked like a regular arm. Interest sparked in her eyes but she said nothing.

Tik-Tok slowly drew the ring, that he'd only just retrieved from Ozma, off his finger. The instant jumble of power inside him pulled a small grunt from his throat, but it was just for a little while. Minutes, at most, though he should've been used to it after the last twenty-two years.

"Give me your hand," he instructed. North slowly held out the one not holding the compass and he slipped the silver band onto her finger. Unlike Ozma, he didn't need to whisper to distribute his magic. He simply pushed a little of his power toward the ring to allow her to share it. Not enough to do any harm should she want to, but enough to get a sense of what magic felt like.

"What's the point of this?" North asked, taking her hand away. "I'm not sure—"

The needle of the compass whirled faster before coming to a sudden stop in North's direction. Tik-Tok's heart hammered in his chest. The compass knew she was the key. *It knew.*

"Do you feel anything?" he asked breathlessly.

North dropped the compass to the bed and tugged the ring off, handing it back to him. "No. Should I?"

Tik-Tok never removed his eyes from the compass as he slid the ring back onto his finger. "I don't know," he admitted. Whether she felt it or not, the compass had responded to her when they shared his magic. "We'll begin training soon."

"Training?"

He made a low *mmm* sound. "How are you with a sword?"

"I trained with an axe."

"We don't have those here. You'll need to learn how to use

a sword, or a dagger at the very least." He nodded to himself. In case there was ever a time someone attacked her and he wasn't immediately there to help, she should know how to stab someone. Perhaps it would boost her confidence too—sometimes it was as simple as the lack of self-assurance that kept a fae's power dormant. There were a lot of things they could try. "And we'll continue to practice with … this…"

"What is *this*?" she asked, sounding a little more nervous.

"Magic." He swept the compass up, the needle spinning once more. "Drink your tea. I'll be back later."

He didn't wait for her to refuse the drink or for her to tell him to stay the hell away from her. Honestly, he couldn't give two shits about the tea that Kaliko prepared. And it was *his* ship. He would go where he wanted, when he wanted, and no spirited—albeit extremely attractive—female would tell him otherwise.

The door to North's room had barely shut behind him before he shouted for Rizmaela. A moment later the dwarf appeared at the top of the stairs leading to the storage rooms. "Man the helm," he ordered.

"Aye, Captain," she said. "Where to?"

"Northeast."

"You sound certain. Did the female have a breakthrough?" she asked, walking beside him to the helm.

"Something like that. For a descendant of Thelia and Reva, her lack of power is surprising," he admitted, spinning the ring around his finger. "Tin has portal magic, so it makes sense that his daughter would too, but speaking truthfully, I'd expected someone with a bit more flare, given her mother's lineage."

"Her father is the assassin?" Rizmaela rasped.

"Former assassin." Tik-Tok shrugged. There was something to be said about a male who could completely turn his life around. The memory of Tin's attack back in the Emerald City made him smirk. "His axe seemed well-kept as he swung it at my head though."

"I see." She placed her hands on the helm, eyes unfocused, and cleared her throat. "Captain?"

"What is it?" He couldn't stop the smile from spreading across his face. This was good. Very good. If he had to pry the lock off North's magic, he would do it.

"Should we go around The Palace of Romance?"

"The Palace of Romance? Why?"

"It's … just that if we head in that direction, from where we are now, it will send us straight through Captain Salt's territory."

Fuck. His old captain—the one he'd stolen *The Temptress* from, along with his entire crew. The fae who went along with the mutiny were long gone, not that it mattered. Not to him and certainly not to Captain Salt. The old bastard was a cutthroat with absolutely no morals, so when Celyna told him to take the ship and leave the overbearing fae behind, it had been no hardship. Disloyalty sat uncomfortably with him for a few years, but once it faded, he had vowed loyalty to himself alone.

But, despite the rumor that Captain Salt had reformed himself, Tik-Tok knew that sailing through his territory wouldn't go unpunished. He already had a metal arm—he wasn't keen on having a matching set, if he even lived through the experience. But going around Salt's territory would take an extra three weeks. *No.* Twenty-two years was long enough.

"It's only a problem if he catches us," Tik-Tok mumbled, more to himself than his first mate. "No detours."

CHAPTER EIGHT

NORTH

North lay in bed, throwing her imaginary axes at the ceiling, only this time it didn't help her fall asleep. She'd been down in this room for a week now, pretending it was her sanctuary instead of her prison.

Only a brownie named Kaliko and Rizmaela had made appearances. Kaliko had dropped off her food then left, while Rizmaela would open and slam the door throughout the day—North assumed to make sure she was still there. But where else would she go? Dive over the ship and swim until she either made it to land or drowned? Whichever came first. North, of course, had thought about it.

Until a few hours ago, she still hadn't seen Tik-Tok since the day she'd arrived. The prick had been as cocky as ever. Still, he stirred something in her that no one else had—not even Birch. She felt *important* around the pirate. There'd been a moment where she believed him, that there could be a touch of magic within herself, that perhaps he wasn't mistaken in taking her aboard his ship.

Then she'd second-guessed everything again after he'd left.

Her mother's magic had been hidden behind a glamour when she was cursed to be a changeling. So it made sense that Thelia hadn't felt her magic until she'd broken the curse.

Maybe North did have something buried, deep, deep down. But then why couldn't she sense it if she wasn't cursed or glamoured?

Focusing on the floating yellow orb above her, she threw a pretend axe at her mark. *Strike.*

With a sigh, she peered up at the door, wanting to clear her head somewhere else. Perhaps she would finally explore the deck, go out into the night to look at the sea and the sky. Breathe the freshness of the outdoors.

Peeling herself from the bed, North slipped on her boots and headed up the ladder. The crisp air rumpled her hair, and the waves beat against the ship's hull, singing a ravenous song. As she passed under the sails, she glanced up to see Kaliko hovering at his post in a circular space with open slits, the top wider than the bottom. He gave her a nod, his dark eyes shining, as she walked beneath him to the railing.

Not another soul was in sight—most must have retired for the evening to prepare for their shifts the next day. She rested her arms over the rail and stared up at the sky, sprinkled with hundreds of stars and a plump silvery moon. One star stood out, shining brighter than the rest.

North felt a body come up beside her, and she rolled her eyes without turning to face Tik-Tok. She wondered how he moved so quietly. "I'm not jumping off the boat tonight."

"I should hope not, North. The hippocampus and other sea beasts will rip you to shreds," a female sang, her voice silky, her body lightly humming.

North squeaked and whirled to the side to find a female, lithe and shapely, matching Tik-Tok in height, standing before her. Her hair was short and almost as red as Tik-Tok's eyes. Silver hoops lined her ears. The lit orbs of the ship made her green irises appear to glow. North found herself mesmerized, focusing on each angle and curve of the female's delicate face. She couldn't look anywhere else, didn't want to look at anything besides this perfect creature forever.

A veil seemed to lift and North's mind cleared. She quickly shook her head and took a step back, her eyes drifting down to an unclothed body. The female was *naked*. Large, perfect breasts, a narrow waist and hips, the longest legs she'd ever seen.

Siren.

North reached up to cover her ears, rip them off if she must, because she knew what sirens would do when they hypnotized someone. She could ask North to slice off her own flesh and North would gladly do it if under her spell.

The siren grinned and yanked North back just as she was about to run.

"That won't be necessary," the siren said, not singing this time. "It was only a test to make sure I could protect myself if need be. I'm Echo, by the way, and I'm with the captain."

North scowled, unable to stop her thoughts from turning to Tik-Tok slowly peeling off his gloves and clothing to tumble this female. She had probably just come from his bed and knew North had tried to entice him the other day.

"Not like that. I'm part of his crew." Her grin grew wider.

North tried to keep her gaze on Echo's face as the siren leaned on the handrail, arching her back against it, making her appear even more alluring. "Why are you out here so late?" she stammered, struggling to collect herself.

"Each night, I take in the sea when the ship is quiet before going back to sleep beside Respen."

"Oh." She and Respen... How did that happen? How had he learned to have faith in a siren? How had Tik-Tok?

"Tik-Tok is a cocky son of a bitch, but you can still rely on him."

"He took me from my home," North bit out. She remembered the horror of seeing her family and all the guests in the ballroom turned to stone. How could she rely on someone

57

who would do that?

"He saved me from mine." Echo shrugged. "There was an invading force in my underwater village. When he found me, I tried to sing him into doing my bidding, thinking he was like the others who'd murdered my clan. It hadn't worked, and he asked me to be part of his crew. That was before I knew he was protected from magic, of course. Try to trust him."

He hadn't given her a reason to. "I'll trust you before I ever do him."

"I'm surprised. I'm usually the last one anyone wants to." Echo pushed off the handrail and stepped past North. "I hope to see you on deck in the morning instead of hiding in your room."

North watched the siren's naked form saunter toward the back of the ship to a door leading below deck, where she supposed the female would curl up beside Respen.

North turned to the water again, shut her eyes, feeling for a possible portal, but there wasn't a single stirring of magic. A splash sounded below and her lids flew open as she shoved her head over the side, thinking she had performed some sort of miracle. But she only caught the scaly skin of a creature's back, jagged spikes lining its spine, and a broad tail as it sank below the swells.

Hippocampus. *Great. Just great.*

Lowering herself to the floor, she propped her back against the railing and let the waves sing their melody while she tried to tap into any spark of magic. Until she was too spent to even head back to her room and drifted to sleep on the deck.

Something nudged North's arm.

She cracked her eyes open to bright light and the tip of a boot beside her cheek.

"Rise and shine, my star," Tik-Tok purred. "Time to train."

She let out a yawn and pulled herself up to a sitting position, the salty air filling her nose.

As her gaze scanned up Tik-Tok's form, she took him in from boot to firm body to wickedly beautiful face. He looked pristine, and she wondered how long he'd been waiting for her to rouse. She hoped a while.

North stared down at herself, appearing as if she just rolled out of a bird's nest. She ran her fingers through her hair to comb out the tangles instead of going downstairs to get her brush.

"Do you want to put on a different dress yet? I can help if you want. I'm quick with my fingers when it comes to unfastening buttons." Tik-Tok grinned, his eyes dancing.

She shot him a glare, and her stomach decided to do the speaking when it let out a loud growl.

"Eat." He tossed her something red from his hand. She tried to catch it, but, of course, she dropped it onto the deck. Arching a brow, he watched as she scrambled to pick up the apple and bite into its juiciness.

She thought of her grandmother while taking another bite— they were her favorite fruit and she always had bowls of them at her palace.

"Here." He fished out a silver flask from his pocket and held it toward her.

She eyed the flask with suspicion but took it from him anyway. She brought it to her face, inhaled the strong scent, and wrinkled her nose. "What is it?"

"Do you not drink alcohol?" He reached to take it back.

She pulled it away before he could think her too innocent, like everyone else did. "I do." *The one time.*

If it were possible, his dark brow arched even higher.

North threw her head back and took a swig of the liquid. And holy gods did it burn as it slid down her throat. It was like fire, lava, and beasts' claws. How did he drink this? She managed to hold back her cough, but she could feel red staining her face.

"That color suits you," Tik-Tok commented with a wink.

59

"I'll have to share my ale more often." Before she could tell him what a bastard he was, Tik-Tok unsheathed an extra sword attached to his waist, then threw it down in front of her feet. "Ready?"

North puckered her lips and stared down at the sharp blade, the golden handle, the sparkling encrusted ruby jewels. "I already know how to defend myself."

"With *all* weapons?"

"Just the axe." And her gods-awful aiming with a dagger and a bow.

"That isn't good enough. Lift it," he instructed.

With or without magic, most of the guards at her palace carried swords. Others, like Birch, used a bow. She thought of him now, already missing his face, his kind words. Even though he was worlds away, she imagined he was speaking to her. *You can excel at anything you want to. You just have to try. Want it bad enough.*

She picked up the sword, its weight heavy in her hands as she held it up, and prepared herself.

"Why are you standing like a hunched hobgoblin?" Tik-Tok motioned to her body with the tip of his sword. "Straighten your shoulders, adjust your feet, bend your knees slightly."

Hobgoblin, indeed... But she nodded, figuring she would learn what she could, take in the necessary skills she was lacking so she could defend herself better. No one had been able to teach her thus far, but she would try again anyway.

North held up the sword, the blade shining beneath the sun's rays. Tik-Tok swung his weapon, striking hers, metal against metal echoing. Her body lurched forward and the sword shot out of her hands, flying to the floor of the deck.

"Pitiful." A grunt came from Rizmaela as she passed them, carrying a large barrel almost the size of her body. "She would be better suited as a prostitute."

North wanted to knock the barrel from her hands and punch the dwarf in her face. Tik-Tok's gaze traveled up North's form, making her feel that he believed Rizmaela might not be wrong.

"I hate you," she said to him as she scooped up the fallen sword.

"Were you planning to tell me that the other night as I made you quake with pleasure?" He chuckled, his shoulders shaking.

She could feel her face heating again, but then she focused on his laughter. It was different than she would have expected—musical, beautiful. Not vicious or cocky, but pleasant. North attempted to block out the sound. "It wouldn't have gotten that far."

"Oh really?" He sauntered forward, backing her up until she was caged in by his arms at the rail. "Tell me, my star, how far would you have allowed your seduction to go?"

Gods. That was a very good question. Would she have spread her legs for him and allowed him entrance? Or would she have wrapped her hands around his length like she had the male in the woods, then realized she couldn't go through with it? She hated that she wondered what Tik-Tok's hardness would look like compared to the one she'd seen, felt.

She shook the image away. Birch. Birch. *Focus on him, even though he doesn't love you the same.*

Tik-Tok was studying her, and she realized that she'd inched closer to him in the cage his arms created around her, her chest brushing his. *She'd* done it. Not him. Realizing their positioning, she shoved him away. "Let's train."

Tik-Tok raised his weapon. She lifted the sword and he swung, and like before, her blade was knocked out of her hands, clanging as it struck the deck.

"Your turn." Not a single bead of sweat dotted Tik-Tok's face or neck, while perspiration was already sliding down her back and forehead. If an axe was in her hands instead, she wouldn't have dropped it, grown tired so easily.

Gritting her teeth, determined, North plucked the sword from the floor. She didn't even step into her stance, and with everything in her, she swung at the blade to take him by surprise. Tik-Tok didn't even blink as her blade gave his a fierce kiss—his hand didn't move an inch. He cocked his head at her, willing her to try again.

Gods, she hated him.

She eyed the gloved hand holding the sword, remembering how the gold had gleamed the night before. It was shaped like a real hand, moved like one, but it had been metal with small bolts attached to the joints.

"How did it happen?" she asked, unable to hide her curiosity about it any longer.

Tik-Tok hesitated, his lips curling into a half-smirk, half-sneer. "I cut it off."

"Why?" She couldn't hide her horrified expression, her gasp. "Was it too far gone from infection to be healed?"

"It was by choice. Because of it, I'm immune to magic and cannot be controlled." He was no longer smirking and had slipped into a neutral expression that she wished she could replicate. "Enough talking. Again." His gaze dropped to her sword.

So again and again she swung. Again and again he blocked. His sword didn't budge. Her sword fell to the floor. Every. Single. Time.

They practiced for the entire day, only stopping to eat or relieve themselves. Though she'd desperately wanted a break, she hadn't asked for one because she'd been so determined to beat him. Knock his sword from his hands just once. Then she could die happy. But she hadn't, so there she was, practically dead, her legs aching, her arms throbbing, and her entire dress drenched.

"One more time," she demanded as Tik-Tok sheathed his sword.

"Go rest," Tik-Tok said while she swayed, her hands shaking and gripping the hilt. "Echo will show you where to get cleaned up. Then we'll try again tomorrow."

North wanted to argue, but her tongue felt thick, and she was too tired to even talk. Echo strolled toward her, dressed in tight leather pants, a shelled top—lined with shimmery pearls, covering her breasts—and knee-high boots.

"You did well," Echo said, leading her to the back of the ship.

What was the siren talking about? North had been awful. It had taken her years to become decent with the axe, but she would never be good with *all* weapons. Especially if it had to do with aiming.

"I'm serious." Echo laughed when she hadn't said anything. "Most would have given up already."

That didn't mean much, because if an enemy came at her with a sword, even if *she didn't give up*, she'd be dead. "I'll be practicing again tomorrow."

Echo lifted the hatch in the floor, then showed her down the stairs to the bathing chambers. Smooth wooden walls surrounded her, and high-back chairs with towels folded in their seats rested at the opposite end. Two large rectangular tubs stood side by side in the middle of the space, while a vanity with an oval mirror and wardrobe took up the wall across from them. Pale yellow orbs swayed along the ceiling, giving off a calming light.

"Some advice?" Echo started as North turned to face her. "I watched you up there this afternoon, and you were driving with emotion. You can't do that. You're small, right?"

North had heard it her entire life. "Yes?"

"Use it to your advantage. With practice, you can be nimble, light on your feet, duck and roll more easily than the captain." She pressed a finger to her lips and smiled. "But don't tell him I told you."

"I won't." North smiled in return.

"Dax already warmed the water in the bath, and there's soap for you to use. I also left you a sack filled with clothing from an old crew member if you need them. They're all about your size."

North had only packed a nightgown and the filthy dress she was already wearing. She normally wanted to look nice, usually for Birch. This time, it would be for herself.

"Thanks, Echo," North said as the siren headed back up the stairs.

The siren glanced over her shoulder before shutting the door, her grin widening as she stared past North toward the sack on the floor. "Don't thank me yet."

North's gaze lingered on the rough material of the sack, her interest piquing at what was inside. She knelt to untie the string, then drew the sack open. She dumped the contents on the floor and gasped at each piece of fabric.

She would never normally wear any of these revealing garments. But they were clean, so she would put something from the pile on. And perhaps, with these, she could revisit her plan to tempt Tik-Tok.

Chapter Nine

Tik-Tok

Tik-Tok tensed at the sight of North walking toward him with a new swing in her hips. Or, perhaps it was the same swing, just no longer hidden beneath flowing skirts. Now, she wore a deep red dress that clung to her curves. The material twisted and pleated in all the right places, accentuating her small waist. Thin gold-braided rope swirled beneath her breasts, looping upward over her shoulders in an intricate design. The sides were cut out, displaying skin down to her hips and the edges of her stomach. Two high slits in the skirt showed nearly her entire leg with each step.

"Why are you staring at me?" she asked with false innocence.

"What are you wearing?" he blurted.

North spun slowly. "Do you like it?"

Like it? He fucking loved it. That was the problem. Everyone on board would be gawking at her previously hidden attributes and thinking exactly what he was: *I want to fuck her.* But that wasn't why she was on *The Temptress.* Besides, if anyone was going to mix business with pleasure, it would be him and him alone.

"No," he growled. "Go change."

North grinned. "Sorry, I rather like this."

"I let you pack a case." He was overcome with a sudden urge to stand between her and his crew so they wouldn't see her looking so delicious. Stepping closer, he widened his stance. "What did you bring?"

"I brought a nightgown. Would you rather I wear that? The material is thin, practically sheer." Her soft lips tilted up. "Or should we end this discussion and begin our training for today?"

Practically sheer. A sudden desire to see the outline of her chest, her rosy nipples hard with the cool sea air, slammed into him. *Shit. Focus.* Tik-Tok swallowed hard and tossed a sword at her feet. "You'd better hope it doesn't limit your movements. I won't go easy on you."

North bent slowly to retrieve the sword, her cleavage begging to be set free as she glanced at him from beneath her lashes. "I'd never expect you to."

His mind filled with the image of her holding onto his headboard as he filled her—as he *didn't* go easy on her. *Damn.* In a desperate bid to rid himself of his mounting thoughts, he lunged into the first attack.

Day after day, Tik-Tok continued to work with North on her swordsmanship. And, day after day, she continued to flail around like a baby bird pushed from the nest too early. His patience was wearing thin. Sure, he had decades of practice, but how hard was it to *block*? To *duck* when a blade came flying toward your head?

Extremely fucking difficult, apparently.

But he had a potential solution. Respen had whirled himself to the market in Merryland an hour ago. The daughter of Tin had practiced with an axe—so an axe she would have. If there wasn't some form of improvement, he would simply chain her to his side for protection and focus on training her magic instead. That was more important, anyway.

"Captain," Respen said from behind him. "I'm back."

"Did you get it?" he asked, spinning to face him. North could only focus on mental exercises to find her magic for so long every day, and he needed to know she could wield a weapon. *Any* weapon. If there was ever a time he couldn't defend her, he needed to know she could defend herself. She couldn't open his portal if someone killed her first.

Respen nodded and held out the handle of an axe. "Merryland is busy today. Should we wait to dock?"

They needed an enchantment to conceal their presence from Captain Salt, and Merryland was the best place to get it. Tik-Tok loathed the crowds with their hustle and bustle, the pickpockets, the loud-ass hawkers, but he would make an exception this time if it meant getting his portal even one day earlier.

"No." Tik-Tok spun the smooth axe handle in his gold hand, his gloves forgotten in his room, testing its weight. It would be another forty minutes or so before they reached land. Maybe the crowd would thin by then. He turned toward the helm where Rizmaela stood, checking her own compass. "We'll go as planned. Who knows how long it will be before we dock again? Let the crew have some fun while I take care of business."

Rizmaela grunted and eyed the axe. "Is that for *her*?"

"Watch your tone, Riz," Tik-Tok replied. "Without her, there's no portal. Naturally, I'm going to take extra steps to make sure she's safe."

His first mate's top lip curled into a sneer, but she said nothing else. Tik-Tok watched her for a moment, swinging the axe gently at his side. *Not jealous,* he decided. There was no reason for her to be, of course, since there had never been anything remotely sexual between Rizmaela and himself. But this reaction was unexpected.

"Straight to Merryland," he said deliberately. "Call Dax if you need him to create enough wind."

"Aye, Captain," Rizmaela grumbled.

Respen caught Tik-Tok's eye, and the elf lifted a brow,

sharing a knowing look. Apparently, they had both noticed the dwarf's unexpected dissatisfaction. "Want me to get North for you?"

"If you don't mind," Tik-Tok answered, returning his glare to Rizmaela until Respen disappeared. "Something you'd like to say now that we're alone?"

"No," she snarled.

But, clearly, there was. He scowled at the dwarf, rubbing his jawline. If she didn't want to tell him, it was likely something he didn't want to hear. Still, he was curious, but not curious enough to push the issue, so he checked his compass instead. *Still spinning.*

"You summoned me?" North said from across the deck.

Tik-Tok ground his teeth at the sight of her in yet another new outfit. Each one showed more skin than the last. If she kept it up, he wouldn't be surprised if she walked across the ship stark naked by the end of the week. Today's outfit was dark green and left a large strip of bare skin across her midriff. A wide golden ribbon circled the top of the skirt and beneath her breasts, bringing his attention straight to her stomach. He wanted nothing more than to lick the expanse of it. To nip and tease. *Damn.*

"It's time to train," he grunted.

North's gaze fell to the weapon in his hand, and her eyes brightened. "Is that for me?" she asked, a hint of excitement entering her voice.

Tik-Tok's chest swelled a little at seeing her happy, the more lecherous thoughts fading. She'd never smiled like that before. "You're shit with a sword so I sent Respen after an axe."

"I thought I needed to learn *all* weapons." Her grin widened, reaching for it.

"Using my words against me, are you?" He released the weapon to her and turned to point at the mast. Shutting his eyes for a moment, he willed away the image of that dress on his floor. Of what she would feel like beneath both his calloused hand and his gold one as he slid the top of her dress off to palm her breasts. "Throw it there," he instructed, his voice rougher than he would've liked.

When the axe didn't automatically soar past him, he crossed his arms and looked over his shoulder. North stood, pretending to toss it, but not releasing when her arm came down.

He waved at the target again in a silent order to let go. "We have other things to do today, my star."

She sighed and, after pretending twice more, let the axe fly. It flipped repeatedly in an expertly thrown arc ... then landed ten feet from the intended target, right between Dax's feet.

"The fuck?" the elemental elf called, his hands frozen mid-air where he was creating wind. The strong breeze he'd already built blew his light blond hair around his face, his vivid blue eyes wild with surprise.

Tik-Tok blinked. Then blinked again. She ... missed. By *a lot*. Whirling, one brow hiked up his forehead, he studied North as if he'd never seen her before. "You..." He rubbed a hand over his mouth, unsure of what to say. Had she missed on purpose? *No*. Judging by her flaming red cheeks, she had actually tried to hit the mast. "Your father is *Tin*."

"I am aware," she said through gritted teeth.

"But..." He watched Dax pry the axe from the deck. "You said you could handle an axe. So I got you an axe..."

She took a deep breath and tilted her head in an attempt at being coy. "I never said I was *good* at it. I said I *trained* with one."

"No shit. What the fuck was that?"

"You told me to throw it," she said with a shrug.

A surprised snort escaped Tik-Tok. "If you were honest with me, you wouldn't have almost killed one of my crew."

"I *was* honest. I simply left out the details." North shrugged. "And I may not be able to throw one, but I can swing them well."

More than anything, he wanted to see her fight well. Not so he knew that she could defend herself, but because it would undoubtedly send blood rushing to his cock. He licked his

69

bottom lip.

"Here, Captain." Dax passed the axe back to him with a withering expression. "Maybe it's a good thing she can't access her power. She'd probably blast us out of the water."

Tik-Tok suppressed a laugh, knowing it wouldn't gain him North's favor. While he enjoyed a good, old-fashioned hate fuck, he couldn't risk her agreeing simply because she had concocted some insane plan to seduce him. It was obvious she'd never sought male attention in this way, but had she fucked many others? Not that it mattered. He wanted her no matter the answer, but he wouldn't take her until she desperately *wanted* him to—until she begged him for release.

"Show me," he dared North, handing her back the axe.

A twinkle lit North's eyes as she found her grip on the wooden handle. Tik-Tok barely had time to draw his sword before she lunged forward. He brought his blade up to block and, an instant later, the hook of the axe twisted it from his hands. The sword clattered to the deck, leaving him wide-eyed, mouth parted.

"Have I shown you enough?" she asked with a smirk. "Or shall we go again?"

Tik-Tok stepped over his sword, into her space, and took in the sight of her. It had been so quick, so skillful, and made him fucking hard. It was all he could do to not steal a kiss right there on deck in front of the whole crew. "Oh, my star, I haven't seen *nearly* enough." When she blushed, he stepped back and reclaimed his sword. "But it will have to wait. We'll be arriving in Merryland's capital shortly."

North scanned the horizon. "I've heard stories of that city. Isn't that where pirates go to sell their stolen goods?"

Mostly. He shrugged. "Until you open the portal, you're my first priority. No one will harm you."

North leaned slightly to the side to see around him. "Are you sure about that?"

Tik-Tok followed her gaze to Rizmaela, who was studying

North with fire in her eyes. "Don't worry about her."

She mumbled something he couldn't quite hear before turning on her heel.

"Where are you going?" he called after her.

"You said training was finished."

Tik-Tok hurried to her side, his gaze stuck on her ass the entire time. "That doesn't mean I'm finished with you for the day. Wouldn't you like to get off this ship for a while?"

North stopped walking and turned to face him, eyes narrowed. "Why?"

"So suspicious." He tapped her nose with the tip of his golden finger. "We're docking soon for food and supplies." *Very specific supplies so Captain Salt doesn't locate us.* "Most of the crew are going into town, and I can't very well leave you here with a couple of brownies."

She folded her arms, inadvertently drawing his attention to the swells of her breasts. They had been concealed before, but this dress clung to them, lifting them, drawing the eye. They were the perfect size to fit in his hands.

"Why not?" she asked. "I've proven I'm capable with an axe."

Because she was too important to risk, even if that risk was infinitesimal. The best way to protect her was to have her beside him. "What if the ship is boarded by thieves while we're gone?" he asked, cocking his head. "How many can you fight at once? The brownies are hard workers, but hardly warriors."

"*Will* it be boarded?"

He laughed at the concern in her words. No, his ship wouldn't be ransacked. Ozma likely had the entire continent looking for them too, but he *dared* someone to try taking North. Besides, his reputation was too great to attract thieves and his stolen treasures well-hidden elsewhere. "Let's use this opportunity to get to know each other," he offered, "since we'll be spending a long time together, it seems."

"We'll see about that." Her gaze locked onto his, seeming to

71

dare him to press the issue.

Tik-Tok grinned and gently pushed her hair behind her shoulders. "This dress suits you," he said in a quieter voice.

And makes me want to rip it off.

His cock jerked at the thought. Of seeing her flesh. Touching it. Listening to the little sounds that he would draw from her. He bit his lip to keep from groaning in anticipation. They were indeed going to be together a long time... It wasn't irrational to think she would end up in his bed. Enough females from the ports had sucked and fucked him on his sheets over the years, but none had made him anticipate the act as much as she did.

"You wouldn't prefer the nightgown?" North asked, matching his tone.

He laughed brightly, genuinely. "You may succeed in seducing me, after all."

"I—"

"Don't worry." Tik-Tok winked. "As I told Ozma, I'm the most gentlemanly of pirates."

"Land!" Kaliko called from above in the crow's nest.

"Land," Tik-Tok repeated with a grin. "Are you coming with me, then?"

"Do I have a choice?" She arched a silver brow.

He held out his gold hand for her to take. "Not really, no."

She placed her hand in his and shivered slightly when her palm touched the cold metal. "Fine, but you're buying me a better axe."

"I'll buy you anything." He leaned closer. "All you have to do is ask."

Chapter Ten

North

North adjusted the axe at her back—it was a little heavier and bulkier than she would have liked, yet the weapon had worked well enough for training. She smiled to herself, remembering the look on Tik-Tok's face when she'd knocked the sword from his hand, then winced when she thought about how she'd hurled the axe and almost sliced off Dax's malehood.

The sun shone bright in the sky, not a cloud in sight, as she walked down to the dock behind Tik-Tok. He was discussing something with Dax when someone slid up beside her, and she recognized the hum Echo's body emitted.

The siren ran a hand through her short red hair and grinned widely. "Who knew you'd be so good with an axe? When I saw you knock the sword from the captain's hand, I almost shit myself." She laughed, draping an arm around North's shoulders. "No one has ever done that to him."

"My father trained me." North thought about him and how, when she was younger, she'd wanted his axe for her own, even though it had been too heavy. Her father had surprised her one day by having an axe like his made, except in her size. After placing it in her tiny hands, he'd wrapped her fingers around the weapon and shown her how to swing. It hadn't come easy, but she'd practiced every morning with him. Not because he'd told her to, but because she'd wanted to. Tears pricked at her eyes, thinking about him. Stone. Her family as stone. They wouldn't be that way any longer, but the image of her father frozen, holding his axe in mid-air to save her lingered in her mind.

"You won't be with us forever, North. The captain needs you to open the portal and then you can go wherever you want," Echo said softly. Her tone lightened again. "I'm glad you decided to wear my gifts."

"I should have known she got them from you," Respen piped in, wrapping his arm around Echo's waist and tugging her to his side.

"Joria's old clothing was still below deck in her sack, practically screaming to be worn by her." The siren's grin grew wider.

North smiled, finding that she liked Echo more and more with each conversation. When it came to clothing, North had never worn anything close to revealing until Echo had given her these. Growing up, she'd always chosen loose, pretty gowns, usually adorned with pearl buttons. The night of Brielle's celebration, when her mother had accessorized North's gown, had been the only time she'd ever dressed differently.

Perhaps North had worn the dresses that she thought would please everyone else, instead of choosing for herself. The tighter fabric felt more like *her*.

As she'd moved with the axe, the slits in the skirt made it easier for her to shift and lunge. When practicing with the sword, she had still perspired, but there'd been better airflow and the material hadn't clung to her flesh like a wet starfish—much.

"Do you want to come with us? We're going to pick up some goods at the market. I'm famished." Echo stepped from the long pier onto a grassy trail leading in two different directions.

"She's coming with me," Tik-Tok answered, as if he'd been

listening the whole time, which he probably had been.

Dax rolled his eyes and sauntered up beside Echo and Respen. "She'll be fine with us. I'll keep her safe."

Tik-Tok glared at him. "You'll keep her safe as you fuck a female in the middle of the market? She doesn't need to witness that horror."

North *did not* want to watch Dax take a female while she stood by, whistling to herself, waiting for him to orgasm. And judging by the direction Respen's hand was venturing on Echo, they would be doing the same thing.

"I'll go with you," North said to Tik-Tok, surprising herself. She'd already spent days training with him alone on the ship, and even though he aggravated her at times—or all the time—it wasn't uncomfortable being around him.

Echo gave her a wave and tugged Respen with her while Dax walked beside them.

"Ah, you can't deny my company, can you, my star?" Tik-Tok grinned. The smile said she would be in for trouble, but good trouble. Did she *want* trouble?

North flicked her gaze from his to the trees surrounding them. *This is the perfect moment to be a little more charming.*

"So," North purred, toeing at the grass. "Where are we going?"

Tik-Tok furrowed his brow. "Something wrong with your throat? We can find a healer."

North sighed at another failed attempt and shifted closer to him, purposely brushing her arm against his. She palmed her forehead when he didn't seem to notice, or did he not feel it in his gold arm?

He lifted his hand and waved her to follow him. "We can't waste time. I'm meeting a friend and getting a real meal while we're at it."

"What friend?"

"Aren't you the inquisitive one?" He fished out a gold pocket watch from his pants, then looked ahead. "The less you know, the less you'll worry."

Of course… But that only made her worry more.

They walked side-by-side down the narrow, grassy trail, and North studied the trees. The foliage there wasn't as lush as the flora across the Land of Oz—it was duller and more muted in coloring. She passed bushes covered with shriveled yellow berries that didn't appear appetizing. Even the small bugs seemed to avoid them, which probably meant their juice was poisonous.

A rustling stirred, shaking the leaves behind her. She turned around, thinking Echo or one of the others had come back. But as she scanned the trail, the trees, no one was there.

"What is it?" Tik-Tok asked. "You stopped walking."

Taking a deep swallow, she squinted. "I heard something."

Narrowing his eyes, he took a step past her, tilted his head, and inhaled. "I don't smell anything unusual. They have all sorts of birds and tree spirits in these parts—could have been one of them."

North shrugged, knowing she was being foolish. She'd heard plenty of rustling sounds in her life. But she wasn't at home. This was an unfamiliar place with more new creatures and fae than she could imagine.

"So," Tik-Tok drawled once they started walking again. "How is it being born of the greats?"

The question always reminded her that she didn't have any magic, but it made her think of all the good things too. "I have everything I could want in a family. They care fiercely about me, as I do them, even though at times we don't always see eye to eye. But in those instances, I've always had Birch."

"Birch?" Tik-Tok lifted a brow. "A lover?"

"No…" She could feel her cheeks heat, and she wished they would stop doing that around him. "He's one of the guards, mostly mine. A friend."

"Yet you blushed when you said his name." Tik-Tok smirked, not one to pretend he hadn't noticed how red she probably was. "Tell me. Who is this Birch, really?"

"Someone who has always seen me as a sister. My grandparents found him when he was a youngling, then sent him to my parents, who turned him into a guard. I recently made the mistake of confessing how I felt to him, but he was about to propose to someone else, so I—"

"Went and found someone else to fuck," Tik-Tok finished for her, giving an all-too-knowing nod.

North's entire body grew hot. She didn't want to reveal all that had happened in the woods after leaving Birch—how she'd acted like a fool when she should have gone home. And she certainly didn't want him to learn how inexperienced she truly was.

In the distance, a light sound drifted closer to her, tickling her ears. Laughter, music, talking. The pleasant aroma of fresh baked bread hit her nose, and she wanted to tear into the food like an animal. All she'd had before meeting Tik-Tok this morning was a piece of dried fruit.

As they curved around the trail, her stomach softly rumbled at the scent of roasted meat. The town was bustling with fae. A group of centaurs trotted beside blue and yellow buildings, carrying baskets of fruit. Tall faeries laughed and danced in the center, their wings not feathered like Ozma's, but smooth and iridescent. Sheer fabric dangled from their wrists.

Shops of different sizes lined a stone path—tall, curved lanterns stood in front of each building, unlit. Everyone seemed to be going about their daily tasks, shopping, eating, or… Her eyes widened at the side of a building where one female was being ravished by three different males, her head tilted back in pleasure.

"A lot of females travel here specifically for the brothels. The male prostitutes are willing to do anything their patrons wish. *Anything*. For a price of course." Tik-Tok's voice came out silky, then he chuckled and motioned her in the opposite direction. "Come on. We're going somewhere quieter."

He led her behind a yellow and blue striped building with a balcony on its second floor. As they rounded the shop to the back, North's gaze fell on an area with four rectangular tables and benches pushed beneath them. A pale pink awning provided the perfect amount of shade.

She could still hear the sounds coming from the other street, but it was less noisy than she would have expected.

"I always reserve this side when I visit." He pulled out the bench for her with his boot.

North took a seat as the back door cracked open. A voluptuous elf wearing a strapless dress of deep blue feathers stepped out. The front of her hair was pulled up into several buns atop her head, forming a neat row, while the rest hung loosely to her waist.

She cast a bright smile to Tik-Tok. "I saw you through the window." She leaned in to whisper something in his ear and he smirked.

Her eyes turned to North. "You have a new guest? I haven't seen this one with you before."

"She's temporary, Drusile."

North frowned. *Temporary?*

"Do you want your usual? Glazed boar and roasted potatoes?" Drusile asked.

"We'll both have a plate and also two bowls of the vegetable soup."

"Maybe I'll bring dessert to your ship later?" She winked and swayed her hips as she walked back into the building.

North knew exactly what kind of dessert she was talking about, and she didn't want to be around for any of that. She avoided looking at Tik-Tok, not wanting to see what expression he'd given to the elf.

"I'm going to step away for a bit," Tik-Tok finally said.

North jerked her head up. He must have not been able to wait for *dessert*. "You're leaving me here alone?"

"I'll be close." He pointed to a garden surrounded by

decorative trees, near enough so he could see her but still far enough away where he wouldn't be able to catch her if she wanted to run. "Will you be all right?"

"I'll be fine." She pointed to the weapon at her back. "I have my axe, remember?"

He leaned forward, his face close to hers, never understanding personal space, but her heart thumped at his words. "Don't worry. I won't have dessert with Drusile, but my door will be open if you feel like something sweet later tonight."

North blinked, and he chuckled.

"I hate you."

"I love hearing those words from you." His face grew serious. "Order anything else you'd like while I take care of this."

As Tik-Tok sauntered toward the garden, Drusile brought out two bowls of soup and set them down on the table. "I always welcome new guests to join for dessert as well." She winked at her, and North choked on her own spit as the elf grinned before heading back inside.

North smacked her chest to clear her throat, and her coughing ceased. She focused on her steaming soup, not wanting to hear any more about dessert, and brought a spoonful to her lips.

"Hot!" North whisper-shouted and dropped her spoon. "Gods!" She should have blown on the liquid or tested it out first. Fanning her mouth, she looked around the table for water, *anything* to cool her mouth. Nothing.

Tik-Tok was already talking to a male with curving dark horns protruding from the sides of his head. He was too far away for her to see his other features.

Just as she was about to push up from the table and go inside to get something cool to drink, footsteps crunched from behind her. North whirled around and reached for her axe, when her gaze landed on matted copper hair. "Oh, it's you, Rizmaela."

The dwarf plopped down beside her on the bench, her expression moody as always.

"I owe your father something," Rizmaela grunted.

"My father?" North's brows drew together.

"I owe him this." The dwarf's hand moved so fast that North didn't have time to blink. Sharp pain sliced at her chest. "For murdering my husband and exchanging his head for payment."

The words sounded far away as blood bubbled up her throat, suffocating her. North peered down at the crimson blooming from her chest where a dagger jutted out. The voice inside her head screamed to grab her axe, defend herself, but everything was growing fuzzy.

Then Rizmaela ripped the blade out. An agonized gurgle escaped North's mouth, and her gaze met Tik-Tok's as he rushed toward her.

The world spun.

And she found herself falling, falling, falling.

CHAPTER ELEVEN

TIK-TOK

Tik-Tok's body moved without thought. His steps were so hard and so fast that he felt the impact of each footfall vibrate through his legs. But his mind—that was suspended. Floating. Frozen.

Before he even finished properly greeting his contact, Rizmaela brandished a dagger. Shoved it into North's chest. Despite the distance between them, North's muted gasp echoed through his head. A low, gurgling sound. Tik-Tok's answering roar ripped from his center and burned up his throat, sending his contact fleeing into a dark alley with the spelled object they needed to avoid Salt.

No, no, no.

Not North. He *needed* her. She didn't deserve such a violent death. And by his first mate? He had vowed she would come to no harm. *Vowed it.* And now that oath was broken.

His hands slammed down on either side of the dwarf's head. One twist, one resounding *crack*, and Rizmaela's dead body slammed to the pebbled ground before she could utter a single word in her defense.

There were no excuses for this.

One of North's hands gripped the table's edge, the other pressed to the gushing wound in her chest. Her eyes fluttered shut and her body swayed. Tik-Tok caught her as she slumped backward, nearly falling from the bench.

"North," he bellowed into her pale face. "You do not get to die. Wake up."

Blood bubbled in the corner of her mouth as her chest heaved. Each inhale was a rasp. Every following exhale, a snap.

"Fuck!" He stood, hoisting her up and cradling her small frame to his chest. *Respen.* They needed Respen—but the elf was on the other side of the market. He could take her to a healer faster than anyone else. Tik-Tok didn't even know where to fucking find one. "I need a healer!" he yelled in desperation.

Drusile burst out the door and gasped, her eyes widening. "What happened?"

"She needs a healer," he barked. His insides twisted and tightened. Panic clawed at his chest in a frantic bid to escape. "*Now!*"

Drusile darted back inside and her shouts seemed far away. He didn't know what the hell to do. Should he wait for a healer? Should he race through the streets until he found one? There wasn't time.

No time!

With each passing second, North grew paler and paler. He refused to look at her chest. Couldn't bear to see it. To watch the life seep out of her, knowing there was nothing he could do to stop it. If he turned her to stone to stop the bleeding, it could make the wound worse. Perhaps he should risk it…

"North," he demanded. "North, please."

"Out here," Drusile called, racing toward him with Respen beside her. He didn't know how she'd found him so quickly—didn't care.

"Move!" An elderly woodland fae shoved between them with a large black, leather bag. Long pale scars and deep pox marks marred his brown flesh, shimmering green wings hung limp on his back, and there was a large depression on the side of his bald head. "Lay her on the table."

Respen knocked the bowls of soup out of the way for him, but Tik-Tok simply held North closer. "Captain," his crewmate urged.

"I want another healer," he growled. If the woodland fae hadn't been able to heal himself, how could the male hope to heal North? No. He needed someone better. *The best.*

"There's no time for this," the fae snapped. "Put her down and step away, or let her die."

The next moment felt like ten as he ran through his options. But there were none. North was dying, her breaths slowing, so he set her on the table. He brushed her silver hair away from her face and didn't budge from his spot. His knees hit the cobblestone beside the table so he was at her level.

"Don't you dare die," he whispered. "I don't give you permission to leave."

The woodland fae ripped the fabric of North's dress to expose the wound and chanted words in another language. His eyes were pressed shut, thin lips barely moving, veins protruding on his forehead. A strong odor—one of death and decay—filled the air, followed by the intense tang of herbs.

But Tik-Tok still didn't look. He didn't listen to Respen begging him to move away so the healer could work. Didn't pay any heed to Drusile's shocked sobs. Instead, he gripped North's freezing hand and continued to whisper that she wasn't allowed to die. Not after he'd waited so many years to find her.

By the time the healer was finished, the moon was rising and a crowd had gathered. The old fae stumbled away from North, wiping the sweat from the back of his neck. "I'm unsure if it will be enough," he wheezed.

"It had better be," Tik-Tok growled.

Respen leaned into the healer's side, pressing a few gold coins into his palm. "Thank you."

"She will need to stay hydrated," he said while Tik-Tok

83

remained kneeling at North's side. He dug through his bag and handed Respen a vial of brown liquid. "If she develops a fever, give her this. The magic I used was strong, but it will still be another day before she's safe from death's clutches. Take her somewhere warm and dry. No traveling via magic."

"Respen," Tik-Tok said in a hoarse voice. "Secure us a room at the Willow Inn."

"Aye, Captain." He hesitated a moment before stepping closer. "What shall I tell the crew?"

Tik-Tok stood, his knees aching from the hard cobblestones. "The truth. Rizmaela betrayed me, paid with her life, and I will return to the ship once North has healed. You're my new first mate." He lifted a tired gaze to Respen. The elf should've been his first mate from the start, especially since he knew the reason Tik-Tok wanted the portal open so badly. But he'd insisted he wasn't ready before. They both knew he was now. "Keep them calm and don't let any of them run off. While I stay with North, you need to find out if Rizmaela was working alone or if there are more traitors on board."

Respen took a deep breath and nodded. "Leave everything to me." Then he was gone.

Tik-Tok carefully eased an arm beneath North's knees and shoulders. She moaned at being jostled as he lifted her, and he offered a gentle *shh*. Finally, with North tucked securely against him, he made his way toward the only decent inn in town.

Respen secured the largest room at the Willow Inn before returning to the ship. Tik-Tok knew Respen could handle the crew. Otherwise, he wouldn't have promoted him. If anyone from his ship started a fight in a tavern or fell overboard after overindulging, that was on them.

North, on the other hand, hadn't done anything to Rizmaela. So why? What caused his first mate to shove a dagger in her chest? And would someone else on the ship try to finish the job? Tik-Tok's mind kept circling back to that thought. Respen would find out—but what if...? Tik-Tok had led a mutiny against Captain Salt. Was this a cruel twist of fate? To have his crew turn on him? But why *now* when he was so close to opening the portal?

Tik-Tok tucked the wool blanket around North again despite the fact she hadn't moved since he'd put her down. She would need a clean dress before they left—one that hadn't been torn open, nearly exposing her breasts. A square, white bandage dipped in healing herbs covered the wound, but once it was removed, her chest would be fully on display.

One day.

The healer said the danger would pass by then. For such a wound, it sounded too good to be true. But North's breathing was now steady and she no longer bled. He'd been too hasty judging the healer by his appearance.

Setting the vial on the small table beside the bed, Tik-Tok eased down to the floor with a grunt. He rested against the bedframe, his head leaning back on the edge of the mattress. The ache in his knees had spread through his body, throbbing most painfully where his golden arm met his shoulder.

He plucked off his blood-stained gloves and tossed them into a corner. His metal fingers clicked against his palm as he made a fist. The pain of losing his arm had left him incapacitated for weeks. In fact, he'd almost died of infection—something the sea witch never bothered to mention being a concern. Only after a skilled healer removed the remaining few inches of his arm, taking it right up to the shoulder, had he healed enough to commission the enchanted arm.

"You can't die," he murmured to himself.

He'd done too much for this portal to fail now. But ... not only that. He genuinely wanted North to be well. To live and sass him another day. Maybe he would even cut her some slack. *Or not.* It was amusing getting a rise out of her. More amusing than usual.

85

With a sigh, he shifted to touch her forehead, ensuring the fever was still at bay, and settled back to stare at the ceiling. His thoughts continued to bounce frantically between North's health, Rizmaela's betrayal, and what was happening on *The Temptress*. Rizmaela's actions were bound to affect morale, if nothing else. It should be the least of his worries. It *was*. But his crew was his family...

His eyes slid shut and he forced them open. Again and again. Until the worries had drained him too much to fight the pull of sleep.

It wasn't clear how long he'd slept before jerking awake. He spun and reached out for North, only to find her staring at him. His hand froze before making contact with her forehead. "North?"

She shifted in an attempt to push up on her elbows, but Tik-Tok placed his palm on her forehead, holding her down. A small huff left her mouth, followed quickly by a groan. "What happened?"

Tik-Tok removed his hand, satisfied that her skin didn't feel overheated, and sat back on his haunches. "You don't remember?"

"I..." North scowled and gingerly poked at the bandage on her chest. "Rizmaela stabbed me."

Tik-Tok nodded. "How do you feel now? Should I call the healer?"

"I feel stiff," she said, moving slightly as if testing herself. "My chest aches like I was punched. Hard."

"Punched is better than stabbed," he said with a smirk.

She glared at him. "Did you know?"

"Know what?"

"That my father killed her husband." Her hands gripped the wool blanket. "That's why she wanted me dead."

Tik-Tok's eye twitched but fought to keep the surprise from his face. Rizmaela only knew that North was Tin's daughter because he'd mentioned it—but the dwarf had known that they needed her. Rizmaela had set her selfish revenge ahead of the portal—a portal that would earn everyone on his crew a hefty payday. Rage filled him, churning and thickening in his veins. He wished he hadn't killed Rizmaela already so he could take his time. Make it hurt. Tin murdered her husband—so fucking what? That wasn't North's fault.

"I didn't know," he said, meeting her eyes. "Even if I had, your father's deeds aren't yours. You're innocent and her vendetta was with him—not you."

North studied him for a moment before nodding. "Where is she now?"

"Dead." His lips curled into a snarl, before he forced himself to calm down. There was no changing what had happened. He didn't want to frighten North with his anger. He peered down at his hands and sighed. "I owe you an apology. You nearly died when I promised you would be safe with me and my crew."

"You also said there was no telling what could happen because you're a good-for-nothing pirate," she grumbled.

A short laugh escaped him. "I'm fairly certain you're twisting my words."

"I'm fairly certain my words are *true*." She looked around the room, licking her cracked lips. "Is there any water?"

Tik-Tok was on his feet in an instant, pouring water from a ceramic pitcher into a glass. Wordlessly, he lowered himself on the edge of the bed and helped her sit up, letting her lean on him for support as she drank. When she finished, he refilled her glass and she drank again.

"Do you need anything else?" He settled her back onto the pillow and tugged the blanket into place, both to hide her mostly-bare chest and keep her warm. "Are you hungry? I'll find whatever you'd like."

"I'm tired," she whispered. "Have you been here with me this whole time?"

He shrugged. "It hasn't been *that* long. Less than a day."

"You must really want me to open that portal," she said with a roll of her eyes. "Where does it lead anyway?"

"I don't know exactly, but I know I need to go. It's the only thing I want." Tik-Tok sat on the floor again, resting his elbows on his knees. Everything he'd done was for the portal. His entire life. He *needed* it open so he could claim his revenge. "But, if you think that's the only reason that I've taken care of you, then you're wrong."

"Then why?" North turned her head, meeting his red eyes with her brown ones. He'd imagined that gaze in a thousand different faces. Obsessed over what silver-haired female would possess them, but somehow, he'd never imagined North.

Tik-Tok ground his teeth. Did he want to tell her? To open up about his own pain? It was dangerous to let this female in when she so clearly wanted to escape him, but he couldn't stop the words from leaving his mouth.

"I told you I cut it off myself," he said in a deeper-than-normal voice as he held up his gold arm. "But what I didn't tell you was I tied a thin iron wire around my upper arm and tightened it with a block of wood. It took hours, and I lost consciousness twice."

North gasped, her hand cupping her mouth. "Why would you do that?"

He gave her a wolfish grin. "I'm a masochist. Couldn't you tell?"

"Tik-Tok," she said, exasperated.

"Celyna—the sea witch—told me I needed to do it if I wanted the portal. Every year she has a vision of what will bring me closer to opening it, and a few decades ago, it was to remove my arm."

Her scowl deepened. "And this year it was to steal me away?"

"A task I gladly accepted—I'd rather keep the rest of my limbs." He continued opening and closing his fist. *Click click click.* "We're getting off track, my star. You wanted to know why I looked after you?" He paused, meeting her gaze. "When I was bleeding profusely, when my arm was infected, when the wound was finally healing but not yet well enough to replace, no one helped. A healer, yes, but only enough to keep me alive. My crew was new at the time and things were … uncertain."

"You—"

"Shh," he admonished lightly. "I don't want whatever pity you're about to give. I'm only telling you this so you know that I understand. I know what it's like to suffer when you have no one you love to comfort or care for you. Besides, there's powerful magic built into the arm, so it worked out rather well in the end despite the fortune I had to give the Tinker Witch who made it."

"Well, then." North's eyes took on a slightly softer edge. "Thank you. For saving my life."

"You're welcome," he said with a shrug.

"Even though I wouldn't have been stabbed at all if it weren't for you." She cleared her throat, taking on a forced arrogance.

"Cheeky," he huffed.

North shifted slightly and he could feel her eyes on his arm. "Can you feel with it?"

"Of course." He ran his fingertips over the woolen blanket, feeling the roughness of the thick fabric. "It's the same as a real arm, only flashier."

"And magical," North added and her stomach growled. "I think I'll take you up on the food now. Something hot. And it had better not taste like what you've been giving me on your ship."

Tik-Tok chuckled softly and rose to his feet. "Anything else, my lady?"

"Clothes." She tugged the blanket higher. "Nice ones. And if you don't get me the axe you promised, I refuse to step foot back on that awful ship."

"Now, now." He took her chin gently and turned her to look at him. "Say what you want about me, but leave my ship out of it."

"Food," she demanded, shoving his hand away with what

might have been a smile.

Tik-Tok bit his lip to keep himself from laughing and left the room to find the innkeeper. Such spunk, even now. Idly, he wondered how far she would push her demands—how far he would let her—and it spurred something in his chest. Such a difficult little star.

His difficult, challenging, spirited little star.

Chapter Twelve

North

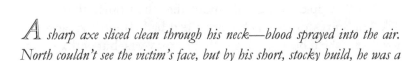

A sharp axe sliced clean through his neck—blood sprayed into the air. North couldn't see the victim's face, but by his short, stocky build, he was a dwarf.

An ear-shattering scream screeched from behind her, and North whirled around, finding Rizmaela watching in anguish, tears flooding her eyes.

North peered down at her hands, where her fingers tightly gripped the axe, her skin coated in bright crimson.

North's eyes flew open and she jerked forward.

"Are you trying to reinjure yourself?" a deep voice rumbled from beside the bed, his hands holding her by the shoulders.

Tik-Tok.

Taking a deep swallow, she slowly leaned against the headboard as he took his palms from her skin.

Rizmaela was dead. The dwarf shouldn't have tried to murder her for something she hadn't done. But North's father had taken someone important from her in the past...

Tin had never hidden his past from North, not once. She knew what he'd done when he was cursed, when his heart was stone. About kills he'd done for money, and how he'd brought

91

her mother to Oz and had planned to take her to Langwidere so the obsessive female could wear her head. North had been horrified for days, but it hadn't made her love him any less. It only proved how far he'd come since then.

But even though she understood his past, it didn't mean the families he'd destroyed could forgive him.

"What are you thinking about?" Tik-Tok knelt so he was eye-to-eye with her, his scarlet irises shining brightly, reflecting the sun's rays that spilled in through the window.

North should have been fearful of that bloody shade, but she only wanted to inch closer, and see the flecks of silver in them.

Shaking off the thought, she flicked her gaze away and lied. "Birch."

"Ah"—Tik-Tok stood and folded his arms—"you still love him."

North would rather talk about that than other things, like Tik-Tok's eyes or the nightmare she'd had about Rizmaela. As for Birch, she'd been in love with him for years, but perhaps that love was meant to fade more easily because it was unrequited, while their friendship was like iron. Over the past few days, she hadn't thought of him or her family much, not while training with Tik-Tok before collapsing into her bed from exhaustion after the long sessions.

"As family." She sighed, pressing a hand to her chest where it still ached from the wound. Her fingers traced the raised scar, finding it smoother than she would have expected.

Tik-Tok nodded, his expression unreadable. "We should get back to the ship. Either I can carry you, or I can retrieve Respen from the shop across the street. He's picking up a few extra things before we leave."

"I can walk."

"You're not walking." Tik-Tok plucked up a long piece of fabric from the back of a wooden chair. He held it up with a smirk, letting the fabric unravel—a dress—hideous. "Respen got this for you. An improvement from your latest choices, don't you think?"

North scanned the bright orange clothing, the different sized beads and jewels covering its entirety, the high-collared neckline. "It's, um…" She chuckled, and the movement made her scar throb.

"I can help you change into it if you want," he said in a low, teasing voice.

"I'll be fine."

"No clever comeback?" Tik-Tok grinned as he handed her the dress. "Where's my star hiding?"

"Go get Respen. I'm not going to let you carry me." She rolled her eyes.

He nodded, leaving the room and shutting the door behind him. As she stood from the bed, her body felt like it hadn't been used in months. She twisted to the side, then stretched and shook out her arms and legs. An unpleasant smell wafted from her body—blood, sweat, and grime.

The dress skimmed the floor after she threw it on, and the material seemed to scratch away a layer of her skin, but it would do for the time being. The door squeaked open, drawing her gaze to Tik-Tok. She hadn't noticed before, but, for the first time, his hair didn't appear as silky as usual and purple circles underlined his eyes.

"Can't you knock?" North cocked her head.

"I *can*, actually."

"That's unproven." Respen pushed past Tik-Tok and entered the room.

"How are the others?" North asked, wishing she could see Echo's face.

"They've been watching the ship." Tik-Tok stepped beside her while Respen stood in front of them.

Respen scanned her over. "Are you going to be all right if I use my magic now?"

She remembered the last time Respen had used his power on her, and how she'd felt as if she'd been riding backward on a stag, consumed with nausea. How there had been nothing beneath her feet, her body filled with the rush of falling. North grasped Tik-Tok's hand without thinking, perhaps because she wanted something to ground her for the short journey.

Tik-Tok peered down at their joined hands and arched a brow. She started to pull her hand away, but he gripped it firmly. Her body relaxed into his touch.

"Close your eyes," Respen said. "It will be easier that way."

As soon as she closed her lids, Respen's hand curled around her shoulder. Not a second passed before the spinning started, and she felt like she was plunging into the darkest pits of Oz. She clenched Tik-Tok's hand so tightly that she feared she would break every single bone in it. And then the world stilled, but her body continued to sway like a flower in the wind.

"You can open your eyes now," Tik-Tok whispered.

"I know. Give me a moment so I don't hurl on your pristine boots." Then she peeled one lid open, followed by the second, after Respen's hand left her shoulder. Her chest heaved as she focused on the deck of the ship. "I want a bath."

"Dax, heat the water!" Tik-Tok shouted toward the elf who was cutting rope across the deck. He turned back to North. "But you're not going down there alone."

North furrowed her brow. "I was alone before."

"You weren't recovering from a stab wound last time."

"I'll go with her," Echo said, sliding up beside her. "And I'll also get her out of this hideous dress. Who the fuck picked this out?"

"I did." Respen tilted his head. "There's nothing wrong with it."

"You have no taste."

"My tongue would say differently."

"No one wants to hear about your tongue," Tik-Tok spat, his hand jerking in hers.

North realized she was still holding onto him and dropped his hand as though she'd been scalded.

94

Echo didn't miss the movement, and she blinked several times before motioning North to follow her. "Let's go."

North didn't so much as glance at Tik-Tok, her cheeks still hot, as she caught up with the siren.

"How are you feeling?" Echo asked. "I was going to come and visit you, but I needed to help Respen and Dax question the crew about Riz. If I had known that dwarf bitch was planning to kill you, I would have sung her a song to rip out her organs."

North's eyes widened, both terrified and impressed at the things Echo could do if she willed it.

The hatch leading into the bowels of the ship was already open and Echo led her down the steps. Dax hovered over the water, his fingers swirling within it. Steam wafted from both metal tubs and he pulled his hand out.

"Water was already in each, so I heated them both. Take your pick." Dax peered up at North, his brow furrowed. "I wish I had taken you to the market, damn it."

"One good thing came out of this," Echo said. "We found out Riz was a traitor sooner rather than later."

Rizmaela could have tried to kill North in her own room, where she wouldn't have had a weapon, where no one would have found her in time. North shook away the image of her lying in bed, drenched in blood with a blade sticking out of her chest.

"Tell me if it's not hot enough." Dax headed up the steps then shut the hatch.

"Let's not waste the heat since he warmed them both." Echo peeled off her clothing and stepped into a tub. "I already brought a dress down here for you. Figured you would want a bath when you returned."

North glanced at the maroon and deep purple fabric folded on the counter beside a stack of towels. Shimmying out of the orange monstrosity, trying not to feel shy about her smaller breasts and narrower hips, she hurried into the warm water. North settled into the tub with a sigh, the liquid relaxing her flesh and aching muscles.

"I've never seen the captain so rattled." Echo tapped the side of the tub with her fingers.

"The portal's important to him." North thought about how Tik-Tok had cut off his own arm for it. She hadn't asked why he wanted the portal open so desperately, but there had to be a good reason if he'd done something so drastic.

"It is to all of us," Echo said as if reading North's thoughts.

"Why?"

"I can't speak on the captain's motive, as it's personal—but for the crew, it's the fortune he promised. It will set all of us up for ten lifetimes."

North nodded, sinking down into the water. She wondered where the portal would lead and what would be on the other side of it. Would the world be like theirs? Would the inhabitants be welcoming, or would it be like the human world that thought no others existed?

She reached for a bar of soap and scrubbed away the dried blood, the sweat, the healing herbs, the day, the feeling of Tik-Tok's hand in hers, Rizmaela's expression when she'd pierced North's chest. She traced the pink scar between her breasts, and relief at being alive washed over her.

Once the water cooled, North got dressed and left Echo resting in the tub. The siren's serene expression made it seem as if she were absorbing energy from the liquid while her hands hovered over her stomach. North shut the door to the bathing chamber softly so she wouldn't disturb her and searched the deck for Tik-Tok. He was nowhere in sight. Two of the brownies were separating buckets of dried fruit and placing them in crates. She gave them a small wave as she passed and climbed down the ladder to her room.

Her body sank onto the mattress and sudden tears surprised her when they rained down her cheeks. So much had happened in such a short amount of time.

North stayed in her room for the rest of the day. She'd been too exhausted, both physically and emotionally, to join the others. Respen had come down to bring her food, then Echo had dropped off a bottle of spirits.

"I brought you a gift to help you unwind." Echo smiled. *"Don't drink too much, though. A little goes a long way."*

She hadn't seen Tik-Tok since the morning, and something bothered her about that. But why should she care? If he hadn't taken her from Brielle's celebration, then she would've been home now, and ... feeling lost. She would have been in the same place, struggling with having no magic. North still didn't have any now, but there was a speck of hope that *maybe* she could.

Another light ache throbbed from her chest. North took a deep swallow as Rizmaela's angry face flashed before her.

What would Tin have done if the roles were reversed? He would have decapitated the fae who dared hurt her mother, not taken an innocent life. If Rizmaela had come after Tin instead, North would have defended him with her axe. She would always protect her family.

Yet, still... The images, the thoughts, swarmed through her, and she needed to clear her head. Get out of this room. Do something... Throwing pretend axes wouldn't help her fall asleep tonight.

North straightened her dress, grabbed the bottle of spirits, and headed up the ladder to the deck. Outdoors, it was only North, the sea, and Kaliko keeping watch up in his spot behind a sail. The salty air calmed her, but it didn't take away everything she felt.

North lifted the spirits to her mouth and took a long swig, allowing the liquid to glide down her throat. She walked to the rail and leaned over, staring down at the sea, the waves. The night sky reflected off the water, making the liquid glisten. She fisted her free hand and concentrated, tapping into her true name. *North Talina Selain.* Quiet lingered. Silence stayed. Not a stir from

97

any hidden magic inside her. Again, North lifted the bottle to her lips, drinking the sweet liquid. More and more. She drank until she felt as if she were floating, as if her mind thrashed like a wave.

North wasn't all right. The alcohol intensified her turbulent thoughts instead of numbing them. Where was Tik-Tok? Why hadn't he thrown open her door without knocking at least once?

She stumbled her way to the back of the ship, curious to see what his room looked like. Grasping the curved handle leading to the captain's quarters, she jiggled it and found it locked.

The door jerked open to a scowling Tik-Tok. "What do you want?" His gaze settled on her and his lips parted in surprise. "North? What are you doing here?"

Her gaze traveled from his face to his bare chest. His skin was golden, his shoulders broad, his abs ripped, and she couldn't stop staring. The only clothing he wore were his pants—even his feet were bootless.

"I want to see your room," she slurred.

Tik-Tok smirked as he sniffed the air. "Who gave you spirits?"

"It was only a single bottle."

"You drank the whole fucking thing?" He drew her inside and shut the door. "I can't have you walking around the ship drunk."

She peered around the room, taking in the cabinets, the desk cluttered with maps, and a large brass bathing tub. And, of course, his bed. White gauzy curtains hung from the four large posts. Silken black and red sheets covered the mattress, which led to a headboard etched with swirled designs. Setting the empty bottle on his desk, she walked to the back corner of the room. North crawled onto the bed before sinking into the mattress, finding it softer than anything she'd ever felt.

Tik-Tok studied her as she patted the spot beside her, remembering what it had felt like when she'd kissed him.

He gave her a sly grin and sat down on the mattress next to her. The room was growing blurry, but he was clear as day. His lips were the perfect shape, and she recalled how nice they'd felt against her own.

"Why didn't you come see me earlier?" She adjusted a pillow behind her back.

"You needed rest and I needed to think."

"I wanted you to come see me."

"Mm. And why is that?" The edges of his lips tilted up.

"I don't know." She lifted her hand and swept a lock of his silky black hair behind his ear. Then she inched closer, her mouth so very near to his.

"I'm not going to kiss you, North."

"Why not?" She jerked back. It was like Birch all over again, the rejection. It made her want to sink farther into the bed, completely disappear.

"You drank a whole bottle of spirits, for one thing." He leaned in, his hand resting on her shoulder. "For another, you were just stabbed."

She couldn't stop the tears from flowing again as she folded herself around his warm body, wrapping an arm around his waist. "What if I could have talked to her? Made her understand that my father was cursed, that he's different now, that so many others had been damaged back then too."

"It wouldn't have mattered," Tik-Tok murmured, tugging her closer. He trailed a finger lightly down her cheek. "Rizmaela made her way to the top by being spiteful. I never cared about other's pasts as long as they shared my goal and were loyal to me. Anyone who's disloyal will die by my hand, and she knew as much. She should've ignored the fact that you are Tin's daughter."

"I want to see him." North cried into his chest, and he held her even tighter. "And my mother."

"I'm sorry." He sighed. "I promise I'll bring you home as soon as possible after the portal is open."

"Why do you want it open so badly?"

Tik-Tok hesitated. "Once it's open, you may understand."

A low growl escaped her throat but she was too exhausted to fight back. She settled on his chest and closed her eyes.

Tik-Tok ran his hand through her hair, tenderly. "After this is over, you won't have to see me again, if that's what you wish."

But a part of her didn't wish that at all.

CHAPTER THIRTEEN

TIK-TOK

Tik-Tok slid himself out from beneath North's sleeping form in the middle of the night. The warmth from her head on his shoulder remained, and the feel of her silky hair made him wish that he could twine her locks through his fingers forever. He gazed down at her, rubbing at the strange new ache in his chest. What was happening? North was his key to the portal—*maybe* a decent fuck if things went that way—but she wasn't someone to get emotionally attached to. She was there for a purpose—a captive who was trying to seduce her way into escaping. If she hadn't been so completely drunk when she'd shown up at his door, Tik-Tok would've assumed it was all part of her grand plan.

Quietly, he lifted a white tunic from where it draped over a chair, and snuck from the room. The salty, cool air bit against his skin as he padded over to the helm. The goblin, Cyrx, stood at the wheel, keeping them on track. Large bottom teeth protruded from his mouth, pressing over his top lip. His deep scars seemed to stand out more prominently against his orange-tinged skin, and his bulging muscles pressed against the tight sleeves of his black shirt.

"Evenin', Captain," Cyrx said in a guttural voice.

Tik-Tok nodded a greeting while tapping his middle finger against his golden palm. *Click, click, click.* "We need to detour to Isa Poso."

Cyrx's eyes widened. "Celyna? Already? Did something happen?"

"No." Just a certain female wedging herself between him and his plan. He didn't hate it as much as he should. Hopefully after fucking Celyna in exchange for a vision, he would be able to think a little more clearly about North. "I couldn't get the shield to keep Salt from detecting us when we docked, so wandering aimlessly through his territory is too much of a risk."

"In that case..." Cyrx turned the wheel, steering them west toward the sea witch.

The crew didn't want or need to be in the middle of Tik-Tok's feud with the fae who had saved him from a life of pain— the fae he'd betrayed. Salt was seeking revenge against his former-first-mate-turned-traitor, just as Tik-Tok was seeking revenge for his past. He understood it, but if Salt caught up with *The Temptress*, there was no telling what would happen. Only that it wouldn't be pleasant.

The silver-capped waves slapped against the hull and a spray of water rained down across the deck. Cyrx wiped the droplets from his face. "You think the witch will give you answers?"

The last time he'd tried to visit Celyna before their yearly appointment, she'd hissed in his face before disappearing into the sea. Tik-Tok scowled at the memory. This time, he wouldn't give her the chance to run off. If she could give him even the smallest of clues, this could all be over soon. All he needed was a clue—something to help him unlock North's power or tell him where, exactly, the portal was. The portal would open, revenge would be had, and North could return home. Then, he could finally rest.

"I have to try," Tik-Tok said, shrugging.

He didn't wait for the goblin to give his opinion on the

matter before striding back to his quarters and shutting the door with a soft thud. North was exactly as he'd left her—mouth open, small snores escaping, her hair spread over his pillow. Her sweet vanilla scent would linger once she left his bed. His heart sped at the thought. *Damn.* What was wrong with him?

Rubbing a hand over his face, he eased onto the mattress and turned on his side to face her. His gold fingers traced the air over the planes of North's face as she slept, never touching, only *almost.* When his middle finger grazed the sweep of her lower lip, she snapped her mouth shut. He whipped his hand back as her eyes fluttered open.

"Tik-Tok?" she mumbled.

One side of his mouth lifted in a grin. "Were you expecting someone else?"

"What are you doing here?" She rubbed a fist against her lids.

"In my own bed?" He lifted a brow. "I *was* sleeping until you decided to join me."

North sat up quickly, eyes darting around the room. "I'm in *your* room?" she asked, despite the obvious answer. She shifted to her knees and peered down at herself. "Why did you bring me in here?"

Tik-Tok's answering laugh was both warm and mocking. "That's rather presumptuous. You came here, *drunk*, because you wanted to know what my quarters looked like. So—" He rolled to his back and motioned to the room behind him. "Are you satisfied? Does it look as you thought it would?"

"Oh." She paused, squinting as if in deep thought. "*Oh.* Echo gave me a bottle of spirits."

Tik-Tok smirked. "And you'll soon regret drinking the entire thing."

"Fairly certain I already do." She rubbed at her temples. "I should probably get back to my room."

"Stay," Tik-Tok said, surprising himself. "You're already here and, besides, I have a gift."

"A gift?" Her brows lifted as she studied him.

103

He rose and crossed to one of the cabinets lining the wall of his quarters. The axe he'd acquired while she was bathing, before they'd departed Merryland, was from the finest bladesmith he knew. It would be easier for her to grip the slim handle, and the metal was nearly weightless. Carrying it back to the bed, he wondered if he should've skipped having the butt of the axe engraved with a star.

"Here." He tossed it onto the bed where he'd lain moments ago. It landed, sinking slightly into the thick blanket. "You can't say I don't keep my word."

She lifted the axe without looking at him, turning the weapon over, examining every inch, her delicate fingers slowly running up its length. Tik-Tok felt her careful scrutiny all the way down to his groin. Felt the imaginary touch of her doing the same thing to him—caressing, admiring. *Fuck.* If she showed his throbbing cock even a fraction of the attention she showed the new weapon, he would burst all over her pretty face.

"It's perfect," she whispered after what felt like an entire voyage across the sea.

Tik-Tok released a small, relieved breath, and joined her on the bed. He sprawled across his half of the mattress and tucked his hands behind his head. "I know."

"It has a star…"

"I know," he said again, closing his eyes. "Now, go back to sleep."

He kept his breathing shallow as he waited for her to decide whether or not to listen. She could return to her room and he wouldn't stop her, but he hoped she didn't. He wanted her to stay. Even after the portal was open, she could choose to remain beside him. The irrational thought pierced him. *No.* She was going home. She missed her family—his enemies. She'd said as much.

Finally, North shifted, leaning sideways over his abdomen. *And she would leave now too.* Of course, she would. Why wouldn't she? But a soft thunk hit the floor instead. Tik-Tok's eyes cracked to find her face hovering over his chest. "What are you doing?" he asked.

"Putting the axe on the floor so we don't injure ourselves." She struggled to balance over him without touching—there was only an inch of space between his hip and the edge of the bed for her to hold herself up. After a moment of trying to shove herself back to her side of the mattress, she gave up and placed a hand on his lower stomach, below his navel. He wished he'd left his shirt off.

Tik-Tok's gold hand immediately landed on top of hers, holding it there. "Careful, my star."

She rolled her eyes and scrambled gracelessly away. When her head hit the pillow, Tik-Tok glared sideways at her, taking in the sight of her in his bed and enjoying how perfect it looked. He would have her there every night if he could.

North yanked at the covers, pulling the material from under his weight, and shimmied beneath them. "Don't get any ideas."

Tik-Tok chuckled. "I should be the one saying that, don't you think?"

"Go to sleep," she said with a tired groan.

"Land!"

Kaliko's call radiated through the walls inside Tik-Tok's quarters—which did, indeed, still smell like North despite her having left hours ago. She had tried to sneak away, but it was impossible not to feel her climb over him. He had kept his eyes closed, however, letting her believe it was all done in stealth.

Grabbing his jacket, he stalked onto the deck. Respen and Dax stood near the helm, working in tandem to bring *The Temptress* as close to Isa Poso as possible, while North used her new axe to spar against Echo and the siren's narrow blade. He paused only for a moment to watch her move effortlessly in a light pink skirt and a brown button-up bodice that showed her stomach. The scar on her chest was hidden beneath the bodice, and the silky skirt was knotted, bringing the fabric up above her knees. Her braided hair whipped over her shoulder as she spun to block one of Echo's attacks.

"The boat's ready for you," Cyrx informed him. When had the goblin come up beside him?

Tik-Tok turned his back on North to find the brownies tying down the black sails. He'd been watching the sparring match longer than he realized. "I won't be long," he said loud enough for Respen to hear, and went straight for the rowboat.

"Wait!" North called. She ran up to him as he stepped into the boat, chest heaving, beads of perspiration clinging to her smooth skin. "Where are you going?"

His red eyes rose to meet her gaze. The look of longing on her face cut straight through him, but he brushed away the spark of pain. Who was she to question him and his methods? She was only there because he'd *forced* her to be. What did it matter if he pleasured Celyna?

It didn't. And North wasn't accusing him of wrongdoing. That was him—putting words in her mouth. Why? Did he feel guilty about what he was going to do?

Absolutely not.

"To fuck the sea witch," he said in a low voice.

The curious spark drained from North's eyes, her cheeks burning bright red.

"Stay put and listen to Respen," he added, then nodded at the brownies waiting to lower him down to the sea.

Once the rowboat hit the silver waves, he untied the ropes and pushed his rising anger into each stroke of the oars. He wasn't doing anything wrong. He and Celyna had their arrangement long before North even existed. A mutually beneficial agreement that in no way involved the female that he'd stolen away to open his portal. He refused to give in to the urge to look back to see if she was still watching. An ache ran along his jaw from how hard he clenched it.

106

After dragging the boat to shore, Tik-Tok took a steadying breath and shoved all thoughts of the silver-haired female from his mind before marching up to the glass house.

Celyna was sprawled on her back in the sand outside the door, naked, eyes closed. The sun glistened along the planes of her lithe body, her large breasts begging to be touched. "You really *did* come earlier," she said with a small curl of her lips.

It took Tik-Tok a moment to remember what she meant. *Ah.* That was right—she'd told him to come earlier next time and he'd forgotten. He laughed. "I didn't want to miss out again."

"Or you hoped to get an extra vision out of me now that you have the female." Celyna beckoned him closer with the curl of a finger. "Luckily, you've caught me in a mood."

"A mood?" he asked, sauntering nearer.

"*Mmm.*" She slid her fingers up her sides, arching her back in a stretch, before running them back down the center of her chest.

Tik-Tok took in her hardened nipples, the heavy rise and fall of her chest, and the slickness coating her inner thighs. A *mood*, if he ever saw one. His cock rose to the occasion and he licked his lips. "Am I interrupting?"

"If that's what you wish to call it." Her black eyes opened and the force of her lust washed over him. "Come to me, pirate. Let's see what the fates have to tell you today."

Tik-Tok didn't need to be told twice. She was giving him *exactly* what he wanted—in more ways than one. As he stepped up to the sea witch, she spread her legs wide. He dropped to his knees between them and leaned over her body, a hand on either side of her head.

She flicked her tongue across the seam of his lips and gripped his jacket, tugging him down onto her fully. He opened his mouth, allowing her access and taking the opening she gave. Soft moans of anticipation rose from her as he met her tongue, thrust for thrust, pulling a groan from him.

Beneath him, Celyna circled her hips, grinding her core

against his length. He responded by sitting up to shuck off his clothes. If he didn't get inside her now, he might not last long enough to make her come. Not when he'd been dying to bury himself in someone else for weeks now. Someone who had been pressed against him last night in the most delicious form of torture. His jacket hit the sand and he pulled the white tunic over his head. The scent of sweet vanilla struck his nose.

And he froze.

It smelled like North. His cock throbbed, his pants straining to contain him. Celyna was exquisite and skilled, but North … was different. And he wanted it to be *her* beneath him now. Her and no one else.

"Fuck," he groaned. "I can't do this."

Celyna ran a hand down his bare chest before squeezing him through his pants. He shook with desire, wanting desperately to unleash himself. But not with Celyna. "You most certainly can."

"Celyna…" he said with a hint of warning.

But she was already untying his pants and pulling him free. Her hand wrapped around his length, stroking in a variation of long, hard pulls and soft caresses, precisely as he liked. His head fell back at the sensation. Maybe he *could*. The vision she could give him would be worth the guilt, after all.

When his eyes fluttered shut, an image of North sleeping in his bed flashed across his eyelids. The way her hair cascaded over his pillow, the soft breaths escaping her rosy lips, and the gentle sweep of her long lashes. How vulnerable she had appeared, hands tucked beneath her chin. Trusting him explicitly as she slept. He jerked back out of Celyna's touch. "I can't," he insisted, tucking himself away.

"You got what you wanted," the sea witch seethed, suddenly on her feet. "She's the key to your portal. Nothing more."

Tik-Tok pulled his shirt back on. "She *is* more."

"Oh?" Celyna walked, hips swaying, toward the ocean. "Perhaps I should make sure she knows her place."

"Don't." Tik-Tok's vision blurred with rage. "Don't go

anywhere near her."

She stepped into the sea and grinned.

"Stop fucking with me, witch!" He snagged his tunic off the sand and stepped toward her.

But she only grinned wider before swimming directly for *The Temptress*.

"Celyna," he yelled. *Shit.* There was no telling what she would say to North, what lies she would spew. He raced back to his boat, shoving it into the water. His hands shook as he rowed faster than he'd ever rowed before. "If you touch her, I'll fucking kill you! *Celyna!*"

Chapter Fourteen

North

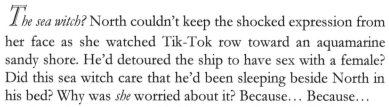

The sea witch? North couldn't keep the shocked expression from her face as she watched Tik-Tok row toward an aquamarine sandy shore. He'd detoured the ship to have sex with a female? Did this sea witch care that he'd been sleeping beside North in his bed? Why was *she* worried about it? Because... Because...

A body pressed up beside her, pulling North from her thoughts. "He goes to visit Celyna every year," Echo said. "They both get what they want when he sees her, but we were here right before he went to the Emerald City. It's too soon to be back..."

Both get what they want? North pushed away the images that slid forth of Tik-Tok bare-chested and unlacing his pants. "He can take a whole troop of faeries to his bed if he wants. I don't care what he does."

Echo arched a red brow.

"I don't." Her voice came out a bit higher than she would have liked. *Gods.*

"The captain's never been interested in anyone outside of the bedroom. But if anyone were to hook him, it could quite possibly be you." Echo grinned. But before North could reply, the siren continued, "I've got some crates to prepare downstairs with the others for when we next make landfall. Go relax for a while, then we can train more later."

"All right." North gripped her axe as Echo headed toward the open door leading down to where the valuables and alcohol were kept.

She wished she had another bottle of spirits—only this time she wouldn't drink the whole thing at once. *Bah.* She avoided the urge to go and ask Echo for one. North didn't feel like heading down to her room, so she padded to the back of the ship and plopped down behind several large barrels.

North glanced down at the weapon in her hand, rotating it around and around, then stopped on the engraved star. Not *just* a beautiful axe, but a thoughtful gift. When Tik-Tok had given it to her, her chest had fluttered. Something about the gift, that mark—she thought there'd been an implication behind it. Like perhaps he was starting to see her not only as a means to open his portal, but, maybe, as a friend. Even when Tik-Tok had first called her his star, it hadn't annoyed her like everything else about him had. She supposed it was because no one had ever given her a nickname before, and she knew, in the mortal world, that the North Star could guide anyone home.

With a sigh, she set the axe aside and unbraided her hair. It was either that or chuck the weapon into the sea at the thought of Tik-Tok and the sea witch. Him sinking into her, her clenching his back as he brought her to bliss.

Closing her eyes, North listened to the waves and hoped their rhythmic lapping would help unlock the possible magic within her. Wave after wave collided against the hull, and she let her veins hum along with the melody. She tried to focus, dipping in to the mental exercises that Tik-Tok had shown her so she could attempt to unlock her supposed power. *Breathe in… Breathe out…*

She didn't know how much time had passed when a soft female voice whispered her name, "North, come here."

Her lids jerked open, but there wasn't anyone around. Had she imagined it? The voice had been so quiet, as if the wind had sent it up to her.

"North." Her name came again, a gentle alluring murmur.

Jolting up from her position, North peered over the edge of the handrail, and her eyes connected with two dark orbs that seemed to glimmer within an oval face. Long green hair floated around a blue-scaled neck and shoulders.

She couldn't break away from the female's gaze, didn't want to. It reminded North of something, someone... But she couldn't recall whom.

You're going to complete a task for me. The shapely dark blue lips on the female's mouth didn't move as she spoke, but North could hear every word inside her head.

Magic tugged at her tongue, pulling an answer out. "Yes."

I know in your heart what you want. You want Tik-Tok, don't you?

"Yes," she whispered.

Why don't you take him? Show him your deepest desire.

A playful grin spread across the female's lips as she ducked beneath the surface of the water.

"North!" a voice boomed. She angled her gaze to find Tik-Tok rowing fiercely in her direction. "Get away from her!"

"Tik-Tok?" North asked, her brows lowering. A throbbing ache pulsed through her head and she rubbed at her temples.

She snatched her axe from the deck and hurried to the middle of the ship as Tik-Tok climbed up the rope ladder. He flung himself over the handrail and hurried over to her, grasping her face between his hands.

"What did she do to you?" he demanded, ragged breaths escaping his lips.

"Who?" North wrinkled her nose, not understanding what he seemed so frantic about.

"Celyna. The sea witch," he rushed out, releasing North and looking out at the crashing waves. "You were speaking with her."

North frowned. What was wrong with him? "I didn't see

anyone."

"Fuck." He slammed his fist against the rail. "She can be a devious bitch when she wants to."

North took a deep swallow and settled her gaze on his rumpled state. The ties at his pants were loose, his tunic backward, his jacket missing.

"I suppose you got what you needed from her, though?"

Tik-Tok drew her to his chest, his eyes focused on hers again. "She's in a … *mood*, and there's no talking sense into her until morning. You'll have to come with me tomorrow so she can remove whatever fucking spell she cast on you."

North rubbed her head, trying to see if she could somehow bring the memory forth. But she couldn't, and Tik-Tok appeared to be telling the truth, judging by the anger rolling off of him. "I'm fine."

"This is my fault. Come with me." He grabbed her by the hand and tugged her in the direction of his room. It was hard for her smaller legs to keep up with his long stride, but she managed it. Opening the door, he brought her inside.

"Why are you acting like this?" North asked, setting down her axe on the floor and taking a seat on the edge of his desk. "Even if she tried to cast a spell, I don't think it worked, because I feel fine."

"That's the thing with her spells. She doesn't cast them often, but when she does, you won't know. Celyna can take your memories and you wouldn't miss them, or she might've told you to drown yourself later tonight."

Could that have happened? And if she had, would North be able to fight the temptation to do whatever the sea witch had commanded? "Perhaps she only wanted you to think she'd done something, and she really didn't."

"She did. I know her." He gritted his teeth as he paced back and forth across the floor.

She'd never seen him so discomposed. "Why would she want to cast a spell on me anyway? I haven't even met her."

113

Tik-Tok stopped and lifted his head to look at her. "Because I didn't fuck her."

North's brows lifted. He hadn't tumbled her... Why not?

"She gets her visions when she orgasms," Tik-Tok continued. "I needed her prophecy, to know where exactly the portal would open, or, if she couldn't tell me that, how to avoid an old enemy. For some reason, I couldn't..." He trailed off but didn't shy away from her wide-open stare.

"Why not?" Her tongue felt thick in her mouth as she asked the two simple words.

"I ... I don't know, North. I don't fucking know. Ever since you..."

"Ever since I what?" she whispered.

He sank down onto the chair in front of the desk and stared up at the ceiling before looking back at her. "I'm in control, North. Me. Not you."

"You're not making any sense."

"I fuck." His hand struck his chest. "I don't do more than that with *anyone*."

North's gaze locked onto his red irises, his powerful expression, and something softer that possibly lay beneath. An urge pulled at her, one nearly identical to what she'd felt last night. She hadn't wanted to acknowledge it then, but now...

Sliding herself from the desk, North stepped toward him, *wanting to*, but it also felt as though an invisible hand nudged her forward.

Tik-Tok didn't say a word, only parted his lips when she spread her legs on either side of his thighs—her skirt riding up above her knees—straddling him in the chair. She leaned nearer, so near. "Why is that all you do?"

His throat bobbed as he ran his metal hand over her hair, entwining his fingers with her silver waves. He drew her head closer until her mouth was dangerously close to touching his. "Because the only one to own me, is *me*."

And then she closed the distance, her lips on his, kissing him.

He didn't hesitate, and their movements were almost savage. She liked it. Liked how he kissed her. North softly bit his lower lip, and she could feel him harden against her core. And she liked that too, how it made her center ache for more. She'd never had someone's length pressed against her in this way.

In one swift movement, Tik-Tok lifted her off him, and she thought he was going to push her away. But instead, he turned her around in his lap so her back was flush with his strong chest, his sandalwood scent enveloping her.

"Tell me how you like it," he whispered in her ear as he swept her hair away, giving him access to her neck. "Tell me what pleases you the most."

"This," she whispered, arching her back and rolling her hips against him.

His hands came to her thighs and opened her legs wider before trailing his fingers up to the exposed flesh of her stomach—the digits of his right hand were cool—the left, warm, both equally intoxicating. He ventured to the top button of her bodice and, with practiced movements, unbuttoned them one by one until they were all undone. Tik-Tok didn't remove the fabric as his hands glided up her flesh, lightly over her scar, to cup her breasts. They fit perfectly in his palms, his fingers expertly pinching and rubbing at her nipples. Breaths uneven, North arched her back even more. His mouth landed on her neck, his lips kissing, his tongue flicking.

There was no suppressing her moan any longer and it escaped through her lips.

"So responsive." Tik-Tok flicked that glorious tongue of his up her neck once more. "What else do you like, my star?"

Bold. Bolder. North interlocked her fingers through his and slid their hands together down between her breasts, to her navel, then slipped them beneath her hitched skirt and between her thighs. She wanted his touch, wanted to know what it felt like to have his warm digits inside her.

She released his hand, allowing his fingers to descend farther

115

down on their own. And he did exactly that.

"You're so wet," he rasped, his digits dancing against her. "For me?"

"Yes." Her voice came out raspier than she'd ever heard it.

She rolled her hips again, and he let out a low growl.

"Keep doing that," he demanded. The palm of his hand circled her clit, stroking, and rubbing as he dipped a finger inside her, then another.

The things he did to her were so wickedly delicious that she burned for all of it. A groan escaped him when she ground against him harder, and she could have sworn his length swelled even more. North leaned back into him and wrapped her arm around his neck. He worked her breasts and center with his practiced hands, while his lips and tongue did magical things behind her ear.

Then something ravenous washed over her, and holy gods, it was wonderfully consuming. As though the sea was surrounding her, the waves crashing, water rising, a purple rush of color collided through her. North gasped as her body shook from the brilliant pleasure.

"That's it," Tik-Tok purred, his fingers not slowing for a moment.

The violet kept blossoming behind her eyes and, even after her body stopped shaking, the color lingered.

"Do it again," North demanded.

With an approving growl, Tik-Tok flipped her around to face him and his lips crashed to hers. Their kissing grew frantic, desperate, their tongues worshiping one another, doing what her body longed to do. He yanked down his pants, then hiked up her skirt to her waist, so she could tear her undergarments down. Then there was nothing between them as she rested against him once more. His hardness was like velvet in between her folds.

"Go slow," she said, lifting herself to give him entrance. "I haven't done this before."

Tik-Tok froze. "You what?" He stared at her as though

maybe he'd heard her wrong.

His horrified expression made her want to take off running, yet that invisible hand urged her to continue talking. "Don't worry. Keep going."

Tik-Tok lifted North off him so fast that she wobbled on her feet. He pushed up from the chair and gripped his hair. "That fucking bitch. I know exactly what she did."

"What?" North cocked her head, not wanting to talk anymore. She yearned to have him pressed up to her again.

He stepped back when she reached out to touch him. "She thought that once I found out you hadn't fucked anyone before, I would return to her. I don't take innocent females to my bed."

North's heart pounded furiously. She knew she should have been embarrassed, but the nudge kept driving her forward. "It's okay. We can continue."

"You're only saying that because of what *she* did." Tik-Tok's jaw tightened. He inched toward her, buttoning her bodice back up with clinical movements.

She swallowed, trying to clear her head. But after tasting him, touching him, she only felt the desire within her.

"We're not waiting until morning—we're going to Celyna now. Come on." He grasped her hand and tugged her out of his room.

"What's wrong?" Echo called, dragging a large bucket across the deck with Dax beside her, carrying thick, heavy rope.

"Celyna spelled North because I didn't fuck her," Tik-Tok spat. "I need you to come with me. You're close to her kind."

"Dax, I may need you," Echo said.

"For what?" He lifted a brow.

"You'll see."

North's clothing felt too tight, and she *needed* to go back into the room with Tik-Tok. But she followed him down the ladder to the rowboat anyway. She was about to settle beside him when he twisted her around to sit across from him. Dax plopped down next to Tik-Tok and Echo's warm hand wrapped around North.

"How far did you go?" Echo asked as Tik-Tok started to furiously row across the gentle waves. "Did you two…"

"No." But the urge was growing stronger, *tightening*—she was aching to have him inside her, even if it was right here in this boat with Echo and Dax watching them.

"Don't look at him." Echo grabbed North's chin between her fingers and turned her head so their gazes met. "I don't want to sing to you, but if you can't control yourself, I'll have to." She turned to Tik-Tok. "And quit growling. Even your voice makes her want to fuck you more."

"It wasn't like this at first." Tik-Tok said. "I didn't realize…"

North tried to stand, to go to Tik-Tok, but Echo held her back.

The siren's nose twitched, seeming to scent the air. "With each passing minute, I can smell the desire in you getting stronger. Close your eyes," Echo instructed her. "Take deep breaths."

North shut her lids while her chest heaved, but within the darkness, all she could think about were Tik-Tok's fingers, his mouth, his length. Echo kept telling her to breathe, and it somehow grounded her enough not to lunge across the rowboat for him.

"Celyna! Get over here!" Tik-Tok roared.

North opened her eyes and her gaze met a naked blue female with scales along her flesh, standing at the edge of the water. Long green hair, black eyes, beautiful. A storm of jealousy plowed through North—she'd never seen this female before, but knew it was the sea witch.

"I was only giving you what you wanted, pirate." Celyna stepped into the water, making her way closer to their boat. "And here you are, as I knew you would be."

"Take the spell off her," Echo said, her voice deadly. "Or I'll bring my mother into this."

"Oh, Siren Princess, I meant no harm." Celyna shrugged. "And why bring your mother into this when we both despise her?"

"Remove the fucking spell," Tik-Tok seethed, his fists tightening at his sides.

Celyna smirked. "You need a vision—so that means I need you."

"It doesn't have to be Tik-Tok," Echo said. "Dax is more than willing to fulfill your fantasy."

Celyna peered at Dax, who seemed poised to leap from the boat toward her the moment she agreed. Licking her bottom lip, the sea witch nodded. "I suppose he'll do." Her eyes gleamed as they trained on North's, and a voice whispered in her skull. *I release you.*

A veil seemed to lift from North and she hunched over, gasping for breath. She remembered Celyna at the ship, then everything that had followed. Her eyes slowly lifted to Tik-Tok's, but she couldn't read his expression. She jerked her gaze away, recalling everything they'd done, him touching her, ravishing her, her liking it too much. How she still liked it. Would even do it again. But he was disgusted by her, that she was *innocent...* Her cheeks grew blazing hot.

A purple flame lit within her, as it had when he'd brought her over the edge, writhing in bliss. That color.

"I feel it," North whispered, her entire being filling with wonder. "I feel my magic."

CHAPTER FIFTEEN

TIK-TOK

North felt her magic. *She felt it.* Tik-Tok's heart nearly pounded out of his chest as he rowed back to *The Temptress*, leaving Dax on the island with Celyna. He'd begun to wonder if North would ever access her latent power or if they would be stuck sailing the seas forever. Waiting. Hoping for something that would never happen.

Echo and North spoke in rushed voices, but his pulse was pounding too loudly in his ears to make out the words. They appeared excited—all smiles and hand gestures. He should be excited too. But he wasn't—he didn't dare let himself hope too much. What if it was something else? Another one of Celyna's tricks. Or... Or fucking *gas* that she mistook as the rumble of magic.

Shit. No. It was definitely magic. The citrusy scent of it was almost too faint to recognize, but it was there, tinging the air.

"Climb the ladder," he told North. Once she was halfway up, he began to follow, stopping after a few rungs to look back at Echo. "Take the boat back and wait for Dax."

Echo wordlessly grabbed the oars and pushed the rowboat

away from the wooden hull.

"You've got this," he encouraged North when she fumbled near the railing. "Swing your leg over."

She listened, disappearing onto the deck, and a moment later he joined her. Respen, Cyrx, and a handful of brownies stared at them in obvious confusion. *Nosy bastards.* Tik-Tok took North's hand and rushed across the deck to his quarters, ignoring the stares.

Once inside, he slammed the door. "Show me," he demanded.

"*Show you?*" she said, trying to catch her breath between words. "How am I supposed to show you a feeling?"

Right. She felt it, but that didn't mean she could *use* it. He tried to even his breaths, calm himself, but he'd waited so long... To have the magic he needed be so close and not be able to access it...

"Are you okay?" North asked.

He met her stare, reading the nervousness there, and unclenched his jaw. "Are *you?*" He looked her up and down, appraising. It hadn't been long enough for the scent of her bliss to dissipate completely from the room. His heart thumped as it reached his nose, creating a direct path to his throbbing groin. *Bad Tik-Tok,* he chided himself. This wasn't the time to get distracted. He rubbed the pad of his thumb along his bottom lip. "Any lingering urges from Celyna's spell?"

North blushed. "No."

Tik-Tok's eye twitched with annoyance. *Calm down.* It wasn't her fault he'd pissed off the sea witch. If anything, what had happened between them was *his* fault. He should've realized North wouldn't have come all over his fingers and begged for more without external help, even if she had planned to seduce him. There was a difference between luring someone in for personal gain and luring them in due to genuine desire. Today had been the latter. So Celyna *knew* North was untouched and that he would never stick his cock in her once he found out.

"Your magic," he said in a tight voice, pushing away the memory of how good it felt to have her on his lap. The heat. How wet she'd been. Each little noise she made when he touched her. He cracked his knuckles. "What does it feel like?"

"It feels…" She paused, brows lowered as she seemed to ponder how to put it into words. "It feels like the sea itself is inside me, like the waves are a part of me. Both calm and thrashing. It's different than anything I've ever experienced."

Tik-Tok paced back and forth a few times before perching on the edge of his bed, leaving a large space between them. "And what brought the sensation to the surface?"

She shifted uncomfortably on her feet. "Is that important?"

"Of course." He set his elbows on his knees and leaned forward, looking up at her from beneath his lashes. "If you know how to tap into that feeling, we can work on manifesting it into something useful."

"Like opening a portal?"

He grinned. "Like opening a portal."

"Can I have a minute?" She rubbed at her chest. "To see if I can find it again?"

Tik-Tok watched her intently as she focused internally. The small line of concern that appeared on her forehead made him want to run a finger over it, to smooth it out. Her silver hair was windblown, strands sticking to her cheeks, and the buttons of her bodice were fastened unevenly—his fault. He hadn't wanted to lower his gaze as he closed the fabric over her supple breasts. His palms tingled as if begging for another chance to hold them.

Stop.

But it was too late—his skin warmed with desire, the sand inside his own shirt suddenly itchy against his too-sensitive skin. He stood, crossing to his chest of drawers, while pulling his shirt over his head. The sand hidden inside the material rained to the floor. Dropping the soiled shirt, he opened the top drawer and dug through his clothes for a fresh one.

Cool fingers traced down his back. Down one of the more

prominent scars. And Tik-Tok froze. "You're supposed to be testing your magic," he grumbled, shifting away from the touch. "Not seducing your captain."

"You're not my captain," North whispered. "What happened to you?"

"What does it look like?" He yanked on a black tunic, hiding the marks given to him by the King of Ev. Of the thousands of lashes he'd received, only a dozen had scarred, compliments of healing potions. But there was a reason these remained. They had been deep, bloody, and gotten infected. He hated that North had seen them—that he'd been too preoccupied with thoughts of her to remember to keep his back turned, like the other night when she'd seen him without his shirt. Facing her now, he kept his gaze on her chin so he didn't need to see the pity likely swirling in her eyes. "Figure anything out yet?"

"Yes." She stepped closer, hand hovering near her mouth, and stared at his chest. "What happened to your back, Tik-Tok?"

He grunted in frustration. Even the densest fae would recognize lash marks and dare not ask about them. Yet he spoke, regardless of how much it bothered him. "I was the ward of the King of Ev for a few years before becoming a pirate. Being young and alone, I was an easy outlet for his frustrations." The faint echo of a cracking whip sounded in his head and he tensed. "Happy now?"

"No," she breathed. "Why would I be happy about that?"

Because she'd gotten her answer. "Stop changing the subject. Your magic—"

"Let's make a deal," she said quickly. "If you tell me why you want to open the portal, I'll tell you a theory about my magic."

"Aren't you the conniving one, my star?" He smirked and stepped back, finding a seat on the edge of his mattress again. Only Respen knew his full past, and that was only because they'd both found the bottom of too many bottles one night. There was nothing she could do with the information to damage his reputation or put him in danger—no upstanding fae thought

123

highly of him anyway and *he* was the one to be feared. He didn't want to divulge his secrets nor relive his pain. He would though—if it meant unlocking North's power. Even if he had to force it out. "Sit."

North padded to the bed and took the empty space beside him. The faint scent of her from his bed didn't compare to the source. Her nearness left him drunk on it.

"There are chairs," he said, throwing his hand out toward the three seats around his desk.

"Do you think that's safer?" she asked, crossing her arms. "If I remember correctly, we slept uneventfully together in the bed, but your chair—"

"All right, all right," he said, wincing. *Stars above.* Did she have to remind him? Twice in one day, he'd gotten worked up, only to have his cock soften, unsatisfied. The ache in his balls grew heavier by the second. "Point taken."

"So…" she prodded.

"Why do I want to open the portal?" He twisted toward her, taking her chin between his thumb and forefinger so she had to look him in the eye. With a deep breath, he answered, "I need to kill my father."

Her lips parted on a gasp.

Tik-Tok chuckled ruefully. "Not what you expected?"

"You… But…"

He snorted, releasing her chin. Of course she couldn't comprehend patricide—Tin had wasted no time swinging his axe in her defense. "Not all fathers are as protective as yours."

"*Kill* him, though? Is that necessary?"

"What does it matter to you?" he asked, genuinely curious. "You don't know him or what he's done. Why do you care if he lives or dies?"

North shifted, squeezing the fabric of her skirt. "You're right—I don't know him. But to go through all of this? You cut off your own arm and took me from my family to murder one male?"

124

A dry laugh escaped Tik-Tok's throat. Yes—he'd cut off his arm. He'd stolen North. He'd betrayed Captain Salt, the asshole of a fae who'd saved him as an adolescent, taken him from a lifetime of slavery to the brutal King of Ev. And he'd done *more*. He *would do* more to make sure his father suffered an excruciating death. Tik-Tok was going to rip the bastard's limbs off, one by one. He would cauterize each stub to keep his father from bleeding out before he was finished. Then he'd carve his chest open and snap his ribs apart. Feed his intestines to wild beasts. Peel his skin from his body as he begged for mercy. *And then* Tik-Tok would deal the final blow.

"My father..." He eyed the cupboard holding his personal supply of spirits and sighed. It had been a long time since he'd talked about this with anyone, and when he was finished, there was no doubt he would need to drown away the pain. "To call him a fucking asshole is an understatement. My father *and* my mother, actually. They were horrendous parents to me and my three siblings. Constantly berating and beating us. My oldest sister escaped through marriage when I was three and my older brother took a job in another town when I was four, which left me and my younger sister to deal with them on our own. If only they had stayed away..."

He closed his eyes, rubbing the lids in an attempt to erase the images of his siblings *before*... Of them alive. Laughing. Protecting him and his little sister from their parents' fury. And then, there was *after*. An ending saturated in blood.

"My oldest sister announced her pregnancy the last time she came home," he said quietly. "She would've made a wonderful mother, given the chance."

"What happened to her?" North put a hand on his knee in what had to be an attempt at comfort. All it did was make his pulse race.

"My parents killed her," he said in a hoarse voice. "And my brother. And my little sister. And ... me..." He glanced sideways to gauge North's expression. Her wide eyes were glazed with a

125

mixture of shock and horror. His lips curled into a rueful smile. "Obviously I was harder to kill than they expected, even at thirteen years old."

"But … *why?*" she asked gently. "Why would they murder their own children?"

"Power." He held up his left hand and let a small spark of red smoke twine around his fingers. "They used a dark spell to steal everything from my siblings then severed their spinal cords, but they couldn't pry my magic out no matter how hard they tried. In fact, their attempt only made more manifest."

He closed his fist around the swirling red magic, extinguishing it. His useless power to scent magic had suddenly been joined by the ability to turn living beings to stone. Then the more volatile ability to crush the hardest of rocks with a mere thought. The new power had exploded from him, fierce and untamed, doing for him what he'd always wanted to do. *Crushing, maiming, in order to free himself.*

He smirked maliciously at the memory. "And I used it to crush every bone in my mother's body. A slow, agonizing death. Instead of helping her, my cowardly father ran off with my brother's portal magic."

"And disappeared through the portal?" North guessed.

Tik-Tok nodded once. "The world on the other side lacks magic, according to the tales told in Ev, and my parents wanted to become gods. My father, I assume, succeeded."

North was quiet for so long that, if her hand didn't still rest on his knee, he would've thought she'd left. He flopped back on the bed, staring at the wooden beams overhead. Anger stirred inside him, clawing, biting, frantic to find an escape. He wanted his father *dead.* Wanted *vengeance.*

"Captain Salt isn't exactly what you'd consider *good*, but he was different toward me. He became something like a father after he snuck me out of Ev. He taught me to fight and, because I saw him doing so many wrong things, I learned to always do the *right* thing." He looked down at his metal arm and felt the scab over his guilty conscious loosen. The right thing *wasn't* to hold a mutiny against Salt. Was Salt the best male? Hell no. But Salt was the best male he'd had in his life while growing up. Perhaps, that one time, he should've simply acquired his own pirate ship another way. Abandoned Salt instead of actively betraying him.

North shifted onto her knees on the mattress and leaned forward, blocking his view of the ceiling. "I don't know why I *felt* my magic, but I know what else I *felt* at the time. Maybe … maybe if we recreate that, it will work again. I want to help you. You should have told me this earlier so I understood."

Tik-Tok's eyes snapped to her face, his gold hand fisting the blankets. Was she seriously going to resume her plan of seduction? *Now?* After what had happened because of Celyna. "North…"

When he didn't continue, she leaned closer, breath shallow. "What?"

He suppressed a groan. Taking an innocent into his bed had always been a hard line for him—the females got attached and he didn't need that kind of trouble. "You need to give yourself to someone better than me. Someone capable of doing more than fucking."

"There are other things we can do," she whispered. "Things we've already done."

Blood surged to his cock. *Yes,* he wanted to tell her. He wanted to have his fingers in her again, have her touch him in places she hadn't explored yet. His hard length pressed painfully against his pants and he groaned in his head. It wouldn't take long. Minutes, if that.

But, as much as he wanted to take her up on the offer of *other things*, he wouldn't. Not if it was simply meant to draw her power out. He'd had enough exchanging of sexual favors for magic with Celyna. North meant more to him than that. He stopped breathing as that realization struck him. *Oh, fuck no.* That was a reality he refused to entertain.

127

If North needed … *something* … to help her release her potential, she would have to use her own hands. Or another crew member. Dax would most certainly be willing, but then Tik-Tok would be forced to toss him overboard.

He gave her a tight smile. "As much as I want to kill my father, I won't use your body like that. There are other ways to achieve my goal—and for you to find yourself. I'm willing to wait a little longer to do this with my morals intact. What's left of them anyway."

She tilted her head, a tinge of sadness in her gaze. "It doesn't have to be about my magic or the portal. It could be … fun."

"Fun," he echoed and lunged up, pressing his lips to hers in a quick, desperate kiss. Then he stood, pulling her with him, and crossed the room. "Forgive me, my star. But I can't." He swung the door open and gave her a gentle nudge. "Go to your room and practice feeling your magic some more, all right?"

North opened her mouth to say something, but he didn't wait to hear if it was an agreement or a refusal. In a moment of desperation to be alone with his feelings—both mental and physical—he slammed the door in her face. He only made it as far as his desk before unbuckling his pants—an illusory image of North on her knees before him—and gripping himself with a low, desperate groan.

Chapter Sixteen

North

North paced back and forth across her room, her arms folded at her chest. She'd been doing it for a while now, trying to draw out that vivid violet magic. Nothing. Not a spark, not a flame, not a single bit of smoke.

But it *was there.*

She thought about the spell the sea witch had cast upon her, and she should have been livid, but she wasn't. Everything she'd done, she'd secretly yearned to do. Wishing her magic came to her as easy as it did to Celyna, she tried again. Nothing.

"Gods, come on," North growled with frustration.

Perhaps it was because she was too wound-up from her earlier conversation with Tik-Tok. There had been so much bottled up inside that male—more than she could have dreamed. The wounds on his back, his parents, the King of Ev... She could tell he hadn't wanted to confess to her any of it, but he'd still confided his past to her. His revelations had unlocked another part within her that had nothing to do with magic. *Feelings.*

And then she'd offered herself so she could find her magic again and help him succeed in his vengeance, even though it wasn't hers to seek. Maybe it was because of what her own family had faced in their past. Tik-Tok's father could've become like the Wizard to another world and brought it to ruins, like Oz had.

Tik-Tok had denied tumbling her, so she'd offered to do other things that could lead to pleasure. She'd wanted him to feel the gratification she had earlier in the day, to return the favor. Instead, he'd slammed the door in her face.

"Bah!" she shouted to herself and threw a pretend axe at the wall. It hit right where she wanted it to. If only it had been real.

Her door swung open and she jerked her head up. She hadn't expected Echo, but was glad to see her, nonetheless.

"I wanted to check on you," the siren said, climbing down the ladder.

"I'm fine, *Princess*." North grinned and sat on the bed.

"Mmm." Echo plopped down beside her. "I stripped myself of that title after my mother fled our underwater village instead of helping to defend against the invading forces. But it needed to be used today to help a friend." She gave North a small smile.

Friends. That was what they'd become. North swallowed, wondering what kind of life the rest of the crew members had faced. She'd had a great one growing up, and her chest tightened over how the small arguments with her parents now seemed minuscule. "I'm sorry."

"I'm better off staying away from her. However, I don't think you're truly *fine*, and I don't think the captain is either. He's holed himself up in his room and didn't answer when I tried to tell him Dax was back. Celyna had a vision that he needs to speak to the captain about. She also wishes to see Dax from now on."

North puckered her lips. "How does Dax feel about that?"

"He said he's more than willing to do his duty." Echo rolled her eyes. "But Dax would hump a tree if it could get him off."

She chuckled softly, unable to stop the image of Dax doing just that from flashing inside her head.

"So, what's really wrong? Is it about what the sea witch made you almost do?"

130

With a sigh, North shook her head. "The opposite."

Echo perked up, her smile growing wide. "Go on."

"I wanted to…" She took a deep breath, her cheeks heating. "I told Tik-Tok that I felt my magic after he … after I…"

Echo blinked. "Orgasmed?"

"No—more like the rush of feelings that come along with that. Feelings for him. I offered to sleep with him, but he doesn't tumble innocents."

The siren's brows lifted all the way up her forehead. "You haven't before?"

"Nope." She wasn't going to go into the story about how she'd saved herself for Birch because that aspect of her life didn't matter anymore. It was strange how quickly things could become clear, how everything could be so unexpected yet feel like the right path.

"Oh…" Echo stared up at the ceiling. "I'm still surprised he didn't take you up on that offer. We all want the portal open, but no one as much as him." Her gaze settled on North's. "I can't believe you haven't. Perhaps it was because I was sixteen when I took my first lover. But I started drowning fae from the moment I could speak."

Echo must have noticed North's horrified expression because she continued, "That was another life, though. It's my nature, what we sirens are born to do, but I didn't want that life anymore. That's why I joined this crew."

"I'm glad you did, Echo." North smiled. "Because I wouldn't have met you otherwise."

Echo let out a low whistle. "Oh, you never know. You could have visited the sea one day and stumbled upon me. Perhaps even been scared at first and held up your axe. You're strong, even if you don't look it."

"It's my size, isn't it?" North chuckled.

Echo smirked and stood from the bed, pulling North up by her wrist. "Come on. Let's go take out some aggression on deck with the weapons. What do you say?"

At that moment, swinging a real axe would be much better than throwing a pretend one. "Sure."

North followed Echo up the ladder. A few of the brownies were doing their usual cleaning duties or taking watch up in the sails while Kaliko and Cyrx stood at the helm. There wasn't any sign of Tik-Tok, Dax, or Respen. At the middle of the ship, near the rail, rested her old axe and a sword, as though Echo had already known North needed this.

As she scooped up the axe, a tinge of disappointment hit her that it wasn't the one Tik-Tok had given her. But she'd left it in his room. After he'd slammed the door in her face, she wasn't going to go to him—he'd have to eventually come to her, if he decided to see her at all. She'd done enough, offered enough, had been willing to give him *everything*.

Echo brought up her glistening sword and North swung her axe against the silver blade, the loud clang echoing across the ship. The ringing in her ears and the vibration in her arms felt good. Echo thrust her sword forward and North easily blocked it.

"Perfect," Echo said.

"Meet me after you finish. I have something for you," Respen called to Echo with a smirk as he made an appearance, carrying a large sack toward the storage space below deck.

"You'll have to wait a while." Echo shrugged, her eyes dancing mischievously.

"I'd wait an eternity for you." He blew her a kiss and disappeared down the stairs.

Echo swung her sword and North whirled out of the way.

"How did you two get together anyway?" North asked, lifting her axe higher.

"Respen tried to woo me for months and I refused his gifts, his conversations, all of it, but then one day, he didn't try anymore. It hit me then that I liked him. If he'd kept trying, I don't think I would have ever changed my mind."

North had never been wooed in her life, and if it had been

132

someone like Respen, she would have probably given in on the first day. She was about to say so but caught sight of something black high up in the sky, drawing closer.

Echo followed North's gaze and craned her neck all the way back. "What the fuck is a bird doing way out here?"

North inhaled sharply as the bird soared nearer. She knew that crow!

Grandfather.

Relief flooded her—this was the proof she needed that her family was truly no longer stone. Dropping the axe with a loud thump, North ran to the end of the ship and waved her hands in the air. "Over here!" she shouted so he could see her.

Her grandfather swooped down and landed on the deck beside her. Black smoke enveloped him and a few feathers floated to the ground as he transformed into his fae form, wearing a dark tunic and pants, and equally dark feathers braided within his hair.

"Who are you?" Echo asked, bringing up her sword. "Step away from her."

Crow released his blades from beneath his bracer, the tips extending over the back of his fingers like talons. "No. *You* step away from my granddaughter, siren."

"What the fuck is this?" Tik-Tok boomed as he made an appearance. He must have heard her loud shouting. "Go home, pheasant. Like I told the queen, I'll bring her back safely once she opens the portal."

"You've had her long enough." Crow glared. "She's coming with me."

"Oh really?" Tik-Tok drawled. "Do you plan to carry her back to the Emerald City in your tiny claws? Or perhaps I should turn you into stone instead?" He cocked his head and raised a hand.

"Wait!" North cried before he could change Crow into an ornament. "Let me discuss things with my grandfather alone. Please. I'm not leaving."

Tik-Tok ran a palm across his jaw and flicked his gaze to Echo, then nodded. "Find me when you're finished," he said to North and motioned for Echo to follow him.

"North." Crow turned to her, retracting his blades, relief written all over his face. "We've been sweeping the seas to find you. Are you all right? No one's hurt you, have they?"

She shook her head. There was no point telling him about being stabbed by Rizmaela. The top of her dress was, thankfully, covering her scar. She was healed and the dwarf was dead, so it would only worry him more than he already was. And it would only make matters worse if she'd brought up being spelled by the sea witch.

"Thank goodness." He exhaled. "I have a plan to bring you home, but I'll have to leave you here to get reinforcements."

Home. But … she couldn't, even if Tik-Tok would allow it. "Grandfather, I want to stay. I know you're not going to understand, but I have my reasons. I haven't been mistreated."

Crow pursed his lips. "Your father will never agree to that."

"He'll have to understand." North folded her arms. "I'm not a youngling anymore and I've found that I do indeed have magic." He didn't need to know that she couldn't wield it yet.

"It's true, then?" Crow asked. "You're able to open portals like your father?"

"I think I can, but I need to stay to find out."

"Reva will have my beak for this," he grumbled.

"Does this mean you're going to let me stay? Grandmother and Father will understand. You and Mother will see that they do, like always." North's mother had once left her mortal home to come to Oz—she would understand more than anyone.

Crow tightened his fists, a low groan coming from his throat, as though he were warring with himself. "You've been old enough to make your own choices for several years."

"I love you." North threw her arms around her grandfather and held him tight, breathing in his calming, woodsy scent.

Crow took a step away from her and lifted a brow as he

134

scanned her clothing. "When you come back, you might want to wear something different. Your father would shit a brick if he saw you in this."

Her smile grew wider. "He'll have to understand this too."

"You give him too much credit." Crow chuckled, then sobered. "I can stay here, if you need me to."

He'd already faced too much in his past, and she needed the chance to grow on her own. "No, go home. Let them know how much I love them." North took a few more steps back because if she hugged him again, she wouldn't let him leave.

"I love you. I've always believed in you." A cloud of dark smoke formed for a brief moment before her grandfather's bird form darted up into the sky with a loud caw.

She watched him as he flew farther and farther away, becoming the smallest of specks, and then he was gone.

Tears fell from North's eyes. She wiped them away and exhaled a puff of air, determined to see this through. Resting her arms over the handrail, she closed her eyes, concentrating. That bright violet was right there, within her reach. She conjured an image of a hand inside her and slowly crawled the fingers forward, trying not to scare the magic away. The closer she inched, the harder it was to keep herself from lunging for that vivid purple sphere, but she forced herself to wait. And then, when she was a hairsbreadth away again, she grabbed it, latched on, and tugged. Her eyes flew open as the burst of power flowed through her.

The silver sea rippled, the waves thrashed, until finally, the water parted, creating what looked to be a whirlpool. The liquid slammed shut, the violent waves calming.

A giddy laugh escaped her as she slapped her palms against the handrail. "Gods, I did it!" she shouted. She would do it again, too.

CHAPTER SEVENTEEN

TIK-TOK

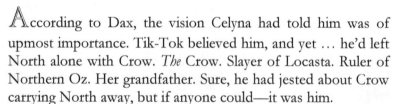

According to Dax, the vision Celyna had told him was of upmost importance. Tik-Tok believed him, and yet ... he'd left North alone with Crow. *The* Crow. Slayer of Locasta. Ruler of Northern Oz. Her grandfather. Sure, he had jested about Crow carrying North away, but if anyone could—it was him.

Dax spoke, repeating the sea witch's words, but Tik-Tok struggled to focus. His mind was full of images of North being whisked away. Hidden from him. Why hadn't he been more specific in his deal with Ozma? He scowled. Would he have a right to take North a second time? Was it breaking the deal if someone rescued her *before* the portal opened?

"Captain," Echo said in a harsh voice. "Are you listening?"

He jerked upright in his desk chair. "Of course I am."

"Then repeat what I said," Dax challenged, crossing his arms with a scowl.

"Shouldn't you be more relaxed after fucking Celyna?" he snapped, angry to be caught pre-occupied with thoughts of North.

Dax threw his hands up in the air. "Shouldn't you be more

concerned with the fact that North could get lost—or worse—if she opens the portal for you?"

"I—" *Wait. What?* Tik-Tok inched to the edge of his chair and put his palms on the desk to steady himself. "Why didn't you tell me this sooner?"

"You wouldn't answer your door," he said in a flat voice.

It was a valid point… He'd only left his quarters when Crow showed up because he smelled the male's magic on the air and heard the commotion on deck. "Repeat what Celyna told you."

"North will open the portal here," he said, tapping at the map spread between them of the Northern Sea. "But there are different possible outcomes. In one, you get your vengeance and return relatively unscathed. In another, when North opens the portal, it sucks her inside and she'll be lost forever. And, if the portal closes once we pass through, none of us will return to the Fae Lands."

His breath caught. Lose North? No—that couldn't happen. He had given his word to return her home, and he didn't renege on his word. "So, we'll make sure it's the first outcome."

"That's the problem," Echo said. "She couldn't see the event that decides which outcome will become reality."

With shallow breaths, he stood, staring at Echo, then Dax. "What are you doing here, then? Get back to the beach and *make* her see it."

"Trust me, I tried. Apparently, *it doesn't work like that*," he said, imitating Celyna's voice. "That's why she only saw you once a year. Decisions had to be made outside of your goal before she could tell you, definitively, what to do next."

That made sense. A lot of sense, if he was being honest. But they would simply have to stay docked right where they were until Celyna *could* see the correct path. *There.* That was a decision.

"What are you going to do?" Echo asked.

She refused to meet his eyes—likely because she was worried that Tik-Tok's desire to open the portal would matter more than North. He wished it did. That would make his life much easier.

"I don't know," he admitted. But first, he needed to make sure North was still on his ship. "I have to talk to North. Alone."

Tik-Tok stood, flew around his desk, and rushed onto the deck. Echo and Dax could leave his quarters behind him. He didn't care if North was finished talking with Crow yet—he should never have allowed them time alone to plot an escape. No matter what he decided, he needed North there. With him.

Scanning the deck, Tik-Tok found no sign of Crow in either of his forms. His heart gave a small, panicked spasm as he searched for North. He wasn't prepared for the sweeping relief of finding her at the rail. The pink skirt hugged her ass where she bent slightly, leaning forward onto her elbows. Jerking himself off hadn't been nearly satisfying enough.

Approaching her slowly, he spoke in a wary voice. "Where's your grandfather?"

"Gone." She tilted her head to look at him when he joined her at the edge of the ship. "I told him I wanted to help you."

She ... what? "Why?" he blurted.

"Because I do."

"And Crow *agreed* to that?" The skepticism in his tone was clear, even to him.

She shrugged. "He didn't like the idea, but I'm grown. You should be happy he was the one who came instead of my father or grandmother."

"I don't doubt that."

North bit her lip, trying hard not to smile. "I did it," she blurted.

"Did what?"

"Used my magic!" She was practically bouncing with excitement. "I made a small whirlpool. It didn't last long, but it's something. I'm sure I can do it again." She spun toward the water. "Watch."

"Wait." Tik-Tok desperately wanted her power unlocked, but did it have to be right now, when he had learned only minutes ago that it could lead to her utter downfall? He sighed and nodded toward his quarters. "Will you come with me? We need to talk about something."

North lifted a brow. "Are you *asking* me?"

"I can demand it, if you prefer," he said, smirking.

Tik-Tok didn't wait for her to reply before heading back to his quarters, and the soft pad of her feet followed at his back. He made sure Dax and Echo had left with a quick glance, then shut them inside, alone.

"Thanks to Celyna's vision, we know exactly where the portal should open." He crossed to the cupboard and took out two glasses along with a bottle of his finest rum.

"That's a good thing, isn't it?" North asked as he poured them each a drink.

"On one hand, yes. I get my vengeance and we all go on our merry way." He tipped back his drink, swallowing, and turned to her with the other in his hand. Before he could extend it to her as he'd intended, he downed it on an impulse, slamming the empty glass on the table beside the first. "On the other hand, if fate goes against us, there's a chance you get sucked into the portal and meet whatever that world has in store."

North stared at him, mouth hanging open. "I don't understand. The only way you'll get to your father is if I…"

"No. They are two very different potential outcomes. In one, we all survive."

North swallowed hard. "So either we all win, we get trapped, or … I die?"

"Celyna didn't say you *died*, necessarily." He grabbed the bottle from the desk and took a swig straight from the source. "Only that you were sucked through and lost."

North opened and closed her mouth a handful of times, forehead creased, eyes glittering with worry. Finally, she met his gaze. "I don't want to get lost anywhere."

"I don't want that either." Tik-Tok slumped so that he sat on the edge of his desk. His whole life had been spent trying to catch and kill a monster. And now that victory was in front of him—*right in front of him*—he wasn't sure he should risk it. Was killing his father worth losing North? For all he knew, his father had already been murdered in the other world and his entire mission was in vain. But he refused to consider that possibility. "Celyna also told Dax that if the portal closes once we go through, none of us will return. That means you would have to stay nearby. We don't know how your magic works yet and we can't risk putting distance between you and the portal." He released a humorless laugh and drank again. "The more I consider it, the more I think maybe I should stop. Let the past go."

"No." North dashed to his side and pulled the rum from his hand, placing it back in the cupboard. "After everything you've told me, I'm invested."

He snorted. *"Invested?* You're willing to die for my revenge?"

"That's only one scenario, isn't it? Everything could work out," she said carefully. "Also, you said I would be lost, not dead."

"North, no." He hung his head. *Fuck.* How could he let her risk her life in exchange for the chance to end his father's? But … how could he not? They would simply have to put off the portal until Celyna could see how to do it safely. After waiting for decades, what was another year? Ironic decision, considering he'd been ready to do anything to make it even a single day sooner. He looked over North, eyes slowly scanning from her feet up to meet her gaze, and resigned himself to the delay. The risk to her life wasn't worth it. "I'm sorry for slamming the door in your face earlier."

North feigned a gasp. "Am I hearing things? It sounded like you apologized, but that can't be—"

Tik-Tok silenced her with his lips. The kiss was so sudden that she froze beneath his touch. Just as he was about to pull away, to apologize again, she moved against him.

He was in awe of the softness of her lips, how perfectly they slanted over his. His kiss was demanding and rough, her answer gentle and pliant. She tasted like fruit sweetened by salt—cherries, and the sea. He cupped her cheeks, held her in place, as her hands fisted in his tunic. The first sweep of her tongue nearly undid him. Groaning, he slipped his own out to meet hers. Brushing and twisting together in an intoxicating dance, each passing moment of it was too much and not enough. He wanted more. Wanted to taste her everywhere.

No. Damn it—no.

Forcing himself to break their kiss, Tik-Tok rested his forehead on hers, still holding her face. "You make me feel things I don't want to feel," he whispered. "How did you get so far under my skin, my star?"

North used his shirt to tug him nearer. Her breasts pressed against his chest, each heavy breath she took going straight to his cock. *Respectable pirate, respectable pirate, respectable pirate,* he chanted silently to himself. When a soft, impatient sound came from her, the mantra completely shattered.

Respectable, my ass.

"Kiss me again." North leaned up on her toes, bringing their faces closer together. Her breath skated across his lips, drawing him in as if she were the siren on board his ship.

Tik-Tok flicked his tongue out, tasting her. "If I kiss you again, I'm not sure I'll be able to control myself. And I don't—"

"It's not like I've never touched a cock before."

"You…" He lifted his forehead to better see her expression. The prettiest shade of pink colored her cheeks, her lips plump and red because of him. "I thought you've never been with a male before."

"I haven't," she admitted.

Tik-Tok studied her, his head tilted to the side, and warred with himself over saying *fuck it.* He wanted to bend her over his desk. Take what she'd offered on multiple occasions. Rip the fabric from her and replace it with his hands. His tongue. His body.

An intense throb in his cock made him shift. *Fuck.* There was no denying this—denying what was between them. His fingertips slipped from where they tangled in her hair and trailed gently down the sides of her neck. In a strained voice, he asked, "How far *have* you gone with someone?"

"I've kissed." North licked her lips, staring at his. "And I've been touched."

"I meant before me," he clarified. "Before I brought you on my ship, how far had you gone?" Trailing one hand down to caress her breast over her clothes, he brushed a thumb over her hardened nipple. "Was I the first to feel these?"

North pushed her chest into his touch. "Yes."

He held back a groan and skimmed his free hand down her chest, over her stomach, to lightly graze her mound. "And this?" He knew the answer—if no one had fondled her chest, they most certainly hadn't explored her tight channel—but he wanted to hear her say it.

"Only you," she breathed.

He moved both hands to grip her hips. "Then, tell me, what bastard let you touch his cock without making sure you were also satisfied? Was it the male you found after Birch rejected you?"

"It wasn't like that." She spoke quickly, her hands flattening over his abs. "I wanted to forget about Birch, so I snuck to a gathering in the woods and found a male. We kissed and I … took him from his trousers, but then I stopped it."

Jealousy nibbled at Tik-Tok's insides. The thought of her delicate hands gripping another fae's length… A small, possessive growl rumbled in his throat. "Will you stop me?"

"I thought you didn't touch innocents."

"It would be a night of firsts for us both." He smirked. It was too hard to deny the attraction sizzling between them anymore. "But only if you're sure you want *everything* from me."

"I'm sure," she said eagerly.

Tik-Tok gripped her chin with his gold hand and forced her to meet his blazing stare. "You need to be *sure*."

"I am," she promised. And he saw the truth of it glistening

in her eyes.

Was he really going to do this? Break his rule. Take the one female that could, if she wished it, destroy everything he had worked for. He was willing to give her a year to ensure Celyna had a definitive vision before deciding whether he should give up on his vengeance. A lot could happen in a year... But he was sure of one thing—one huge, terrifying thing: North meant something to him. More than any other fae ever had.

"If I do anything you don't like, or if you want to stop, you need to tell me immediately," he told her, tightening his grip on her chin to make sure she understood he was serious.

"I will." North looked up at him from beneath her lashes. "First, I want to return the favor from last time."

Last time. When he made her come all over his fingers.

If she kept looking at him like that, he would come in his pants. Closing his eyes, he kissed her deeply, delving between her lips with his tongue, crushing her mouth to his. Then he brushed his lips across her cheek to her ear. "Get on your knees for me."

North's breath caught and she sunk down in front of him, eyes locked on his.

He forced himself to tear his gaze away. If he did look—did see her in front of him like that with her wide brown eyes and just-kissed lips—he was certain things would take an embarrassing turn. His seed would end up across her face before she even touched him.

The moment he unlaced his pants, his hard length sprung free. North's sharp inhale made him pause and wait. He was larger than most and, for someone who had only briefly encountered a cock, it had to be intimidating. But, instead, she reached up tentatively and wrapped her fingers around his shaft.

"Oh shit," he hissed, hips jerking. Had the simple touch of another's hand ever felt so good? "Wait." He covered her hand with his. "I want your mouth."

"I ... don't know how," she said softly.

Slowly, he moved her hand up and down as he spoke. "Open

143

your mouth and cover your teeth with your lips." When she did, he slid her hand down to his base. "Now close your mouth around the tip."

White light flashed across his vision when the warmth of her mouth touched the head of his cock. Precum leaked from him as he resumed moving her hand.

"Use your tongue," he rasped. In answer, it ran across the ridge and he fought the urge to fist her hair and shove his way into the back of her throat. There would be time for that if she wished—after she was used to taking him like this. Releasing her hand now that he'd established a slow rhythm, he tilted his head back and groaned. "Just like that."

North worked him with clumsy strokes and repetitive swipes of her tongue, but it was absolute bliss. Every tiny twitch of her fingers had him on the very edge, the buildup of heat from her mouth making him feel as if he were on fire. Because it was *her* that was doing it. And she was fucking perfect. A tingle started in his balls and he backed out of her grip before he could come. There were too many things he wanted to do first.

She wiped her lips with the back of her hand. "What—"

"My turn." In one fluid movement, he had her off her knees and spread across his desk— maps be damned. Kneeling between her thighs, he shoved the fabric of her skirt up to her waist and slowly slid the undergarments away. The sight of her, of the fluid covering her entrance, nearly sent him over the edge. "So ready for me," he said with a grin.

Leaning up on her elbows, she looked down at him, panting with lust-glazed eyes. "What are you doing?"

"Do you want to stop?" he asked. He would. It would be monumentally fucking difficult, but he would. When she shook her head, his grin widened.

Tik-Tok maintained eye contact this time as he leaned forward and flicked his tongue over her clit. North's head flew back on a moan, giving him all the encouragement he needed. With his tongue, he circled her bundle of nerves. He gently pressed his gold palm against her abdomen, keeping her in place, while his other hand found the slick entrance.

Using two fingers, he worked her with languid strokes, curling and twisting his digits until she grabbed the edges of his desk to steady herself. Thirty seconds more was all it took for her walls to clench tightly around him. The entire crew must have heard her cry out as she came, and a part of him enjoyed the idea. North was his.

"Gods," she said between gasps for air. "That was…"

Tik-Tok stood, licking her sweetness from his fingers as she watched. His cock was painfully hard now. From where he stood between her knees, it was so near her entrance that it wouldn't take much effort for him to rub the head in her wetness. The last bit of North's innocence … protected by half a step.

Damn. Fucking close. So fucking close.

"Don't stop," North said. She must have noticed his hesitation as he fisted himself and stared. His free hand gripped her bare thigh.

"Not here," he forced himself to say. Pulling her toward him, he lifted her against him, her legs immediately circling his waist, and he carried her across the room. "The bed." North shivered in what he read as anticipation. But what if it wasn't? His mind was too fucked up to tell the difference. Gently, he set her down on the edge of the mattress. "There's no going back once it's done. We can do *something else*," he said in a questioning voice, repeating her earlier offer to him.

North's reply was a playful smile. With quick fingers, she unbuttoned her bodice and tossed the material to the floor, then she peeled off her skirt and kicked it away. Tik-Tok drank in her completely naked form on his blankets. The soft curves. The lean muscles. Pebbled nipples on firm breasts, the light pink scar between them. The glistening reminder of her orgasm coating her inner thighs. *Shit.* He was done for.

North scooted backward, laying down. "Are you coming?"

About to—in more ways than one.

145

He prowled toward her, placing one knee on the mattress, and leaned over her. "You're *sure?*" he asked in a tight voice.

"I swear, if you ask me that again, I may have to get my axe." She grinned, gripping the hem of his shirt, and slid it over his head.

Tik-Tok settled over her then, nestled between her thighs, his cock resting against her lower belly. And he kissed her. Slowly this time. Softly. Even though his body demanded he *take her now.* "It might hurt," he whispered. The thought of hurting her was enough to stamp down his primal urges. "I'll be gentle, but…"

"It's okay." North brushed away a loose piece of his dark hair from where it clung to his lashes. "I trust you."

She trusted him? A new kind of peace settled over him. He'd been trusted by crewmates before, but North was different. She had come to him with hate, and now… Now it was different. Tik-Tok buried his face in the crook of her neck, kissing and nipping, as he continued to hold his weight off her. She trailed her fingers down each individual scar on his back.

Then he lined himself up with her core.

The first press inside her warmth made him fist the blankets. When he'd gained an inch, North inhaled sharply. He paused, shaking with the exertion, and covered her mouth with his own. His tongue nudged hers, mimicking the slide of his cock into her.

He took his time sinking into her, letting her adjust to his size before going a little farther. North's groans vibrated against his mouth where he kissed her, pulling a heady growl from him. If it weren't for her nails digging into his lower back and the way she urged him to move when she was ready, he would've risked her axe to his throat to make sure she was still all right.

Finally, after what felt like hours, Tik-Tok was fully coupled with North. The rumble that escaped him came from somewhere deep inside. Their breaths mingled, heavy, as the kiss continued. This was usually when he thrust hard and fast, fucking a female into oblivion, but, instead, he shifted slightly. Another time he would show her hard and fast—but not now.

"Tik-Tok," North mumbled against his lips. "I want to feel all of you."

He swallowed hard. "Are you—"

North bit his lower lip hard enough to silence him. "Stop asking that and *move*."

He chuckled, pressing another lingering kiss to her lips, before setting his forehead on the pillow. His gold hand cupped North's breast, eliciting a pleased gasp from her. Rolling his hips as gently as he could, he pulled back until the tip of his cock was the only thing left inside her. And glided back in. Laboriously, exquisitely unhurried.

North wrapped her legs around him. "Again. Faster."

Who was he to deny her? He began a steady rhythm, faster, but still tender. The tingle returned to his balls as they tightened, nearing release. But she still hadn't come again. He slid a hand between their sweat-slick bodies and rubbed tiny, quick circles over her clit.

"*Oh*." Her back arched, her breath quickening.

Tik-Tok smiled against her neck. The way she responded to him, the sounds she made, it was a perfect symphony. All leading to a remarkable finish. His thrusts became irregular with more power behind each one, but North didn't seem to mind. In fact, her walls fluttered. She gripped the sheets tightly, her chest pressed hard against his, and her hips shifted upward to meet each thrust.

"Come for me," he urged. *Begged*.

A satisfied scream tore from her as she clenched around his cock, nails biting into his skin.

"Oh fuck!" he roared as his own pleasure barreled through him. His cock jerked with each powerful release. "Fuck," he repeated on a harsh exhale.

He'd never come that hard in his life.

Chapter Eighteen

North

North's chest heaved as she stared into Tik-Tok's scarlet irises, no longer the color of blood, but beautiful as the deepest red rose. Her thoughts were scattered while she continued to stare up at him. She'd known the act of tumbling another must be at least somewhat decent—otherwise, why would so many fae do it? But, *gods*, she couldn't string words together to describe it, or all the emotions flowing through her.

Tik-Tok furrowed his brow as he studied her. "Are you—"

"My axe is still in here if you finish that sentence. I'm wonderful." She chuckled, cradling his warm cheek. "Are *you* okay?"

"I'm … I don't know what I am, my star. But I *do* know I want to keep you in my bed forever." He settled beside her, his breaths heavy.

With a smile, she grabbed his wrist and rolled to her side, then draped his arm around her.

"What are we doing now?" he purred in her ear, his chest and body aligning perfectly with her backside. "I'm happy to give you seconds, but I'll need a moment."

"Cuddling." She glanced over at him and arched a brow. "Do you not do this?"

"No."

So he would only tumble females, then leave. Something about being an exception to this made her heart swell.

"Well, you do now," North said with a smile.

"Whatever you want." He pressed his lips to her jaw.

"Even the portal? What if opening it is what I want?" She had to ask—she was going to convince him to go. After everything he had faced, he deserved to avenge his family.

"We're not going yet." His tone was an end-all to the question, but it wasn't to her.

"Tik-Tok," she started. "Will you at least get the crew to take us there and help me practice my magic in the morning? That's all I'm asking, for now—to go to the location and check it out. If you don't agree, I won't stop asking you." But once they were there, she was going to open that portal, regardless if he said no. If others in another world were at risk, then why procrastinate?

Even though she wanted to open the portal, that didn't mean she wasn't nervous. It wasn't only the possibility of death that had her on edge, but the unknown waiting on the other side of the portal and potentially getting lost there, never finding her way back. It wasn't even a living enemy she was facing, like her family had in their past adventures. It was a hole in the sea—just a tear in the fabric of reality. Would it be easier, or far worse? Yet, she'd chosen, and there was no turning back. It was the right decision, even if he didn't realize it yet.

Tik-Tok sighed. "I suppose I can do that." He eyed her suspiciously. "Just practice. We should arrive by midday tomorrow if I tell Respen to hoist the sails soon."

She smiled and turned to face the wall. Tik-Tok had at least given in on something. "Shouldn't you go tell him, then?"

"Later." His teeth grazed her neck, then nipped at her ear. "I like where I'm at right now."

Behind her, North felt him harden. "Already?" she asked

with a laugh.

"If you want my cock inside you again, then you need to say it," he cooed, his voice demanding.

She did want it … very much. "I want your cock inside me."

"I like how you say *cock*." Tik-Tok kissed her right below the jaw again. "It rolls off your tongue quite nicely."

She turned to face him, capturing his mouth with hers. His lips moved in a sensual manner, his tongue slowly flicking. He cupped her breast as he buried himself inside her in one stroke, filling her once more.

"Try again," Tik-Tok instructed. "Focus."

North tightened her grip on his metal hand as she looked out at the sea. She'd been outdoors with him for only a little while, but her magic didn't seem to want to come out and play again.

Closing her eyes, she thought about her night before with Tik-Tok, the rush of elated emotions she'd felt. North relaxed for a moment before opening her lids. The violet magic within her swirled, and she reached inside herself to grasp it. Her hand passed through it. Taking a deep, steadying breath, she tried again and latched onto the magic tightly, holding firm.

She studied a small wave, and stretched out to it with a stream of purple. Her body quivered with exertion as she tried to stabilize it. At last, the wave stopped mid-motion, frozen. Her heart kicked up at the sight and she grinned.

"Good," Tik-Tok said. "Now split it in half."

"Easy for you to say," North muttered.

Brushing against the magic holding the wave, she concentrated and watched as her power divided into two tendrils with fingers peaking from their ends. Before she could pull the wave apart, it flattened back into the sea with a crash.

North growled in frustration.

"Keep your shoulders loosened. Try to relax your body,"

Tik-Tok said, releasing her hand. "Perhaps I can help with that." He walked behind her and swiped her hair over her other shoulder. His lips came to her neck, and he kissed up her jaw, his hands trailing down her waist to her thighs.

Her stomach tightened for a reason other than the magic. "That *isn't* helping."

He chuckled in her ear. "Try now. Then after, spin the water."

She peered out at the waves as his arms folded around her and he set his chin on her shoulder. With a deep breath, she pushed out two violet tendrils and watched them drift forward, halting a wave. Jaw clenched, she dug the magic's fingers in and ripped it in half. Her heart practically skipped a beat as she pushed the two tendrils back together. Dipping the magic below the sea's surface, she worked the liquid, spinning it around and around. She was doing it!

Tik-Tok whirled her to look at him with a smile on his face, her magic snapping back inside herself. "Perfect, North." His lips came to hers in a single, blissful kiss.

She itched to try more, so she took her gaze to the sea once again and started to churn the water. Then she clenched a wave, yanked on it, making it increase in size. She could feel the entire ocean tuning into her magic's call. It wasn't only a small area of water she could control, but the entire sea if she wished.

North wasn't sure how much time had passed as she practiced again and again. Her mouth was parched when she finally decided to stop, her body aching. Kaliko had brought them water earlier, and she walked with Tik-Tok to the pole where their drinks had been left. Lifting her glass, she chugged the water down as Dax approached.

"Captain, Respen and I need to discuss some things with you," Dax said, raking a hand through his rumpled blond hair.

Tik-Tok gave him a brief nod and turned to North. "I'll meet with you later."

North set down her empty glass and went to scoop up her

axe to go and take a bath, when Echo came up beside her.

"Someone reeks of sex," the siren drawled as she drew her sword from its sheath.

North peered down at her feet and blushed before making eye contact.

"Don't look so embarrassed. I have to bathe soon myself, but first this." Echo swung her sword forward and North lifted her axe, blocking it. "Excellent."

The sparring with Echo was another way for her to distract herself from what was to come, so she decided to linger on deck a little longer.

She and Echo exchanged blows with their weapons for another hour before they were both drenched with sweat and decided to go down and bathe. Dax had heated the water so it was extra warm, as though he knew her muscles ached. And it wasn't just the ones sore from the training, but from Tik-Tok pressing inside of her. The second time he'd had his way with her, their tumbling had lasted even longer, as if he'd wanted it to go on for an eternity. She hadn't wanted it to end either.

After bathing and throwing on a silky deep blue dress, North went to the deck and sat alone for a while, eating jerky and a dried plum.

A shadow fell over her, and she glanced up to find Tik-Tok peering down at her with a smirk. "Avoiding me?"

"No. I was thinking." She shrugged, rolling the plum in her hand. But she had been—she hadn't wanted him to realize how antsy she'd become about the portal. Her lack of eye contact and twitchy fingers were bound to give her away.

Tik-Tok lowered himself beside her and plucked the fruit from her palm, then sank his teeth into it.

"Hey, that's mine." North took it back from him.

"We share." His grin grew wider while he chewed.

Rolling her eyes, she tossed it to him. Her stomach was starting to feel queasy, knowing they were approaching the portal's location.

152

Tik-Tok continued to munch on the plum. One of his legs was straightened, the other bent, with his arm lazily dangling off it, and his head leaned back against the wall of the ship. He appeared composed, as if it were just another day sailing across the sea.

"We're not far from the portal," Tik-Tok finally said. "I'm considering turning the ship around before you do anything we'll both regret." His relaxed composure started to unravel as he eyed her. He knew her plan…

"Why haven't you turned it already, then?" North replied, holding his stare.

"I should." He pursed his lips. "I should take you home right now."

"But you won't."

"Not unless you say so."

"I won't. I'm doing it. Once I figure out how to open the portal, I'll keep it open once we pass through—for however long I have to." She clasped his hand and inched closer to him. "Are you worried about facing your father?"

"No. Not in the slightest." He furrowed his brow, his grip on her hand tightening. "I'm more worried about you disappearing into the fucking portal."

She was too, but she was still going to face it. "There's no changing fate, and I'll try my hardest to make everything go smoothly. Besides, you'll make sure this other world doesn't end up the way Oz was before I was born." If opening the portal didn't go their way, it would be one life sacrificed to save everything that lay in the world beyond. But if she wasn't close enough to keep the portal open, it would mean Tik-Tok and the rest of the crew could be trapped.

"Celyna saw different outcomes, but I'm only willing to accept one." It took a moment for him to speak again, as though he was having an internal struggle with himself. In one swift motion, he scooped her off the floor and settled her in his lap so they were face to face as she straddled him. Her eyes widened and she glanced behind her to see if anyone was watching.

His fingers caught her chin and turned her face toward him, their gazes trained on one another. "It doesn't matter who watches," he said. "This moment is between us." Tik-Tok's mouth claimed hers, his lips moving in a soft caress. He pulled back from the kiss and hugged her to his chest, his calming scent enveloping her. "Fight like hell, my star. Fight to stay with me when we get there. That's all I want. All you have to do."

Tears pricked at her eyes as she folded her arms around him, gripping him so tight that she thought she might be hurting him. She loosened her hold on him a smidge while resting her head on his shoulder. There were so many words she could say, but this said it all, was more than enough.

A throat cleared behind them. When neither moved, it sounded again.

"Not now, Respen," Tik-Tok muttered.

"We're here, Captain," Echo said.

They had arrived. Echo and Respen stood beside each other while a few crew members were scattered across the ship. North released Tik-Tok and pushed up out of his lap. He peeled himself from the wall and rose beside her.

"North's going to open the portal." Tik-Tok peered out at the sea, and from his face she couldn't tell he was worried in the slightest, although she knew he was.

A brownie wearing a green smock freed the anchor into the sea with a loud splash.

Respen stepped up to North and placed his hands on her shoulders. "Whatever happens, you're one of the crew. Echo and I will be by your side the entire time."

Tears streamed down her cheeks and she swiped them away. "Let's begin."

"There's no rush," Tik-Tok said, his lips pursed.

"No use in waiting either." North moved out from Respen's grip and turned toward the water. She placed her palms against the handrail.

154

Tik-Tok came up behind North, his body caging her in as he set his hands beside hers. Perhaps he thought it would prevent North from being torn away. And maybe it would.

"Keep your eyes open the entire time," Echo told North, coming up on her right while Respen took the left. "There might be another way back if you're looking for it, if you do get lost. Don't give me that look, Captain. I'm only saying this in case something *does* happen. So she'll be prepared."

"I'll keep them open," North whispered, clenching the rail. "I'm ready."

"If you need to stop," Tik-Tok said, "then you stop. Don't force yourself to keep going. Listen to what your body needs and don't overexert yourself."

She nodded and looked at each of their faces—faces that had become familiar. These were her friends, and she wanted to do it for all of them.

Exhaling, North settled her gaze on the silver waves, their gradual movements. Her violet magic stirred, as if it could feel the portal already. With invisible fingers, she pushed down inside herself to the swirling pool of purple and snatched it. The power unfurled from her body like a tree blooming with new flowers. As it spun from her and stretched out to the sea, her body shook slightly. Tik-Tok inched closer to her, his chest brushing against her back, keeping her grounded.

The violet tendrils touched down on the surface of the water, and the waves' light movements kicked up, becoming stronger, forceful, thrashing. The sky above them darkened, thunder booming. Was her magic doing that too?

She kept her eyes trained on the water, squinting at the waves. The magic formed into its smoky hands, their fingers digging into the liquid, then peeled it slowly back. A jagged line opened so deep that there was no seeing an end. Her magic vibrated, erratic. The waves crashed together, the ocean's surface whole like before. Her heart pounded harder and beads of sweat dripped down her face. She didn't know if she could truly do

155

this. But she remembered her earlier training with Tik-Tok—she hadn't gotten it the first time then, either.

North shook her head, finding focus once more as she plucked out the magic from within herself. She kept her eyes wide open this time too, and the waves rose as she pushed her magic out in their direction, their swells growing taller. The ship jostled.

Her body shook harder when her magic dug into the water again. It was as if she might be torn in two.

Tik-Tok's arm left the rail and wrapped around her waist, holding her in place, grounding her. It gave her a new drive as she concentrated, pushing her power forward. A dip in the silver water formed and liquid around that center started spinning in a circular motion. The slow movements churned, growing faster and faster until the sight before her blurred.

North felt herself being pulled away from Tik-Tok and toward that silver shimmer. Her feet rose of their own accord so she was on her toes, her hair lifting around her head, the waves sounding like the world was cracking in half. Tik-Tok's grip tightened as her heart accelerated, pounding against her rib cage.

She didn't know which path was currently being chosen for her, but she kept going anyway, holding onto the magic so tightly that she knew, if her invisible hands could bleed, they would.

With an ear-piercing scream that burned her throat and rattled her chest, she thrust out all the magic she could at the churning center, only this time, more controlled. A heavy, all-consuming force slammed her backward across the ship, colliding with the floor on top of Tik-Tok.

"North!" Tik-Tok lifted her in his lap.

"Are you all right?" Echo asked, crouching beside them.

Everything spun and her body was limp. The magic had reeled itself back inside her, and she was too exhausted to even speak, let alone try to open the portal again.

"She did it," Respen breathed, rushing to them with his eyebrows up his forehead.

North must have had energy left after all because she leapt away from Tik-Tok and darted for the handrail. Below, the spinning circle was no longer silver, but glowing bright violet.

"I *did* do it." She smiled, her voice coming out faint. North's body drooped to the side and Tik-Tok caught her.

CHAPTER NINETEEN

TIK-TOK

The moment North collapsed in Tik-Tok's arms, a loud *boom* echoed in his ears. Not from the newly opened portal, but from behind them. He knelt and curled his body over North's as the ship jerked sideways. The explosion blocked out the sound of choppy water slapping the ship's hull, and a rain barrel crashed against the railing, splintering apart.

"Incoming!" Respen yelled from somewhere close by. "Get down!"

Oh, shit. Tik-Tok clutched North harder against him, holding so tight she would likely have bruises. But no fucking way was she going to be knocked overboard and dragged helplessly into the spinning vortex—to be lost through the portal like Celyna warned. *No fucking way.* He stormed toward his quarters despite the violent rocking of *The Temptress* and threw open the door. Stumbling around the now-crooked desk, he hurried to lay North on the bed. If there was another attack, she probably wouldn't stay there, but he'd rather she fell to the hard floor than into the sea. Swiping his sword from where it had landed near his desk, Tik-Tok rushed to join his crew. He hated leaving

North alone, but he couldn't hide inside while his crew fought for their lives.

"Who the fuck is attacking us?" he asked, joining Echo at the main mast as the brownies scurried below deck.

Another ship, wholly undetected before the first explosion, with huge white sails, plowed through the water, straight for them. White light flashed, and another boom sounded. Tik-Tok grabbed onto one of the ropes to keep from falling as the bright magic hit the side of the ship.

"Not sure, Captain," Echo said after the violent swaying of the ship had ceased.

"Dax!"

"Up here, Captain," he called from the crow's nest above.

Tik-Tok squinted at the enemy ship. "Send wind to keep them from getting closer." He scanned his crew. "Echo," he ordered in an even tone, turning toward her, "steer the ship away from the portal before we're accidentally knocked through it." She bolted toward the wheel to do as instructed, and Respen replaced her at Tik-Tok's side in a flicker of magic. Before he could speak, Tik-Tok commanded, "go see who we're dealing with."

Respen was gone and back in less than a minute, eyes wide with worry over whatever he saw on the enemy ship. "It's Salt. He's got three elementals with him—two water and one wind."

Motherfucker. How were they supposed to withstand that kind of power? Dax blowing them in the other direction was like a bird trying to fly against a hurricane. If Rizmaela hadn't stabbed North, this wouldn't be happening now. Tik-Tok would've gotten his cloaking device in Merryland, and his old captain would never have known that *The Temptress* sailed through his territory. *Gods damned dwarf.*

"What are we doing?" Respen asked.

What are we doing? They were absolutely fucked. What *could* they do? For all Tik-Tok's arrogance, he was still a single—albeit powerful—male. He could turn Salt and his crew to stone, but

159

they had to be close enough first. From this distance, there was no stopping the powerful blasts of magic.

"Parlay," Tik-Tok said with a grimace. After he killed his father, after North was safely home, he and Salt could fight to the death. But now, too much was left undone and unsaid. Not to mention the portal swirling far too close to the ship for his liking. They needed a parlay—a meeting where both parties negotiated under the understanding that neither were harmed. "Tell him we need to parlay. Bring him here."

Respen vanished again, traveling to Salt's ship to follow his captain's orders.

"Dax," Tik-Tok called. One elemental against another was fair, but not one against three. Dax may need to use his wind to get them out of there if the parlay went poorly. "Save your strength."

Gnawing on his bottom lip, Tik-Tok watched Salt's ship inch closer and closer. The blasts of magic had temporarily ceased, but a hum remained in his ears. Each second that ticked by only served to speed his pulse a little more. Respen wasn't there to chat—only grab Salt and return. Anything more would put him in danger.

Respen reappeared, and, beside him, the male who'd saved Tik-Tok from the King of Ev. It was strange seeing him again after so long. Oddly nostalgic. Bitter. The fae reminded Tik-Tok of too many things: his whippings, his betrayal, and his father. Or, what his father *could've* been if he wasn't a deranged murderer.

Captain Salt swung a fist toward Respen's face, but the blue-haired fae dodged the blow, shoving away. Salt's short white hair showcased a handful of jagged scars along his scalp and the tip of one of his ears was missing. His gray eyes held none of the affection they'd once had for Tik-Tok. Instead, they swirled with the force of a thousand storms.

"Long time, no see," Tik-Tok drawled. "Bit of a dramatic reunion though, don't you think?"

160

"I didn't agree to parlay," he snarled.

Tik-Tok shrugged. Respen had undoubtedly made sure Salt's crew knew that was the reason he took their captain. They wouldn't attack when Salt was on board *The Temptress*, regardless, because it would put him at risk. "You don't have to agree."

"Ungrateful bastard!" Salt stormed forward, hands balled tight. He was nearly as tall as Tik-Tok but broader with a patchy beard. "Out of pity, I snuck you out of the palace in Ev, raised you like my own son, made you my first-mate, and how did you repay me? *Mutiny.*"

All of it was true. He'd even felt guilty for a while about betraying Salt and stealing his ship to seek revenge. Then the captain had begun hunting Tik-Tok across the Nonestic Ocean. Completely understandable, of course. If anyone understood the need for vengeance, it was Tik-Tok, but he couldn't feel bad for someone who wanted him dead—the circumstances were irrelevant. If he had wanted Salt dead, he would've killed him during the mutiny, but that was never the goal.

Until now.

"Parlay," Tik-Tok reminded him as Salt lifted his fist.

"Fuck you and your parlay." Salt bared his teeth, swinging his fist down across Tik-Tok's face. Knuckles cracked against his cheekbone.

Tik-Tok spat blood onto the deck, his cheek stinging like a motherfucker, and slowly turned his gaze to his old captain. *A punch to the face?* He felt slightly offended that Salt hadn't done something more damaging. Pack a bit of magic into the fist, at least. "Feel better?" he sneered.

Salt lunged at Tik-Tok but a strong wind blasted him sideways. He landed flat on his back beside the rail.

From above, Dax called, "Parlay, ya old coot."

Tik-Tok snorted in amusement and stalked toward the prone male. He crouched beside him and lifted a brow. "I have one deal to offer. Take it or leave it."

"Leave it," Salt growled, sitting up.

161

"You haven't even heard the terms." His smile was cold as ice. "There's an open sea portal on the other side of *my* ship. We're going through it and you're not going to stop us. In exchange, when we return, I'll agree to fight you to the death. Get this whole sordid thing over with once and for all."

"A portal?" Salt barked, the sound ending on a disbelieving laugh. Then, when he met Tik-Tok's steady gaze, he sobered. "You don't have an elemental on board causing the whirlpool?"

He gave a small, mirthless chuckle. "I betrayed you, Salt, but did I ever lie to you?"

Salt spat in his face. "No deal."

Tik-Tok stood, forcing his rage down, and wiped the saliva from his cheek. He hadn't come so far—betrayed Salt at Celyna's bidding to gain a ship and a reputation—to fail now. Calling on his magic, Tik-Tok pursed his lips and pushed the rough-edged power outward. Gray immediately crept over Salt's sun-darkened skin, locking bones in place, solidifying organs. He gasped, the sound a mix of shock and fear, and the stone froze his old captain's expression in place. Eyes narrowed, nose wrinkled in disgust, revealing anger that Salt's voice hadn't.

Ah, hell. Salt couldn't attack him now, but if Respen returned him as a statue, the crew would blow *The Temptress* into a million slivers. If they dropped him overboard, he would eventually return to flesh and bone when Tik-Tok was far enough away for the magic to fade … and then he would drown before ever seeing the sun again. There was bad blood between the two fae, but not even Salt deserved that torment. The entire feud was Tik-Tok's fault, so the least he could do was give the male a clean death.

"Take him back," he told Respen, flicking a hand at the stone fae.

Respen didn't hesitate to obey, but there was a distinct line of confusion between his brows. His confusion was fine. It was his silent trust in Tik-Tok that sent a twinge of gratitude through his chest. Moving behind Salt, Respen grabbed his stone shoulders and used his magic to whirl them both away.

162

The moment they disappeared, Tik-Tok looked to Dax. At some point, while the two captains spoke, he had climbed down from the crow's nest. Tik-Tok's shoulders slumped slightly. "They'll sink us for this," he said matter-of-factly.

"Then why take him back?"

Tik-Tok groaned, unsure if it had been the right thing to do. "Because if he doesn't return, or if we start sailing away with him still on board, his crew will catch up. They won't dare follow us through the portal—Salt's too superstitious about them. Let's hope seeing him that way startles the crew enough to make them turn around completely." The wind stirred and Respen reappeared, alone. *Shit.* That was fast—not that his first-mate would've stuck around for the fallout after dropping a stone Salt at their feet. "Sail into the portal. *Now.*"

Everyone on deck fell deathly silent. Dax, staring at Tik-Tok as if he'd misheard, Respen opening and shutting his mouth, and Echo and Cyrx frozen in shock where they stood at the helm. Another blast of white light lit the air, then a *boom* sounded, and a brutal crash of magic hit the side of Tik-Tok's ship. The waves lifted the vessel on sudden swells, shaking it like a youngling's rattle. Wood creaked beneath the sea's force and Dax was flung into Respen, taking them both to the ground.

"The portal!" Tik-Tok shouted. "Go!"

Echo spun the wheel so fast that when Dax blew wind into the sails, the ship jerked to the side. Tik-Tok gripped a rope circling the mast, keeping himself steady, at the same time a small shriek came from his quarters.

Fuck. North was awake. If she came out now, there was every chance she would fall into the portal—alone and without a ship to keep her from drowning. Celyna hadn't been specific enough about how North would be lost. The simple act of opening it could've pulled her in when the magic had lifted her from the ground, or was it something afterward that sent her tumbling through?

The knob turned slowly. Tik-Tok lurched forward,

struggling to remain upright and shoved the door inward.

North stumbled back into the cabin wall, pale and wide-eyed. "What's going on out there?"

"We're going through the portal," he said, slamming the door behind him. "Salt found us … if we don't go, he'll sink *The Temptress* and everyone on it."

"I can control the water if you need my help against him," she said, holding onto the heavy furniture as it began to slide across the room.

"I don't care if you can break the ocean in half." He felt around the door in search of the handle. "Stay here, no matter what you hear."

North's head whipped toward him. "I can help."

"If you leave this room, North, I swear—" He found the handle, opened the door and slipped sideways through it, pausing before the last step. "I'm sorry, but I told you there's only one outcome I'm willing to accept."

He shut the door with a thunk and held on another moment as the ship rocked, tilting precariously on its side. His boots slipped out from under him, sending him skidding across the deck. Echo caught his metal arm through the spokes of the wheel before he could careen into the water.

"Brace yourselves!" Cyrx bellowed.

As if it would make a difference. Tik-Tok gripped the wheel, nodding his thanks to Echo, and held on tight as the ship entered the edge of the spiraling water.

The water grabbed onto the hull, whipping the ship into its rapid revolution. Spinning, spinning, spinning, drawing them closer to the center at an alarming rate. Sea water sprayed the deck, soaking them all. Wood creaked and groaned. The portal hummed louder and louder until it roared. The sound of perfect chaos.

And there was no escaping it.

Chapter Twenty

North

North stood inside Tik-Tok's room, gripping the edge of his desk as the boat jostled side to side from the choppy waters. She wanted to go outside and slap him across the face for telling her to stay here. Though she understood why he had. If North chose to, she could easily walk out of the room, but she wouldn't risk something happening to her—for his sake. There'd been fear in his eyes, an emotion that had reflected her own. If the portal separated her from the crew, how would Tik-Tok get the ship back, if she wasn't there to control it? She'd made a promise to remain, and she wouldn't break it until they sailed through the gateway and returned safe.

The boat jerked forward, and she felt it skim the waves as it rocked harder. North didn't huddle in fear. Instead, she held Tik-Tok's desk harder and kept her eyes wide open, preparing herself for the unknown.

Tik-Tok had mentioned Salt when he'd rushed into his quarters to check on her after she'd woken. Salt must have found them while she'd been unconscious from overusing her magic. Yet the portal had stayed open, still connected to her. If she hadn't been so useless, she could have been out there on deck, helping to protect the crew from Tik-Tok's enemy. It was a male he'd betrayed, but she was on Tik-Tok's side regardless.

North's magic pulsed inside her veins, her heart thrumming in sync with it. Her power expanded inside her, and she felt the portal, alive and looming, growing nearer, even though she couldn't see the Nonestic Ocean as they crossed the barrier. Every fiber, every nerve, twitched while the ship sailed through the maelstrom, rattling, vibrating, as if the wood might crack in half.

North's hair rose again around her head, her feet lifting up to her toes, the sound of waves thrashing pounding in her ears. She couldn't tell if the cacophony was from outside the ship or inside her own head. Glass shattered, furniture scraped the floor, and her entire body vibrated.

As if the ocean itself had frozen within her, the movements ceased, her silver hair pooled back around her shoulders. She released her death-grip on the desk. Everything was still and quiet.

They'd gone through the gateway, and she was still here, in one piece. The portal stayed open, churning in a steady circular motion. She could feel her tenuous connection to the magic that kept it in existence. If she wanted it to close, all she needed to do was shut off the violet magic. But she left it on, and she would let that light continue to shine bright until they were ready to go home.

North sucked in a sharp breath as she peered around— fragments of broken glass were sprawled across the floor near the cabinets, Tik-Tok's bed was now near the middle of his room, and papers from his desk had scattered everywhere. She rushed to the door and flung it open at the same time Tik-Tok seemed to be reaching for the handle from the outside.

His wild gaze locked on hers. "You're safe."

"I think so." Her eyes widened when she took in the dark gray sky filled with black clouds. A putrid smell hit her senses, like rotting meat. She cupped her nose and mouth with her hand. "What is this place?"

"My father's home." He motioned at the air. "It fits him rather well."

North brushed past Tik-Tok on the slick, debris-free deck, and made her way to the handrail.

Her lips parted as she peered down at the water. The sea was so blue it was almost black. The liquid rippled—small bubbles popped at the surface, oozing a deep brown. North was certain the foul odor was from the sea itself, which appeared to be a thicker consistency than water.

As she looked out farther, the dingy green shore stretched across the horizon. A dark forest filled the land, and black smoke curled up from the tops of the tall trees. She squinted to see if she could see anything between the slits of the trunks, but the ship was too far from shore.

Tik-Tok's boots sounded behind her. He pressed up beside her, letting one arm dangle over the rail as he clutched his compass in the other. Holding it out, he watched as the arrow spun and spun, never slowing, until it did, right at the shore before spinning once more. "Now that we're here, I don't want to waste any time finding my father. It's dangerous to stay too long."

"I wish I could go with you." She stared out at the portal, still swirling a few yards away, its purple light shimmering. Within the dark water, it appeared like a beacon, waiting for fae to be drawn in. The sea witch had told Tik-Tok that if the portal didn't remain open, they would never return to Oz, and that thought made North's heart beat harder—she didn't want to let Tik-Tok and the crew—*her* crew—down. She took a deep swallow, steeling herself.

"No, you don't." Tik-Tok clenched his jaw. "My father ruined my life. I know I've made vile choices in my past to seek revenge, but I can't apologize for it."

"Even for taking me from the Emerald City?" North arched

167

a brow.

"Especially that." He smirked.

North's cheeks heated. But a part of her felt awful for it because the fae of Oz had all been worried, searching for her. At least Crow would have told them to halt the search after he'd spoken to her. Perhaps sometimes it was all right to be selfish, though.

"What about Salt? Are you worried about him?"

"Don't worry about him." Tik-Tok sighed. "As soon as we go back through the portal, he'll be there, waiting. I may need you to use the ocean against him, so we can make a clean break."

"I can do that." North smiled at the thought of being useful instead of sitting back and doing nothing. As she realized what Tik-Tok would be doing next, a scowl formed on her face. "You're not going alone, are you?"

"I am." He nodded toward the ropes holding the rowboat.

A squelching sound came from somewhere within the sea's depths, and she suppressed a shudder at what might be lurking below the surface. He couldn't take the small boat without knowing what lay hidden in the murky waters. It could be nothing, but it could also be *something*.

"You're not rowing," North said, her voice serious, leaving no room for argument. "Take Respen. He can whirl you to the shore and then to your father. It's faster than walking the entire world to find him."

Tik-Tok chuckled. "I didn't know you were captain of this ship."

"I know you don't want to risk anyone," North started. "But if you need an escape, Respen can easily bring you back here, then we can sail through the portal. Please."

He clucked his tongue. "Fine. I'll take Respen, but no one else."

North nodded. Her heart pounded through her rib cage at the thought of him leaving. It truly hit her then, what Tik-Tok's father had done to his family. Years had passed since he'd seen

168

the male, and no matter the powers that Tik-Tok held, his father's could be greater. Tik-Tok could die… But North would never tell him to stay, not after they'd gotten this far. He would face his own enemy, the way North's own family had.

"Before I find Respen, come with me. We have ten minutes to spare." He grabbed her hand and pulled her toward his room, his pace quickening. She frowned as she kept up with his long strides. What was so important that he couldn't tell her right then?

He opened the door and kicked it shut behind them.

"Tik-Tok, what—"

Spinning around to face her, he slammed his mouth to hers, silencing her with a kiss. Tik-Tok backed her up against the wall, and she let out a small squeak before kissing him in return. He hoisted her up and wrapped her legs around his waist as his mouth coasted over her lips, tasting, taking. She could feel his hard length pressing against her core.

"I know this is wildly inappropriate given the circumstances, but there are so many things I want to say before I leave. There isn't time though. There's only this, my North Star." His voice came out raspy, thick, as he rubbed himself against her. A whimper escaped her lips as sensations pulsed through her from each grind of his hips.

When he'd called her his North Star, a different kind of warmth spread through her. She couldn't find the right words to give him in return, so she caught his bottom lip between her teeth and sucked on it, then lifted her dress to give him access.

She rested her forehead against his as he unlaced his pants and freed himself. Tik-Tok lowered her a fraction so she could feel him against her once more. With those wicked fingers of his, he pushed her undergarments to the side, not even taking the time to remove them. He then slid inside her with one perfect stroke, making them both groan in pleasure while he filled her. Her hands tightened in his hair as she took in a deep breath.

"You feel so fucking good," Tik-Tok purred, thrusting his

169

hips forward, her back striking the wall.

He increased his pace, rattling her entire body with rapture. She was pretty certain they were shaking the entire boat, but she couldn't be embarrassed about this, this wildness, this animalistic side of him, of her, of them together. She'd loved when he'd taken her sweetly, loved it even more in this moment when he was pounding into her with ferocity. That pleasureful feeling was inching closer and closer and *closer*, each of his movements fueling her into oblivion. Everything within her shattered when he brought her over the edge, her head falling backward as she whispered his name. The orgasm had been so overpowering that she didn't even have the strength to shout it.

Both their chests heaved as she brought her head back down, their gazes connected.

"I need to go," he murmured.

"Don't make his death an easy one." She kissed his lips, hoping this wasn't their last goodbye. "He doesn't deserve it."

Tik-Tok lowered her to the floor and she straightened her dress as he tucked himself back inside his pants. He opened the door and led her out to the deck, neither saying a word to each other about what had happened between them. But from his deep breaths, she knew he was still reeling from the aftereffects, same as she was.

They made their way back to the crew, who were all huddled in a discussion.

"Respen," Tik-Tok said, "I'd like you to come with me. Can you bring us to shore so we don't have to worry about a boat?"

"Yes, Captain." Respen nodded. It was only briefly, but North could see the flicker of worry in Echo's eyes. Perhaps North shouldn't have suggested he take Respen, but anyone else wouldn't be as safe or as fast. This way, they could easily get away from lurking danger.

Tik-Tok instructed Dax and Cyrx to sail the ship and leave this world without them if they had to. North wouldn't let them leave without Tik-Tok or Respen if it came down to that, and she didn't think Echo would either.

Tik-Tok turned to North, his expression unreadable. "No goodbyes." He tucked a tendril of hair behind her ear, then walked away from her, toward Respen. The first mate placed his hands on Tik-Tok's shoulders. A cool wind kicked up and a yellow light gleamed, then they were both gone.

Echo jogged to the end of the ship and North followed, meeting her at the handrail. On the shore, in the distance, stood two figures she could barely make out.

"No goodbyes," North said softly as she watched them disappear inside the forest, the black smoke continuing to rise into the sky.

"Are you all right?" North asked when she noticed Echo was still watching the empty shore.

Echo pursed her lips, her arms folded over her stomach. "With this life, you have to be. But that doesn't mean your heart still won't ache at times."

North's chest tightened. What if they didn't come back? How long would she and the crew have to wait here? North knew Echo would try going after them if it took too long, and she would too. But if North left the ship, she would risk the portal closing. For now, she had to drown the worry and focus on her own task.

"I'm going to grab you some water and fruit. You need to keep your strength up." Echo pushed off from the handrail and headed toward the door.

North didn't think she would be able to eat anything without throwing it back up. She was too full of knots. A swishing sound came from the direction of the portal and North jerked her head up. The magic within her shifted as if something heavy were moving through her.

Not her...

The *portal*.

She gasped and her heart thundered when a massive ship with large white sails rose out from the flashing portal. The ship

171

was completely dry as the portal churned it in a backward motion. The gateway slowed, then the ship stilled, pushing off from the entrance, and headed toward them.

Chapter Twenty-One

Tik-Tok

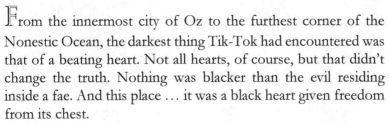

From the innermost city of Oz to the furthest corner of the Nonestic Ocean, the darkest thing Tik-Tok had encountered was that of a beating heart. Not all hearts, of course, but that didn't change the truth. Nothing was blacker than the evil residing inside a fae. And this place ... it was a black heart given freedom from its chest.

Alive. Corrupt. The air carrying an ominous vibration.

It sent a shiver down Tik-Tok's spine as he and Respen walked farther into the strange land. The anticipation was almost too much for him to handle—being there, where his father was, after all these years of searching, made him want to crawl from his skin. Celyna's visions led him here and, back on the ship, his compass had pointed in this direction—he knew his father was alive. The phantom pain of broken ribs and dislocated shoulders assaulted him. His stomach twisted as if anticipating a *special* tart baked by his mother and force-fed by his father. The poison she'd used wasn't strong enough to kill them, but enough to make him and his siblings violently ill for days. Swallowing hard, he focused on how sweet his revenge would be.

The world looked like Oz when a raging storm approached, darkening the skies. Towering trees with needle-like branches gave way to steam rising from soil and a village nestled into the bottom of a ravine. It had only taken a short walk to find this place. They were barely past the trees, which led Tik-Tok to believe it was a fishing village. Some sort of port town, perhaps. This close to the sea, it was the most logical conclusion.

Soft white lights glowed inside the large homes—or what he *assumed* were homes. Sloping roofs topped the two-story dwellings, and fences, far too short to do more than decorate the grass, surrounded them. The structures were arranged in squares of four with gravel paths running between each. Beneath their feet, the dirt path turned to ground-up rock.

"Do you think the creatures living here are friendly?" Respen asked.

Tik-Tok shrugged and flipped open the magic compass in his palm. "I think I don't give a fuck."

The needle of the compass whizzed in clockwise circles before slowing, pointing directly ahead, only to whip back around to point behind them. Toward *The Temptress*. Where North waited. He hated leaving her—leaving all of them—when everything about this world was a mystery. There was no telling what may happen while they were tracking down his father.

Tik-Tok shook the nagging thoughts away and focused on his father again, urging the compass to direct him toward *that* desire instead. It moved, almost reluctantly, back toward the homes.

Respen removed a long, narrow blade from inside his boot. "Just in case," he said, surveying the quiet village streets.

With a grunt of agreement, Tik-Tok pulled his sword out, but held it in a relaxed position, its tip pointed at the ground. There was no sense in provoking the locals. If there were any *to* provoke. "Everyone seems to be inside," he mused.

A young female stepped from between two buildings as if his words had summoned the nearest resident. Her eyes landed first on Respen, then Tik-Tok. She froze, her face draining of color, even under the gray light, and a bucket of water fell from her hands with a loud *sploosh*. The following seconds melted together as they all held their breath, each waiting for the other to move. Her dark hair was drawn back, giving prominence to angled features, and overly large, orb-like eyes. If it wasn't for her rounded ears, he might've mistaken her for some sort of fae. Black fabric wrapped around her neck, twisting down her abdomen where it tied at her waist, hanging around her legs in loose, flowing panels.

Then she screamed. A high-pitched, frenzied cry.

Respen was behind her in a snap, cupping a hand over her mouth. "Shh," he urged. Her response was, naturally, to flail in an attempt to escape his grasp. "We aren't going to hurt you."

Fuck. She was making too much noise. They didn't need her family or friends coming to investigate, only to find two strangers accosting her. "Stop it," Tik-Tok demanded quietly, stepping forward. He would've turned her to stone, but she might have useful information. "I don't have time for your antics."

Tears gathered in her eyes, spilling out in inky streams. A defeated whimper left her, and Respen eased away. "P-p-please, Your Exalted Eminence," she begged between tiny hiccups. "I didn't realize you had recovered a-and you frightened me, is all."

What the fuck is she talking about? Tik-Tok frowned. "Well, that's one way to greet me. Much preferrable than *Your Mediocre Majesty.*"

"A Paltry Prince, if I've ever seen one," Respen quipped.

The woman looked between them, chest rising and falling in rapid breaths, and cried harder. *The fuck?* "You didn't hurt her, did you?" Tik-Tok whispered to his first mate.

"Of course not." Respen cocked his head, watching her curiously, and stuffed his blade back into his boot. "We mean no harm."

Her gaze dropped. "No one was aware of your visit, but if you'll give me a moment, I'll make sure everything is prepared

175

the way you like it."

"I'm *extremely* confused," Tik-Tok admitted with a small smirk. "But since you're so eager to accommodate, I'm looking for my father." Not that he expected the first town they happened upon to be the *right* one, but perhaps she could offer a hint at the fae's whereabouts.

"Lizbet, what's taking so long?" A younger girl, no more than ten—if the beings there aged the same as fae—scampered down the street and latched onto the terrified female's hand. "You've been out here for—"

Lizbet drew the girl tight, shifting to hide her behind her skirts. "*Please*," she pleaded. "Let her go back inside. I'll do anything you ask."

The two pirates exchanged a quick, bewildered look, then Tik-Tok furrowed his brows. "I don't give a rat's ass what she does—or you for that matter." Assuming she didn't attack them, but that seemed extremely unlikely. "Unless you feel like obliging me with a bit of information."

"Go," Lizbet urged the younger girl. "Hurry. Tell Father that Glarondal is here and to ready the finest sacrifices."

Tik-Tok felt the blood drain from his face. *Glarondal.* His father. They thought *he* was his father. He bared his teeth, eyes narrowing. "I am *not* that piece of shit fae."

The female slapped a hand over her mouth. "Blasphemy!"

"Blasphemy?" Tik-Tok snarled. "Who the fuck do you think Glarondal is? A *god*?"

Shifting backward, feet dragging in the gravel, she eyed them both through a suspicious squint. Using quick movements, she covered her chest with both palms and brought them outward in a wide arc as if performing some sort of ritual. "Glarondal is *the only* god and may he strike you down for your insults."

Respen snorted. "Weren't you terrified a moment ago?"

"Come now," Tik-Tok drawled to his first-mate. "Fear and worship often go hand-in-hand."

The girl made the same motion over and over with increasing

speed, mumbling words too low for them to make out. Each time she repeated the movements, Tik-Tok's chest tightened in anger. Blindingly violent wrath.

"Enough," he snapped. Whipping out his compass, he checked the face. This time the needle was steadfast, leading deeper into the village. He was in *no* mood to traipse through the entire fucking world searching for his father. For all he knew, they were on opposite sides of this universe.

"You okay?" Respen asked as Tik-Tok stormed away from the praying girl.

"Wonderful," he snarled. There was nothing quite like finding out you looked like the fucker who murdered your family. Except, perhaps, being mistaken for him. And that he was worshiped as a god.

"Let's make this quicker," Respen said, gripping Tik-Tok's shoulder. The world went fuzzy, whizzing by, until it suddenly stopped. Respen had whirled them out of the village and into a field with deep green, ankle-high grass. Large creatures stood on four legs. Light gray scales covered their gangly legs and long snouts, and black fur sprouted from their bulbous bodies. "Any closer?" he asked.

Tik-Tok glanced at the compass. It still pointed ahead, only slightly to the left. He tilted the tool to show Respen, who still had a grip on his shoulder. Again, they traveled with Respen's magic, stopping only to check the compass. Again and again. Appearing in glittering cities and bogs and outside of steam-powered factories.

Until finally, in the middle of a massive mountain range, surrounded by stony cliffs and climbing vines, the needle glowed gold. Sleet pounded down at an angle as Tik-Tok and Respen walked cautiously to the mouth of a dark cave. Water dripped somewhere inside, splashing softly against the stone ground. A wet cough accompanied it before trailing off into a wheeze. Tik-Tok slowed his steps, holding his sword at the ready.

Something was in there. His father, according to the

compass, but perhaps he wasn't alone. Glarondal used to talk about this place—how it was ripe for his intentions. Others had visited long ago, returning with tales passed down through generations—tales about how it lacked magic completely. Even the mortal world where Thelia came from had traces of it, but this place had *nothing*. When Tik-Tok's brother realized he had the extremely rare power to open sea portals, his father had pounced. No one since Tik-Tok's brother had held the ability to open portals in the sea, not until North.

So, unless his father had brought any fae with him—and Tik-Tok was sure he wouldn't have risked any potential power struggle—it wasn't much of a threat. Especially with a cough like that.

"You don't have to come with me," he offered Respen.

He shrugged. "I'd rather watch him die, if it's all the same to you."

Tik-Tok grinned and took an orb from inside his jacket pocket to cast a small amount of light. It created shadows along the walls where jagged rocks reached out and up like spindly fingers. Water trickled from the ceiling, following the path worn by years of erosion, though in other places, it dripped straight down into hollowed pockets on the ground. Easing around sharp spikes, the two pirates descended farther and farther with light footsteps, and the darkness swallowed them from behind.

If it weren't for another round of hacking, Tik-Tok would've thought his compass was broken. Respen paused suddenly and nodded to the side. Tik-Tok cocked his head to listen and scowled. The sound was coming ... from inside the wall.

Magic. It had to be. Tik-Tok reached out with his golden hand and brushed it across the rock. The wall gave beneath his touch, springing back like the top of Cook's warm pastries. He narrowed his eyes, scanned the wall, and sniffed the air. Traces of sweet berries, warm sunlight, and burnt wood mingled together.

"Fae magic," he concluded.

"Do you know how to get through?" Respen asked.

Tik-Tok's lips curled into a wiry smile and he lifted his sword. It was fae magic, but weak. Brittle. Otherwise, it wouldn't have given beneath his hand, and the sound of coughing would've been contained. With a quick bash of his sword's hilt, Tik-Tok smashed through the barrier. It fell silently, the illusion toppling like a stack of blocks, before disintegrating on the ground.

Inside was a large, squared-off cave full of gold furnishings. Most prominent was a throne-like chair, wide enough for two to sit in comfortably, with etched patterns across the back. An elaborate bedframe with rich brocade blankets and pillows sat in a corner, and a floating chandelier glowed brightly with attached orbs like the one Tik-Tok held. Even the wooden dining set sported shimmering leaves, and the rug was woven with golden fibers. A feast spanned the table, extravagant enough for the Queen of Oz herself.

And yet … everything was covered in dust and mildew. The food was blackened with age.

"What are you doing here?" wheezed a male, hidden somewhere in front of them.

Tik-Tok sniffed the air again, trying to scent the magic, but it *all* smelled of his father. He would never forget the bitter flavor of his magic—the way it oozed around him during every beating, the way it had nearly suffocated him during their final interaction—the day Glarondal and his wife had murdered their children.

Snarling, Tik-Tok stuffed his orb back into his pocket, keeping both hands free. "Venture a guess," he suggested.

Respen shifted uncomfortably beside him, but Tik-Tok refused to show the bastard an ounce of discomfort. If whatever shield he used was as weak as the barrier, it wouldn't last long.

"Your magic glows bright," the voice said, crackling. "Strong magic. I've seen that color before."

"Have you now?" Tik-Tok said through clenched teeth.

A body suddenly flickered into existence, slumped in the

throne. The elegantly wrought chair with its fine designs held the vilest of beings. Glarondal's hair hung in thin, black clumps, patches of his head bald and bleeding. Brown spots dotted his dry, waxy skin. The rusty brown of his eyes was hidden beneath a blue film, and a large sore grew on the corner of his mouth. The body Tik-Tok had once feared beyond all things was now hunched, fingers bent at wrong angles, limbs little more than bone.

How? Fae didn't age like this. They stopped showing their years once maturity was reached, and only began again when they were in their final century or so. Even then, it was never like this. Never so ... mortal.

"How did you come to my kingdom, fae? Is there another who can open the portal?" He coughed and blood spurted from his lips. A darker, dried crimson covered the white tunic he wore. "If there is, bring him to me and I will reward you handsomely."

"I will bring you no one," Tik-Tok said without an ounce of leeway. *No one,* but especially not North. He walked slowly into the room, skimming his golden hand over the backs of the dining chairs. "After all the trouble it took to get here, I'm surprised you would want another portal."

"This place will drain the magic from you," Glarondal spat. "So gradually that you won't notice until it's too late. You can't stay—take me back with you."

Tik-Tok smirked. Seeing his father this way, hearing the desperation in his voice, was the sweetest gift. Even sweeter than his mother's dying screams had been. "Oh, I have no intention of staying."

Glarondal pushed up on the arms of his chair in an attempt to stand, but fell back in his seat. "We should leave for the Fae Lands immediately."

"What will you do there?" Tik-Tok grimaced at the small white worms slithering through a bowl of fruit. "Will you rejoin your family?" He wasn't sure why he asked, but he was curious. Not of his plans, but if he had an ounce of remorse in his abhorrent body.

"My family was murdered by my son," he wheezed. "Hateful youngling."

Tik-Tok froze. *What the* fuck? Was he serious? All thoughts became suspended as he stared down the worthless male. Even emotions failed him. For a single moment, he felt nothing—not anger, not fear, not glee or disgust.

Then it all came rushing back tenfold.

His eldest sister, cradling her stomach, protecting the life inside, even as their mother dragged the very essence from her body. His older brother, leaping in to save her. Their father meeting him, midair, with his sword, spilling his brother's guts. The screeching cries of Tik-Tok's younger sister as Glarondal stalked toward her with blood dripping from the blade. How he'd severed each of their spinal cords to make sure they stayed dead. And the way it felt to be held immobile by magic, watching, *knowing* he would be next...

Tik-Tok lunged forward and, in the span of a breath, he held his sword against his father's throat. "*I* killed them, Father?" he seethed. Glarondal's mouth dropped open in shock. "I seem to remember it differently. Please, do tell me what happened."

"Tik-Tok." He drew a loud, gasping breath. "You've come for me."

He pressed his blade a little deeper and a line of red trickled down Glarondal's veined skin. "I've come to *kill* you, you wretched blackguard. For *decades*, I've hunted for someone to open the portal. I made sacrifice after sacrifice to be here so I could chop you into tiny pieces and feed you to the sea. Even then, that wouldn't be enough to pay back all you did to me and my siblings."

"You can't kill me." Glarondal laughed, but it quickly turned into a cough. Tik-Tok eased the sword away so the bastard wouldn't kill himself and rob him of his vengeance. "I'm a *god*."

Respen laughed from across the room, but quickly shut his mouth when Tik-Tok shot him a glare. "Sorry, Captain. It's

181

just. . ." He gave Glarondal a scathing look.

"Captain?" Glarondal said, and latched onto Tik-Tok's sleeve. "Who would follow a vermin like you?"

"Who would worship a piece of shit like *you*?" Respen shot back.

A spark of magic suddenly zapped Tik-Tok's golden arm, tingling, and he yanked it away from his father. "Did you try to steal my magic?" he spoke quietly. Too quietly. Making it louder than the blasts from Salt's ship.

"What happened to your arm?" Glarondal croaked, rubbing his hand as if it stung.

It probably did—his arm repelled any magic, including having it stolen, and his father had been foolish enough to try while touching it. Only one other had attempted it before, and the dryad had quickly become engulfed in flames, all from one small spark of protection. Tik-Tok leered down at his father. "I don't think I'll kill you after all," he said slowly. "I think there's a better end for you."

"Wh—"

Tik-Tok motioned Respen over with a nod. "Take us back to the first village."

"Aye, Captain." Respen lifted a brow and gripped Tik-Tok's shoulder. "Hold onto him."

Tik-Tok grabbed the dying male by the throat, eliciting a panicked gasp, and Respen's power dragged them from the cave, directly back to the crossroad where they'd stood only an hour ago.

Dropping his father, Tik-Tok strode up to the house that the young girl had exited earlier. He squared his shoulders and pounded on the door. Eagerness built in him as he waited for someone to answer. All this time, he'd wanted to savor his revenge, and this was how it needed to happen.

A portly being swung the door open and gasped. He was square-jawed and hairless—at least what wasn't hidden beneath loose black robes that covered him from neck to ankle. "Your

Exalted Eminence," he said with a bow. The confusion on his face was hard to miss. His daughter had likely told him how *blasphemous* he'd been before, striking doubt into the whole family. "It's an honor. My daughters told me you'd arrived, so we prepared—"

"Enough." Tik-Tok closed his eyes for a moment before he lost control of his temper and punched the innocent man. "Bring your family outside to bear witness."

Tik-Tok whirled around and went back to Respen's side. Glarondal wheezed on the gravel, frantically searching for something, though surely, he couldn't see more than shadow with the blue cataracts coating his eyes.

"What are you planning?" Respen asked with a curious tilt of his head.

"I'm becoming a god," Tik-Tok replied with a disgusted grin. When he turned again, the two girls from earlier stood behind the patriarch, along with two older women, a young boy, and an elderly man. They strongly resembled each other in the face— dark eyes, darker hair, slightly upturned noses—but it was as if every day they lived had visably aged them. The wide-eyed, younger children cowering behind the grown beings were the exception, but likely not for long.

"You've worshipped a false god all these years." Tik-Tok's voice boomed, and he loathed pretending to be the cruel god that his father had created. "This ... creature..."—he shot a glance at his cowering father—"has taken my likeness as his own and fooled you all."

"What are you doing?" Glarondal snapped, pushing to his knees. "Don't listen to him. He's a great deceiver!"

Tik-Tok forced himself not to scoff and instead met each of the locals' gazes. "Would a god decay as such?" He swept a hand out. "Deal with him as you would deal with any *deceiver*. Punish him well or I will turn my wrath to your world."

"Liar," the young girl from before shouted.

Though the old woman pushed her further behind the

group, he saw the defiance burning in her youthful eyes. "Am I?" Tik-Tok asked. "Shall I prove it?"

Before any of them could tell him no, he shoved the roughest of his magic outward. It hit the patriarch straight in the chest, sliding over his body, turning it to stone. The girl who'd called him a liar screamed so loudly that his ears rang, and the oldest woman fainted, collapsing onto the graveled street.

"Perhaps I will leave him here as a reminder," he mused.

"No," Lizbet whispered, stepping away from the group, repeating the ridiculous hand movements *again*. "We believe you. Please, Your Exha—"

"Shh," he hissed, a finger to his lips. Then he released his power from the man so he could return to his true form.

Respen shook with silent laughter when Tik-Tok grabbed his forearm.

"Not a fucking word," he said under his breath.

The entire family, unconscious woman aside, replicated the Lizbet's motions. Hands pressed to their chests, arms sweeping out, words mumbled with reverence. And they weren't the only ones. Other doors opened, more families coming into the streets.

Hell fucking no. Tik-Tok tightened his grip on Respen. "Let's get back to the ship."

"You don't want to stay and watch?" his first mate asked.

"No." This wasn't the revenge he'd envisioned, but his father was going to die slowly, painfully, desperate and alone. Truly alone. Those terrorized into worshiping him would take their own revenge for the awful things he'd surely done.

And Glarondal would leave this world—*all* worlds—hated. Despised. Powerless.

No. It wasn't what Tik-Tok had dreamed of. Not what his siblings with their kind hearts and fiercer love would have wanted. There was no battle to be won or bloody vengeance to exact on their behalf. Glarondal was already too far gone for that. But this ... this was better. Tik-Tok smiled down at the male as he crawled toward his boots.

"Goodbye, *Father*," he whispered blithely as Respen's magic swept him back to *The Temptress*. To his home and to his future. *North.*

Chapter Twenty-Two

North

"The bastard followed us!" Dax shouted, racing toward the middle of the ship and snatching North's weapons from the floor.

North whipped her head up, her gaze landing on the ship that had sailed through the portal. Once fully in the new world, the ship fought its way clear of the vortex and barreled straight for them. Its large white sails cracked like thunder with the wind, and its glossy wood coloring reflected from an obscured sun. This ship was as grand as Tik-Tok's, towering and looming. Several fae stood on deck, but she couldn't see their faces clearly. Her hands shook and her heartbeat increased. Tik-Tok was gone, and she wasn't sure what was happening. But she needed to retrieve her axe from Dax.

"Not again!" Echo growled withdrawing her sword as she stomped across the deck. She turned to the brownies who were hurrying into place, their expressions determined. "Remain here to defend your captain's ship—your home—if need be."

They nodded and stood in a huddle, most holding broomsticks and makeshift weapons.

Dax jogged to North with her axes in his hands, his nostrils flaring. "You're probably going to need them both."

As she reached to take the weapons from him, a familiar boom roared, making her jump. It was the same sound that had woken her after she'd passed out. A bright white light soared toward them, disrupting her vision. Magic struck the boat, slamming her body into the handrail. A sharp pain throbbed at her hip and a squeak escaped her lips.

"Is this Salt?" North asked, her heart thudding rapidly.

Dax yanked her down beneath the handrail so they were protected by the ship's barrier. He set her axes in her lap. "Yes. Tik-Tok turned Salt into stone during a parlay so the crew is probably pissed."

"What?" North's brows rose up her forehead. Did this all happen when she'd been unconscious? "Tik-Tok didn't think to mention these details to me before he left?"

"No one thought Salt's crew would follow us through the portal."

Another hard blow struck the ship as if a giant godly hand whacked it. The impact lurched North forward, rattling her entire body.

Dax stood, facing Salt's ship with his hands held in front of him, ready to use his elemental power.

North pushed up from the floor, her lips parting when she focused on Salt's ship. It was practically beside Tik-Tok's now and it would only take a quick row for Salt's crew to board *The Temptress*.

A light breeze drifted off Dax's palms, ruffling his hair. His wind took no time to pick up, quickening its speed. North gripped the handrail, her locks whipping around her face, *The Temptress's* black sails flapping harder. With a single shove, Dax thrust his power across the water toward Salt's ship. Two of the masts cracked in half. They fell to the deck, splintering wood and breaking the pristine railing with a deafening smack.

Two males sprinted to the front of the ship, their faces

187

contorted in rage. They stopped near the broken handrail and settled their gazes on Dax, Echo, and North. One, a male with stark white hair and a patchy beard covering the lower half of his face, wore bronze cuffs on each arm. The other fae was a tall, slender elf with golden hair and black tattoos covering all of his exposed flesh.

"Where's your fucking captain?" the white-haired male seethed from his ship.

"You shouldn't be here, Salt," Echo shouted, her hand slapping against the rail. "If you proceed any farther, you will all die."

Salt bared his teeth. "It's you and your crew who will die, whore."

North's blood boiled in her veins, her eyes narrowing at the male. Tik-Tok may have betrayed Salt, but what had Echo ever done to him? Nothing. No one else on this crew had either—they weren't the original crew who'd betrayed him. She had to do *something*.

Focus. Focus. Focus on Salt. Your target.

Lifting her old axe, North kept her gaze locked on the male's face. She pulled her arm back, then hurled her weapon forward. It flew through the air, swishing and slicing, and planted itself with a hard strike in the face of the golden-haired elf. Right in between the eyes. Blood spilled down the elf's face as the force sent him careening backward, his body flopping to the deck, undoubtedly dead.

"Gods." North blew out a hard breath. She'd missed her intended target, but regardless, it was the first time she'd killed. She felt ... sick. Even if it had been Salt that she'd hit, she would have felt the same.

"You took down their strongest fae." Dax slapped her on the back. "That bastard was always an asshole."

"You bitch!" Salt roared, his piercing gaze targeting North. "You'll be the first to die."

"She's trying to board the ship!" Cyrx pounded across the

188

deck and rushed near the end of the ship. A female maenad leapt from Salt's side onto Tik-Tok's deck, landing perfectly on both hooves. Her antlers bobbed as she ripped her sword free of its sheath, but Cyrx was fast as he ducked from the blade and tore her head off her body. Blood oozed from the wounds and North watched, wide-eyed, as Cyrx threw the head and body overboard. The water splashed below.

"You're going to pay for that!" Salt bellowed.

"With the elf dead, I could blow the ship back through the portal to Oz, but they would be able to cross again." Dax shook his head and glanced at Echo. "Echo. I think you need to end this. None of them know what you are, what you can do."

A deep line settled between the siren's brows as if she were warring with herself. Perhaps even thinking about her past, when she'd brought males to their knees and killed them. Then she nodded. "Let's get this over with." Echo tilted her head to the side and popped her neck. "Salt first."

North held up her axe, the one with the star engraved from Tik-Tok. She wanted to have it ready in case she needed to protect her friend.

"I suppose you wish I were your whore, don't you?" Echo shouted to Salt, grinning.

"How about this?" Salt called back, his gaze locking onto Echo's. "You suck my cock as soon as I'm finished sinking your ship."

Echo opened her mouth, not to speak, but to let a song pour forth from her lips. The entire world seemed to freeze. Everyone. Even North. A light melody, full of magic and tales, darkness and light, alluring and deadly, like nothing North had ever heard before. A true siren princess of the sea. North was captivated, wanted to dance and spin in it. She wanted to live in the song.

Salt's eyes appeared glazed, his expression neutral, his movements stiff as he drew his sword from the sheath at his hip. His arm didn't shake when his own blade pressed against his throat, nor did he blink when it glided across his flesh. Bright scarlet poured down his neck, and he didn't release so much as a gasp or parting of lips before his body folded and collapsed to the deck with a thud.

Three of Salt's goblins ran toward their captain's body, taking in his still form. Their heads jerked toward where Echo was standing, and they withdrew their swords.

"I'm going to them before they have a chance to come here," Echo said.

Before North could free herself of the siren's spell and stop her, Echo leapt from the ship and landed in front of Salt's crew.

North leaned on the handrail as Echo's song came again, holding her in place. The low aria unfurled from Echo, growing higher and higher in pitch. North watched as she moved toward the three males, singing, persuading, taunting. The three goblins lifted their blades to their throats as Salt had done. Three bloody red smiles appeared on their flesh.

A deafening squelch rose from the ocean's depths, interfering with Echo's song. The familiar noise that North had heard earlier when she'd been out here with Tik-Tok grew louder and louder until it was a crescendo of its own. The sea shook, the ship quaked. Something from below was rousing, but North couldn't see anything within the water. Her heart beat so hard that it was about to burst from her chest. Echo's song had ended and North exchanged a glance with Dax, who seemed to emerge from his own spell.

With a resounding watery explosion, a creature shot up from the sea's surface. Water rained down on North while she watched in horror as it threw back, not one, but two heads, revealing razor-sharp teeth as it let out a powerful roar. The blast made her ears ring, and she cupped one while clenching the axe in her other hand.

Ghastly twin heads, with coal-colored orbs peering out from its sockets, hung from the creature's long, thin neck. Sharp, scaly thorns covered every inch of its massive alabaster body. Pointed teeth the size of North lined its open mouth. Two arms on each side of its body ended with curling claws, and a tail lined with spikes extended from beneath the water.

A dagger flew from someone on Salt's ship, the tip of its blade bouncing off of the creature's thick flesh. The beast released a shrill screech and smacked its long tail against the ship with a loud *thwack*. North jerked up her weapon, trying to figure out what to do. Her axe wouldn't make a dent in that thing, but perhaps she could do something with the water.

"They're only riling it up," Dax said, his arms falling to his sides. He glanced at her and shook his head. "Don't use your magic yet."

The creature wrapped its tail around the enemy ship, tightening. With a boisterous creak and groan, the beast dragged the entire vessel beneath the thick, churning water. The sails seemed to give a farewell wave before the ship was fully pulled under. Bubbles rose to the surface, and the water slowed, perfectly still, as if an entire ship hadn't been hauled away by a massive beast.

What if the creature decided to take down *The Temptress* next? North scanned the ship for Echo. But she wasn't there. Had she not leapt back?

"Echo!" North shouted down to the water, searching frantically. There was no sign of red hair anywhere. Only the dark water and the violet whirlpool.

"There!" Dax shouted. North followed his gaze and found where he was looking as a head pushed up from the sea.

Another creature jutted out from the water, smooth and slender like an eel, with hungry green eyes. It dove back beneath the murky liquid, and in seconds, Echo was pulled under. The water was so dark, but North could have sworn it became darker ... *blood*.

"Gods!" North didn't think—she gripped her axe and leapt over the side of the ship. Her heart lodged in her throat as her body smacked into the freezing water, a sharp pain shooting up her spine.

She opened her eyes and a slight stinging sensation pierced them. Everything surrounding her was black. She kicked her legs and swam upward through the thick liquid that weighed her down. When she broke the surface, another form shot up. The eel-like creature hissed and flicked his black forked tongue, tiny spikes covering the tissue. With a single swipe, she tore the axe across its body. Dark scarlet bubbled from the wound.

Another head broke through the water, and North was about to swing her weapon again, when she recognized the short red hair.

"Echo." North sighed, lowering the axe.

"Go!" She shoved North toward where Dax dangled a roped for them to grab.

North clasped the rope—it burned her hands as she climbed up. Her teeth chattered and the putrid odor of the sea clung to her.

"You shouldn't have risked your life like that!" Dax spat, grabbing her by the back of her dress and dragging her on deck. "Captain is going to be pissed."

"He'll have to deal with it," North said, her chest heaving.

Echo came up next and dropped to the floor on all fours. Dax knelt beside her and placed his palm to her shoulder.

Bright red blood dripped on deck, mixing with the water pooling beneath the siren. North gasped as she realized it came from Echo's abdomen. "You're bleeding!"

"It's fine." She sat back, her knees planted against the wood, and pressed a hand to her stomach wounds. "They'll be fine too."

North furrowed her brow. Echo must have been delirious.

Dax took in a sharp breath. "Respen doesn't know, does he? And you risked your life like that?"

"Know what?" North asked.

Crimson seeped in between Echo's fingers. "I'm with child."

CHAPTER TWENTY-THREE

TIK-TOK

After leaving Tik-Tok's father to his ill fate, Respen's magic dropped them onto *The Temptress* to a flurry of brownies, armed with brooms and mops, rushing toward the edge of the ship as it rocked violently back and forth. Dax and Cyrx knelt over someone at the center of the deck. They spoke in harsh whispers, expressions hard. Crimson blood coated the rail, more of it running in rivulets across the wooden planks.

Tik-Tok's heart stopped.

North.

Where was North? He took a single step forward and caught sight of Echo's pale face. The relief that it wasn't North was short lived as the realization hit—Echo was badly injured. If not dead already.

Cyrx lifted his head, dark eyes wild, and caught sight of Tik-Tok and Respen. "Captain! Thank the mother!"

Respen shoved his way through the brownies and slid to his knees. "Echo!"

"Shit," Dax said under his breath. He glanced at Respen, still leaning over her body, and met his gaze. "I can't fix this."

193

Tik-Tok's chest grew tight, each inhale a struggle, and his feet refused to move. He'd seen his siblings die up close—he couldn't watch his friend potentially do the same. "What happened?"

"Got everything!" North shouted from the stairwell.

His head snapped toward the sound of her voice. North burst from the door leading below deck and stumbled across the rocking ship with an armful of towels. Blood stained her skirts and exposed forearms. When her gaze locked with Tik-Tok's, she gasped. "Thank the gods you're back."

"What happened?" he asked again in a rough voice.

North ignored him, going instead toward the form between Dax and Cyrx, and dropped to her knees. Dax scrambled backward, his entire front soaked in blood, so she could apply pressure to the wound with a cloth.

"Echo!" The rawness in Respen's voice rattled Tik-Tok to his very core.

"I'm sorry, Res," Dax said in a gravelly voice. "I don't know what else to do."

North lifted her stare from the stained towel in her hands. "She's with child."

A desperate wail left Respen. The hair on Tik-Tok's arm stood on end. Echo was with child? With a wound like that... His stomach twisted.

"You have to risk taking her to land," Cyrx told him.

And it was a risk. Respen's power could potentially make her wound worse, but it wouldn't improve by waiting until the ship arrived at a port. How skilled were the healers here? Without magic... Tik-Tok didn't move. Couldn't move. Echo was bleeding out. There was too much blood for her to survive whatever injury she'd suffered. He swallowed hard and turned his gaze to North.

As if sensing his stare, she looked up. Her eyes were dilated, and dried tears stained her cheeks, with more threatening to fall. "Salt followed us through the portal, but something destroyed his ship."

If Tik-Tok thought, even for a moment, that Salt would've followed through the portal, he never would've left. The ass was somehow both fearless and superstitious. Crossing into other worlds would *anger the gods*, or so he'd claimed. He swallowed hard.

"Destroyed by what?" he asked.

"Whatever is in the water. It attacked, and Echo dove in to save us and…" The ship gave another violent jerk. "We have to go back to Oz before it sinks us."

The first squelching sounded. *Fuck*. He ran to the helm and grabbed the spokes of the wheel. "Dax, wind!"

A large gust slammed into the sails, jerking the ship forward, toward the swirling vortex of the portal. The masts creaked against the force, the sails snapping as the wind caught at different angles. The spinning water swept them up, dragged them closer, swallowed them whole. Tik-Tok's stomach lurched with the rapid movement despite the years he'd spent on the water. Cyrx had braced Respen and Echo, keeping them from sliding across the slippery deck, while Dax held onto a mast and North caught herself on a rope. Kaliko and dozens of brownies skidded across the deck, some bouncing off the railing before sliding the other way as the ship twisted in the current.

"Hold onto something!" But the roar of the portal drowned out Tik-Tok's shout.

A moment later, the portal spat them back out. With a blue sky overhead, glittering silver waves below, and a gentle sea breeze, they were home. It was over in a single breath, but left Tik-Tok winded and disoriented. Once he regained his senses, a quick headcount told him that three brownies were missing. "Fae overboard!" he yelled, abandoning the helm. Dax continued with his wind, blowing them away from the portal, while Cyrx sprinted to the side of the ship, looking for their lost crewmembers.

"They're gone, Captain," Cyrx called. "No sign of them anywhere."

Of course they were—the portal was still wide open. There was no way the brownies could swim against the current. A heavy pang hit his chest as he realized Cyrx was right—they were *gone*. But if he let himself dwell, let himself mourn their loss... *No.* He had to focus. Other lives still depended on him.

Jolting to North, he hauled her up from the deck by her upper arms. "Close the portal." There was no warmth in his voice, though he hadn't intended to sound so callous. He had to act like *Captain* Tik-Tok now, not their friend. Had to take charge and leave no room for questions about his orders. That's what kept things running smoothly in a crisis. He whirled away from North to return to the helm. With a quick glance at his compass, its needle pointing him in the direction of the nearest land, he spun the wheel to the left. "More wind!"

Dax rotated his hands through the air, churning the breeze into something stronger, and used it to fill the sails, sending *The Temptress* soaring over the silver sea. Behind them, there was no trace of the portal.

"I'm taking her to the Isle of Phreex," Respen yelled, his voice cracking with fear as he scooped Echo off the floor. Blood dripped freely from her abdomen, joining the pool already on the deck. "They can help her there."

Tik-Tok checked his compass again, adjusting slightly in favor of the right isle. "We'll meet you there as soon as we can," he promised.

Then Echo and Respen disappeared as he whirled her toward a healer.

"North," Tik-Tok called. She stumbled to his side, wiping her hands down her ruined dress. "What happened while I was tracking down my father?"

"I told you. Salt followed—"

"No." He inhaled deeply, readying himself. "Spare me no details."

The Isle of Phreex was a paradise—all sandy beaches and lush meadows with a picturesque mountain range—but the inhabitants were another story. The kinglet was an arrogant prick and the females loved luring males in, hypnotizing them until they went mad. There was also a large steam machine with one wheel that rolled around the island, crushing buildings and terrorizing fae. Then there were the different groups of cutthroats, like the Brotherhood of Failings, who wouldn't hesitate to snatch newcomers.

Respen used to *be* a member of the Brotherhood. The eight—now seven—males were outcasts who'd found somewhere to fit in. With each other, they had a family and a home, but they remained the bane of the island. What unsupervised younglings wouldn't cause trouble? The brothers simply never grew out of their mischievous ways. All except one.

Tik-Tok had met Respen by chance. A dice game in a tavern, the stakes, a challenge meant to be nothing but good fun. When Tik-Tok won, he had dared Respen to do something exclusively for his own happiness. Something Tik-Tok figured was open-ended enough not to piss off the Brotherhood so he could restock his ship and get the fuck out of there.

But he'd decided to join Tik-Tok's crew instead.

Respen assured Tik-Tok they would still treat him like family. *The Temptress* hadn't sailed back to the isle to test that theory, however, since it wasn't worth the trouble.

Tik-Tok stood beside North at the ship's railing, watching fishermen go about their business as if a pirate ship hadn't cast their pier in shadow. Their cargo of sea life was only a cover for something more nefarious—trafficking fae or stolen goods, perhaps even dealing with dark magic. Tik-Tok knew fellow pirates when he saw them. Their confident strides, the not-so-casual way they avoided fae who belonged to a different ship, and the gentle way they set down certain crates. No one took that much care with *shelled nuts*, if the stamps on the boxes were to be believed.

But somewhere beyond the pier, amid the uneven, chaotic rows of thatched buildings leading up to the three-tiered palace, was Echo. Fighting for her life, and that of her child, with Respen by her side.

"She'll be okay." Tik-Tok spoke to himself as much as he spoke to North. "Respen has an extremely skilled healer in his circle."

"Shouldn't we go into town instead of waiting here?" North asked.

Tik-Tok shook his head. "Respen's friends blame me for his leaving. While they can forgive him because he's family, I'm a *good-for-nothing pirate.*" He forced a small smile and winked. It was better to stay on the ship and avoid any potential disasters. "Dax will bring us news when he has it."

North nodded, keeping her gaze outward. "And you?"

"What about me?" He leaned his elbows onto the rail, stretching forward to peer at the water lapping against the side of the ship. It needed repairs after Salt's attacks and the journey through the portal, but not here. The damage was small enough, thanks to the magic wards he'd commissioned years ago, that it could wait until they reached a safer port.

"Are you okay? You haven't said a word about what happened in the other world." She paused and his silence filled the air between them. "I told you everything, but you didn't even mention to me that you'd turned Salt to stone."

"Bastard deserved it," he murmured. "Attacking my ship like that." Tik-Tok couldn't bring himself to give a fuck that his old captain was dead.

North lightly set her hand on his forearm. "You're avoiding the question."

"I'm fine, my star." *A lie.* Soon, she would be gone from him too, and it might be the thing that finally broke him. After losing so much, emptiness consumed him, and North was his only flicker of hope. He would need to extinguish any trace of it now before that spark spread. If he didn't, if he let it grow, the pain of losing her would destroy him. "My siblings are avenged, and my father lives no more."

"You killed him?" She squeezed his arm a bit.

Tik-Tok shifted his eyes to meet her inquisitive gaze. "You could say that."

"Wh—"

He leaned in and placed a chaste kiss to her lips. A *final* kiss. "I don't want to talk about death now. Not while Echo is fighting against it and I've lost three of my crew on the way back through the portal."

"We can talk about it another time." North looked up at him when he remained silent.

"Someday," he agreed, and his heart weighed heavily in his chest. The time he and North had together was almost over. Her family expected her to return home—*she* expected it. He'd given his word. "If the wind ever blows us into each other's path again, I will tell you."

North's face paled, her grip tightening. "What do you mean?"

"As soon as Echo's well enough, you're going home like I promised." He pushed up and away from the railing. "I need to rest. Wake me if Dax returns with news."

Without waiting for North's opinion on the matter, he walked away. Each step took more strength than he felt he had. What he truly wanted was to bring North along with him, settle into his bed with her nestled beside him, and sleep, long and hard. His life's mission was complete, but instead of feeling vindicated, a ... hollowness filled him. Numb. And the only thing he could imagine replacing the new emptiness with was North.

But he didn't want to be selfish. Even though he'd never cared about that before.

Unlike Tik-Tok, North had a family who loved her and wanted nothing more than her safe return. And she loved them too. Far more than she could ever care for someone like him. What could he offer her—or any other female, for that matter? Life on a ship wasn't meant for everyone. It was more than that, though. A male needed a purpose, no matter how small, and his purpose was finished. How could he drag North aimlessly around with him as he searched for a new one?

Kicking the door to his quarters shut with his heel, Tik-Tok shed his filthy coat and muddy boots. He should've taken a bath in his private tub, but he was too tired. Too ... *nothing*. The desire to be clean paled in comparison to his *need* to sleep.

He flopped on his bed and rolled to face the wall. Instead of holding North like he wanted, he tucked the pillow that smelled of sweet vanilla, of *her*, beneath his chin and closed his eyes.

Today, his father got what he deserved. But three brownies and Echo got something they *didn't*.

Tik-Tok had won. He'd also lost.

And soon, he would lose more.

Chapter Twenty-Four

North

The next three days seemed unending—they connected and spanned an eternity. North tried to sleep, but every time she did, the sight of blood from Echo's stomach filled her mind, causing her to jerk awake.

Kaliko and a few of the other brownies had already scrubbed the deck, but North stood at the handrail, studying the now-empty spot. She had tried to visit Echo, but Dax refused to take her to see the siren.

Her gaze flicked back to Tik-Tok. He stood near the end of the ship, alone, his arms dangling over the rail.

Dax brought a pear to his mouth and came up beside her. "You keep staring at the captain."

North had tried speaking with Tik-Tok, but he'd been distant, different. He gave one-word answers and chose to eat alone in his quarters. She wasn't angry about it—she didn't know how she felt. Whatever emotions spun through her were her own issues to deal with, so she gave him the space he seemed to need.

"You should go talk to him," Dax suggested as Tik-Tok tilted his head in their direction.

"I've tried." She turned away from him and studied the opposite side of the empty ship.

"His loss." He shrugged as he chewed.

"I'm surprised you haven't ventured off to enjoy Phreex."

"This is the one place where my cock shall remain in my pants."

North had heard the story about a clan of females there who would lure strangers to their bed, and in return, the males would end up chopping off parts of themselves to feed to them.

"Don't talk to her about your cock," a deep voice drawled from behind her. She hadn't heard Tik-Tok saunter up.

Dax smirked and pushed off from the rail, leaving Tik-Tok and North in silence.

"So…" she said, toeing the floor, trying to figure out what to ask first as she gazed at his beautiful face. But he was staring past her at the sails. "Gods, why won't you at least look at me?"

"North, you—"

A shuffling of feet sounded behind her, and she whirled around to find Respen coming onto the ship. He looked as though he hadn't slept in days. His blue hair was rumpled, purple bags rested beneath his eyes, and even his normally straight body hunched forward.

"They're both going to be all right." Respen sighed, and there was such relief in those words. "She's asking for you, North."

Tik-Tok gave a slight nod. "Don't let her walk through town. It's too dangerous, and they don't want me there. Bring her back once she's finished so I can speak with her before you take her home."

"Yes, Captain."

"And, Respen? I think it goes without saying, but anything you or Echo needs is yours." Tik-Tok turned and headed back toward the front of the ship.

Respen studied him as though he wanted to say something else. Instead, he placed his hands on North's shoulders and blew out a breath. "I wouldn't let you walk through town either."

Based on the rumors, she wouldn't want to anyway. "I'm perfectly fine with that." As soon as she closed her eyes, the rush of falling blasted through her, her stomach dipping, but only for a few seconds this time.

North opened her eyes. She stood outside a small silver and gold cottage made entirely of metal. Large boulders hovered off the ground and leafy trees brushed the sky overhead. She glanced over her shoulder and gasped. They were on a mountainside, at the edge of a cliff—a woozy feeling shot through her as she peered down, finding the base of the mountain terribly far away. Huts and cottages were sprinkled all over the town, and in the center was a massive palace, each of its three tiers a different shade of gold. The hues flickered underneath the sun, making the palace shine like it was enveloped in fairy dust.

Respen knocked on the door, and a gnome with white locks of hair to his waist and a scruffy beard the same length, answered. The gnome came to about North's belly button, and deep wrinkles etched his flesh.

"Lou, I brought someone to see Echo." Respen ducked while stepping inside.

Lou eyed her with suspicion as she lowered her head and followed behind Respen. Herbs and something musty enveloped North as she pushed into the simple sitting room. She straightened and the ceiling brushed her head. A rocking chair stood in the corner with a fur blanket sprawled across its back. Misshapen glass bottles filled with colorful tinctures were scattered across a nearby table.

"This way." Respen remained hunched as he guided her toward an open door.

Echo lay on the floor atop a pallet of stacked wool blankets. An empty bed, too small for anyone besides the gnome, took up one of the corners. Echo's head turned to face them, and a weak smile spread across her lips. Sweat drenched her red hair and beads of perspiration lined her forehead. The siren appeared feeble, but she was anything but that.

203

"I'll give you two some time alone," Respen said softly. "Let me know if either one of you needs anything."

"Eat something," Echo told him.

"For you, I will." He held Echo's gaze until disappearing from their view.

The siren focused on North and her smile remained. "Don't even ask how I am. I feel as though I've been stabbed in the stomach."

"I wouldn't dream of asking you that." North smiled back and knelt beside her friend. "Why didn't you tell anyone about the child?"

Echo took several breaths before answering. "I didn't want to be treated as though I were fragile."

"You aren't." North grasped her friend's hand and gently squeezed it.

Echo bit her lip, tears filling her eyes. "I secretly feared they would have left me behind. That Respen wouldn't have wanted me any longer."

"Of course he would still want you!"

"I've never had anyone like him before. He's happy. Scared, but happy." Echo paused. "Once I'm healed, we're planning to return to the island near my old home. I can't risk the child's life again by living on a pirate ship. It doesn't mean we'll never come aboard *The Temptress*, though."

"I'm going home after this, too," North whispered, twisting her hands. "I won't be on the ship when you do return."

A crease formed between the siren's brows. "Do you want to stay?"

"He hasn't asked me." North was told she would go home once she'd opened the portal for Tik-Tok. But a part of her thought, after everything, that he possibly would've wanted her to remain.

"You can always ask him." Echo grinned. "Remember, he hasn't done this sort of thing before."

"Perhaps." If she asked him if she could stay, then he might feel pressured into saying yes, and she wouldn't linger unless he truly wanted her to. North knew her family wanted her home, but she wasn't entirely sure what she yearned for anymore.

North continued to chat with Echo about the siren's future for a while longer until her friend's lids closed and her breathing became even. Trying not to disturb her, North slowly rose from the floor and met Respen back in the sitting room. He leaned against the wall in a crouched position, fiddling around with Lou's tinctures. The gnome paced at a shelf, rearranging tattered books by color.

Respen set down the glass vials and pushed himself up to stand. "Ready?"

"Yes." She smiled. "Thank you for bringing me to see her."

"No." He placed his hands at her shoulders. "Thank you for saving her. She told me what you did by distracting the creature and killing it."

"I would have done it for any of you."

"I know," he said, a warm smile tugging at his lips. "Ready?"

North nodded and closed her eyes, sucking in a sharp breath as he whirled them back to the ship. When she opened her lids again, Respen had brought them to the front of the ship where Tik-Tok stood, facing them.

"Let me know when she's ready," Respen said, taking his hands from her shoulders before walking toward the middle of the deck.

"You're not going to take me home?" North's gaze flicked to Tik-Tok's, her voice coming out more desperate than she would have liked. But she assumed he was at least traveling with her to the Emerald City.

"I feel bad enough asking Respen to take you, and he's too exhausted to take us both. Besides, something tells me your family wouldn't enjoy seeing my face again." Tik-Tok picked up her luggage beside him and handed it to her, along with her axe in a strap. She attached the weapon to her back as he pushed his hand into his pocket and drew out something red and shiny. A stone heart. Tik-Tok dropped the object into the center of her palm. "Return this to Ozma. Tell her I didn't need this after all."

She stared down at the stone, knowing what it was because her grandmother had one that was exactly the same. It was a stone which could prevent curses. Reva had used hers for protection while helping to defeat the previous Northern Witch, Locasta.

He took a step back and spun to leave.

North's eyes widened and confusion jolted through her. "That's it?" she called.

"Have a safe journey home," he added without glancing over his shoulder.

Tears didn't come. She didn't feel hurt or sad, only *angry* over the most dismal farewell she'd ever had. Fury stormed through her veins. The magic within her touched down on the waves, making them rise in anger too, until they sprayed over the edges of the ship to the deck. "I hate you!" she yelled. It was pitiful. She should have cursed at him, but that was the most she could force out.

Tik-Tok stilled and glanced over his shoulder. "Back to that, are we? Good." His red irises shifted away from her as he resumed walking.

Her jaw clenched. "You're a coward." With a scowl, she turned to face the water, the waves choppy but slowing. She hadn't suffered in her past like he had, but, had their roles been reversed, she still would have given him more words, more emotion, more of a goodbye.

The sound of heavy boots thudded across the deck, and a growl escaped Tik-Tok as he spun her around. His face was inches from hers, his crimson eyes blazing, his expression as angry as hers had been. "I may be a selfish bastard, but I'm not a coward." He gripped the nape of North's neck and crashed his mouth to hers. His lips fit perfectly with hers, then he parted them with his tongue and pushed it inside, kissing her senseless.

When he pulled back, the anger was no longer on his face,

and in its place was something else she couldn't read. He reached into his other pocket this time and fished his compass out. With gentle fingers, he opened her hand and placed the object on her palm, then he tenderly wrapped her digits around the cold metal. "It's yours. Go home. Think about it. If you fail to see sense and want to find me, use the compass."

She sucked in a deep breath, her eyes wide as she stared at his beloved object. "Tik-Tok…"

"Don't argue with your captain." With the finality of his words, he walked off again. And this time, she didn't stop him as he went inside his room. He didn't ask her to stay—he'd left her a choice instead.

"Well, that was interesting." Respen cleared his throat as he came up beside her. "Do you need more time?"

North studied Tik-Tok's closed door, then looked down at the compass. She opened her luggage and placed the two objects he'd given her inside. "I'm ready."

Respen nodded and grasped her arms. When she closed her eyes, nausea bubbled through her entire body with the longer journey, and the falling seemed to last and last until everything was still.

As she opened her eyes, bright green shone around her. The flickering emerald brick road, the glistening shops, the sparkling palace.

At the Emerald City Palace gates, every guard's stare locked on her and Respen. Her hands shook as she threw her arms around the pirate in a quick hug before releasing him. "Go!"

With a smile goodbye, he vanished just as an arrow whizzed past her to where he'd stood, flying through empty space.

"North!" a familiar voice shouted. *Birch.*

She turned to him as he lowered his bow. "I'm fine. You're still here?"

Birch wore his chestnut-colored uniform, his hair ragged as he pulled her into a tight hug. "We all are. Once Crow came back with news of finding you, we decided to wait for your return."

He hugged her tighter. "I wish I could have done more at the celebration. I wish I had known Tik-Tok was coming."

"It's fine." North hugged him back, and none of the old feelings she had for him surfaced. She was simply relieved to see her friend. "No harm was done to me." At least not from Tik-Tok or any of his crew besides Rizmaela.

"Let's get inside so everyone can finally be calm. Your father and grandmother have been impossible to live with since you were taken. Even after Crow returned with word, the two of them have continued to rant."

North knew they both would've struggled with her decision to stay on *The Temptress*. With a sigh, she walked beside Birch past the floral gardens and into the palace. The entrance was mostly quiet except for a few servants cleaning the high-backed velvet chairs. They all looked at her and gasped, halting their movements as she proceeded past them into the throne room.

It was strange seeing the bare area now, when the last time it had been full of celebrating fae, frozen as statues after Tik-Tok had turned them to stone.

"Wait here while I get your parents," Birch said.

Ozma and Jack shot through the open doors before he could take a single step. Brielle was nestled close to Ozma's chest, her eyes shut as she slept.

"North, I'm so sorry. I had wondered if you were the one Tik-Tok wanted, but then you never manifested magic. So I was sure you were safe," Ozma rushed out, gently passing Brielle to Jack. She grabbed North and drew her to her chest. "Crow told us everything … that you wanted to stay."

North nodded. "It's all right, Ozma. If anything, I have you to thank because I was able to discover my magic. As for Tik-Tok, he isn't a villain. He went through the portal to save another world." She wouldn't confess all his reasonings to her family because those were his stories to tell. North knelt and opened her luggage to retrieve the red stone, then stood and handed the object to Ozma. "He wanted you to have this back."

Ozma's lips parted as she took the stone from North. Jack frowned, like he didn't believe Tik-Tok would do a good deed for no reason.

More hurried footsteps echoed throughout the throne room as her mother and father burst in with Birch. Thelia's chest heaved as she crushed North into a fierce hug, and her swollen belly pressed against North's.

"I knew you would be all right." She stepped back and tucked a lock of silver hair behind North's ear. "My strong, brave daughter."

Tin folded his arms around her next. "I've been worried out of my mind."

"I'm fine, Father." She squeezed him in return. "You don't have to worry so much."

Tin cocked his head, eyeing her, as if he knew something, could read all that had happened within her. Before he could say anything else, her grandparents rushed into the room with rumpled hair, untucked shirts…

Gods. She could feel her cheeks heating at what her return had so obviously interrupted.

"I can't *believe* you sent Crow home after he located you." Reva narrowed her eyes and crossed her arms.

"I had to find myself." North shrugged.

Her grandmother's gaze softened. "We all have to do that from time to time."

"Did Tik-Tok turn you to stone at all?" Jack asked.

After his question, more fired off in all directions about Tik-Tok—she had to explain over and over that he had treated her well and not once had he turned her into his personal ornament.

Birch must have noticed her drooping frame because he grabbed her arm and pulled her toward the door. "I think North wants to lie down for a little while."

"I needed that," she whispered so only he could hear.

"I could tell." He chuckled.

"I'll take her from here, Birch," Thelia said, wrapping her

arm around North's shoulders. She led her out of the room and up the long emerald stairs.

North stayed quiet while her thoughts churned inside her head. Stay home? Or return?

"Are you really all right? Is there anything I can do?" Thelia asked as she opened the door to the room where North had been staying at the Emerald City Palace.

"I … I miss him already." She'd hugged so many people today, but she needed her mother. Her arms enveloped her and she cried, ugly, wretched tears.

And she told her mother *everything*.

That night, North warred with herself. Her mother had understood everything she'd confessed. After all, Thelia had left her mortal world and stayed in Oz with a male who everyone had once feared. And no matter what North chose, her mother would support her.

North lay in bed, rotating Tik-Tok's compass in her hand. She didn't know what to do, but it wasn't as if she could never return home if she chose to go back to Tik-Tok. There was one person she didn't want to hurt, who might not understand.

A knock came at her door, and she sat up in bed. "Come in."

As if he'd heard North's thoughts, Tin walked through the door, a scowl on his face.

"What did the bastard do to you?" her father demanded, taking a seat at the edge of her bed, the mattress dipping below his towering frame.

"Nothing." North rested her back against the headboard.

"You're different. I could see it as soon as you arrived."

She flicked her gaze toward the window. "I miss the sea is all."

"Be honest with me." His tone was serious, leaving no room for argument. He was good at reading anyone, but especially her.

Blowing out a breath, she turned to face him. "I miss him. I miss Tik-Tok."

He pressed his hands against his head before bringing them down to his knees. "I fucking knew it. I knew that look on your face. The sadness. The longing. Is it a spell? Please tell me it is, and we can get someone to remove it." It wasn't anger she saw in her father's expression, but worry, so much worry.

North pressed a hand to her chest, where her scar rested beneath the fabric of her nightgown. She'd thought about telling her father what had happened with Rizmaela, but she couldn't let him hold onto any more guilt. He knew what he'd done in his past, and this would only make him believe that it was his fault she'd been stabbed. She wouldn't hurt him like that. While she might not be able to hide the scar forever, he didn't need to know about it tonight or tomorrow.

"It's not a spell." She sighed. "He didn't even ask me to stay. He told me to go home and decide if I wanted to come back to him. But if I do go back, I don't want you to hate me."

Tin stared at her for a long moment, an eternity longer than any she'd ever faced. "North." He broke the silence and scooted closer. "I was one of the most hated males in Oz. Do you think your mother gave a fuck about who would hate her if she were with me?"

"No…" Crow hadn't stood in his daughter's way when she'd chosen to be with Tin.

"While I want you to remain nearby for the rest of my life, it doesn't mean you have to. Regardless of what you choose, you will always be my daughter." He held up a finger. "But if you do choose him, I will end his life if he treats you wrong. The bastard already pissed me the fuck off when he turned me to stone."

Tears fell down her cheeks and she launched her arms around him. "I love you, Father." She remembered how he would carry her on his shoulders when she was a child, throw her into the air, swing their axes together in sync, and had even let her slip flowers into his hair. "I thought you would hate me."

"That's an impossible feat."

CHAPTER TWENTY-FIVE

TIK-TOK

———◆—⊂·······⊃—◆———

Large white sea birds cawed overhead as Tik-Tok busied himself with swabbing the deck. He'd fought off the brownies for the chore, just as he'd peeled vegetables for Cook earlier. Anything to occupy his time now that he'd gotten his revenge. Perhaps he needed to visit Celyna so Dax could fuck her and get him some insight into what to do next.

"Captain?" Dax approached with light steps and a wary expression. "We're heading into town. Are you sure you don't want to come along?"

Tik-Tok gripped his mop tighter. If he left the ship to venture onto the Land of Ix, he would get drunk at any number of taverns and then, when thoughts of North returned to plague him, his mood would *truly* sour. "No. Go enjoy yourselves—you deserve it."

Dax hesitated for a moment. "Cook left you a plate in the kitchen if you get hungry later."

"I'm not a child," he snapped, then winced, hating himself for being such an ass. It didn't stop him from tacking on a grumbled, "I can feed myself."

With a stiff nod, Dax walked backward to where the rest of the crew waited. "We'll return after the performance."

Quavo, a renowned minstrel, was visiting the Land of Ix, but it didn't interest Tik-Tok in the slightest. It was good for the crew, though. Not only had everyone suffered recently, but Tik-Tok wasn't the most pleasant fae to be around since North had left three weeks ago. Part of him wished he'd never sent her home, but another, more rational, part knew that it was the right thing to do.

Fuck being right.

As the crew filed down the pier and into the city, Tik-Tok's heart lurched. *Alone,* it seemed to say. When was the last time he'd had *The Temptress* all to himself? Had he ever? He wasn't entirely sure he liked how lifeless the ship felt without them. The yawning emptiness inside him widened a fraction, making him bone-weary. A nap would soothe the ache...

Another fucking nap. He wasn't *that* gods damn old.

Instead, he shoved the mop into the bucket of now-muddy water and tilted his face up toward the sun. The warmth of its light barely registered as he closed his eyes and sighed. What was North doing now? Did she also stand beneath the sun, or was she holed up inside a palace doing ... whatever it was she did before he came along? He should've asked her—found out what her days were like. It was too late now. She was home with her family, where she belonged.

Damn. This was disgraceful. He was a grown-ass male, not a sappy youngling, and he had to snap out of it. With a low groan, he rubbed his temples. But, combined with his new aimlessness, the sting of North's absence refused to fade. "What the fuck is wrong with me?"

Maybe he *should* join the others in town. Order Cyrx or Dax to keep him far from any sort of ale. The minstrel might even be as talented as the rumors say, which could lighten his spirits. The performance was hours away, though, which left too much free time on his hands. Time he could spend drowning his ... *feelings.*

214

He scowled. If his cock worked anymore, he would even consider sticking it in the nearest willing female, but North seemed to control that from afar.

Bending, he dragged the bucket to the far side of the ship and hefted it up to the railing. Brown, soapy water sloshed out when he tipped it on its side, sending the liquid straight into the silver sea. A squeal sounded as it splashed against something solid below, and he leaned forward to see what it came from.

Gliding across the gentle waves was a small rowboat covered in soapy water and ...

North. The soapy water had just missed her, hitting the front end of the boat instead.

Tik-Tok's chest expanded at the sight of her rowing the last few feet toward the hull. Dressed in a casual, deep green gown, she slid the oars gracefully through the calm water. The sun glinted off her silver hair, making it appear as if she glowed. He blinked a few times, sure that he was imagining things. But she was still there. Still rowing.

"North?" he called out. Was it really her? Why would she leave her family again so soon? Not that it mattered. She was *here*—exactly where he wanted her.

"Hold on," she called back, her cheeks flushed. "This kind of thing always works better in my novels."

A small, amused smile tugged at his lips, and he leaned forward, dangling his arms over the rail. "What is it you're trying to do, my star?"

"Rowing."

"Is there a reason for it?" There was a perfectly good pier she could've walked down to reach *The Temptress.*

"I was trying to be *romantic,*" she said with a glare. "Throw me the ladder."

Tik-Tok simply watched her little boat bob along the silver swells. If he left to get the rope ladder, if he took his eyes off her for even a single moment, he worried she might magically disappear. And then what?

215

Then I would find her and bring her back again.

He shut the idea down immediately, determined to let her make her own choices, and reluctantly stepped away from the rail. It took mere seconds to grab the ladder, hook one end to the rail, and release it. The rope hit the side of the ship with a heavy *thwack*. He chanced a look down again and North began her ascent.

She's really here.

Something nudged at the emptiness inside him. Heat. A pulse. Sparks that weren't quite magic but might as well have been. Every second he waited for her to reach the top of the ladder was torture. He beamed down at her as she climbed. "Seems like you've made a decision."

"Stupid dress," she muttered to herself, ignoring his comment.

As soon as her hands curled over the top of the railing, Tik-Tok grabbed her under the arms and hoisted her over the edge. Chest heaving, she blew a strand of hair from her face and smoothed down the front of the dress. The fabric was covered in small, embossed flowers and gold ribbons crossed through eyelets, holding the panels of her bodice tightly together. Finally, she stopped fussing and met his gaze. "Hi," she said quietly.

"Hi," he replied.

She smiled, holding up his old compass. "I found you."

"I see that." He swallowed hard. "Why, exactly?"

The smile faded, replaced with uncertainty. "You don't seem happy to see me."

"Why are you here?" he asked, voice cracking. He knew, deep down, she'd come back to him, but there was still a new, uncertain feeling inside him. Only hearing her *say* it would alleviate the twisting nerves.

She tilted her head, examining him, and he was suddenly very aware of his appearance. Rumpled clothes, hair tied into a messy knot at his nape, stubble on his cheeks. It was a fucking miracle he'd bothered to bathe that morning.

"I want to stay with you." North bit her bottom lip and looked at him from beneath her lashes. "I came back to be with *you* … if you'll have me."

Fuck. Me. He would do anything to have her. To keep her. She was his North Star, his new purpose, and he would be damned if he let her slip through his fingers again.

Tik-Tok moved to her then, his lips capturing hers. His kiss was desperate and rough, his fingers tangling in her hair. With one swipe of his tongue, he parted her lips, and she let him in. A sigh escaped him as he tasted her sweetness. He felt himself come alive against her mouth as he took from her and gave everything he had in return.

She'd come back *for him*.

Her fingers tugged up the hem of his shirt and he broke away only long enough to pull it over his head. The sensation of her fingers trailing down his chest, over his abdomen, toward the tie on his pants, had him groaning with anticipation. His cock pressed painfully against the fabric, and he tightened his grip on her hair. With his other hand, he pressed against her lower back until she was flush against him.

The feel of her body, even through all the layers, made him moan into her mouth. "North," he breathed.

"I know. I need you too."

Tik-Tok groaned and backed her up against the outer wall of his quarters. With deft fingers, he began untying the front of her bodice. Each tug loosened it a bit more, exposing smooth skin beneath. The curves of her breasts peeked through the ribbons, teasing him. He cupped one of them over the fabric and slipped his thumb inside, running the pad down the small crease of her cleavage. Goosebumps rose on her skin in response, and he licked his lips.

"Wait," she breathed, her eyes widening. "They'll see us."

"Everyone's gone into town." After everything they'd done together, she was still so innocent. It made him impossibly hard knowing he was the only one who had seen her writhe in pleasure—pleasure *he* gave. "They won't be back for hours."

With a final tug on the ribbons, the bodice gaped open, revealing her breasts. The hard, pink tips pressed over the fabric like an offering. His cock throbbed at the sight, his tongue yearning to trail across each slope of her body. Sliding his hand inside her top, he gave the soft flesh a gentle squeeze.

She sighed and arched into his touch. He grinned at her, eyes sparkling, as he sucked a stiff nipple into his mouth, rolling the other between his fingers. North grabbed his head, holding him there as she rolled her hips into his.

"Patience," he murmured, though he was hanging on to his by a thread.

North slipped the tips of her fingers into the band of his pants and tugged him against her. "Gods, you make it hard."

Tik-Tok licked his lips and stared at her, seeing his own lust mirrored in her eyes. A sinful smirk played on his lips as he slowly—so *painfully slowly*—slipped her skirts up around her waist. His breath hitched when he found her bare beneath. "How presumptuous," he teased.

"You forget I rowed here, and it was hot." North panted.

"Uh-huh." He pressed his lips to hers again, breathing in her sweet scent, as he opened his pants to give her full access. When her fingers wrapped around his length, he inhaled sharply, leaning into her further. "Fuck," he said, tearing himself away from her lips. Locking one of her legs around his waist, he lined himself up with her entrance. "Hold on to me."

The moment her hands wrapped around the back of his neck, Tik-Tok pressed inside her warmth. His body quivered with the strength it took to hold back. He wanted more. Harder. Faster. Wanted to *claim* her as his.

"Do you know why I came back here?" she breathed into his ear.

"To be pleasured by me?" he said in a strained voice, thrusting languidly.

North huffed. "No..."

"No," he agreed. "You came back because you love me."

Her eyes locked onto his. "Yes, and I would row back to you again if I had to."

His hips moved faster at her admittance, breaking free of his careful control. "I love you too, my star. More than anything that this world or any other has to offer," he told her. He never thought he would love anyone. Not after his siblings died. But then he found *her*.

One hand gripped North's ass, pulling her forward to meet his every thrust. He reached between her legs, stroking her where she needed it.

"Gods, keep doing that." She leaned into his touch, taking all she needed. As he removed his hand, her heel pressed into his lower back, urging him to let go.

Tik-Tok leaned in to nip at her ear. "Whatever you need." His resistance snapped. He buried his cock as deep as it would go. Again and again and again until North threw her head back, panting his name in a way that showed she cherished him. He gave a low growl as his release followed quickly, but they remained there, chests heaving, for what felt like ages.

"Do you have your axe?" Tik-Tok asked when he finally remembered how to speak.

North raised a brow. "It's in my luggage, which I left in the rowboat. Why?"

Tik-Tok smirked. "I wanted to make sure before I asked if you were okay."

North shimmied a bit until he released her leg and she stood on both feet again. Stretching onto her toes, she gave him a lingering kiss. "You're lucky I'm too exhausted to retrieve it." A huge grin spread across her perfect face.

Tik-Tok leaned his forehead against hers and closed his eyes. "I missed you."

"I'm sorry it took so long to come back." She cupped one side of his face and ran her thumb over his cheekbone. "It turns out that traveling on land without Respen takes forever."

219

He chuckled. "Why do you think I have a ship?"

She spun and took a few steps away. "You know, after all that rowing, I'm second-guessing my fondness for traveling on ships too."

"*Try* leaving again," he warned playfully, tugging her back to him.

North laughed as she faced him. "I want you." She snuggled in closer, laying her head on his bare chest. "And I want the sea."

Tik-Tok wrapped his arms around her, holding her resolutely. *North* was his family now—not the ship, nor the sea, but her. Contentment washed over him for the first time in his life as he hugged her close. "Then you shall have it."

EPILOGUE

NORTH

TWO MONTHS LATER

⚜ ⋯⋯ ⋯ ⋯ ⋯⋯ ⚜

"Ow!" North squeaked.

"Fuck!" Tik-Tok scooped her off the floor and placed her on the edge of his bed. "This isn't going to work."

"It will if you *practice*." North rolled her eyes as he removed her boot and inspected her foot. "It's fine. It's the tenth time you've done it, so I'm used to it by now."

"The only dancing I want to do involves far less clothing." His lids were hooded as he peered up at her from beneath his thick lashes. "Are you sure I have to behave myself until we return?"

North laughed and leaned forward, cupping his face with her hands. He tilted his head back and closed his eyes as she ran her fingers through his hair before she pressed her forehead to his. Since she'd returned, he continued to challenge her, woo her, love her. And she loved him, more than she could have imagined. He'd wanted to learn more about her life before she came aboard *The Temptress*, so they'd shared their lives and stories while he'd taught her how to steer the ship, raise the sails.

"Keep touching me like that and I can't guarantee you'll look this pristine when we dock," he purred.

Her hair was pinned into two buns atop her head with a few loose tendrils hanging down the front. She wore a long, dark pink dress, its skirts pleated with silver jewels lining its length.

North itched to remove his tunic, his pants, until he was bare before her, but they would have to wait. "After the celebration." She didn't pull back, leaving her forehead kissing his. "Are you ready to properly meet my family?"

Tik-Tok arched a dark brow. "I'm thrilled."

Her grin grew wider. He was doing this for her and wouldn't dare step foot in the Land of Oz otherwise. Crow had sent word that there would be a celebration in the South with food and dancing in honor of North's new brother.

"Have you decided where we're going after we visit Echo and Respen?" Once they left her parents' territory, they would be headed there.

"First, I want to read the romance book that made you think rowing was romantic." Tik-Tok stood and picked up North from the bed. She wrapped her legs around his waist as he carried her over to his desk before he set her on the cool wood. He spread her legs apart and pushed closer to her warmth, causing her breath to catch. "Then I want to watch you peel off each piece of clothing." He kissed the corner of her mouth. "Very slowly." Another kiss to the other side. "I think you know what happens after that."

With a smirk, he leaned in, her body heating. Her heart thumped wildly, and she was about to give in to temptation when his hand brushed past her. A shuffling of papers sounded as he picked up a folded map from his desk. Taking a step back, he opened the map to a picture of all of the Fae Lands and took a seat beside her. Across the yellowed paper were numerous black circles within the seas.

He pointed at each one of the markings near the South.

"These are the portals I've learned about over the years that lead to different worlds."

Tik-Tok motioned at the map with his chin for her to choose where she wanted to go. When she'd learned there were more portals she could potentially open and explore, she'd wanted to discover what else was out there. She studied each marking.

"How about this one?" She pointed at a dark circle directly in the middle of the sea.

"As long as it isn't infested with bloodthirsty fiends, then your wish is my command, my star." He paused. "Before we go to your parents, I have one more thing to show you." A crease formed between her brows as he clasped her hand and drew her out the door of their room to the deck. "What? I'm full of surprises."

"Sometimes," North drawled, taking in the salty scent of the air, "those surprises involve long training sessions."

"You did tell me you wanted to learn how to aim." He grinned. "You'll get there eventually."

She hadn't gotten any better, but she would never stop trying. The extra time spent with him was worth it.

Tik-Tok stopped in front of the handrail and drew off his glove. His golden appendage flickered beneath the suns' rays. He peeled off the magic ring he'd placed on her finger once before.

"Give me your hand." Tik-Tok cocked his head, the edges of his lips tugging upward.

North held out her hand and he slowly slid the ring onto her middle finger. She watched as the band changed from silver to the purest of golds.

"There," he said, locking his gaze on hers. "In case you ever need it, while my heart still beats, you have my magic."

"What if I want to share my magic with you instead?" She peered up at him, blinking, her chest feeling fuller than it ever had.

Tik-Tok stood behind her and entwined their fingers, his nose nuzzling her neck. "You already have."

Did you enjoy Tik-Tok?

Authors always appreciate reviews, whether long or short.

Check out Rav, the Vampires in Wonderland prequel!

You think you know Wonderland. But you don't.

Imogen, the Queen of Hearts, is known for taking the hearts of those who betray her, including her servants. Her king, Rav, ventures to the mortal world to lure in new prey to replace their dwindling help. One bite, one simple exchange of her blood is all it will take for a mortal to become one of them. And this time, Rav chooses a girl named Alice.

TURN THE PAGE FOR LION'S PREQUEL TO THE
FAERIES OF OZ SERIES.

LION

CHAPTER ONE

LION

Green light coated everything in the Emerald City twice a day—once at dawn and again at dusk. Lion avoided stepping out during those times if he could help it. He hated that it made everything look sickly, but a summons from the Wizard of Oz was never optional. Though, if Lion were being honest, a gnarled troll banging on his door when it was nearly dark was intriguing. He rarely had visitors, and if he did, they were *never* from Oz's personal guard. Things had become far too monotonous since the Wizard marred Tin's face with iron—even the cursed pixies that tortured the residents calmed down after that stunt—but perhaps that was about to change.

Lion had his courage.

What he needed was something to do with it.

The troll led him through freezing green glass corridors. His footsteps echoed through the dim hall, then again off the impossibly high ceiling, as they made straight for Oz's private chambers. Two expressionless elves guarded a massive, scrolled doorway. When the troll approached, the elves swung the doors open without a word. The moment Lion was inside—they slammed the entrance shut again. With a scowl, Lion tucked his long blond hair behind his ears and scanned the seemingly empty bedroom. His top lip lifted in disgust as the putrid smell hit him like a stone wall.

The bed was bare, a single blanket and stained pillow tossed haphazardly onto the mattress. Feathers spilled from a few holes and garbage littered the floor. The room itself was opulent—hanging crystal lighting, floor-to-ceiling windows, hand-crafted furniture. The emeralds and diamonds embedded in the headboard had to cost more than Lion's entire home. Dark curtains hung crookedly from their rods. The embroidery was stitched with mermaid hair and embellished with crystallized nixie tears, but the sparkle of both was hidden beneath a thick layer of dust.

Lion's boot crunched over a slice of moldy, stale bread, but that was the least of the food problems. Rotting fruit cores were scattered around the room, the sickly scent permeating the air. What the hell happened in here? Surely there was a mistake. Oz couldn't have gotten this bad with his faerie fruit addiction without someone interfering on his behalf...

"Wizard?" Lion called, his tail flicking nervously behind him.

Something banged on the other side of the bed followed by a soft *oof.* "Lion!" Oz's head popped up over the far side of the bed, scratching his scabbed scalp. The unmistakable gleam of red faerie fruit juice glistened on his lips when he gave a smile full of blackened teeth. His thinning white hair stuck up at different angles as if he hadn't brushed it in days, and his wrinkled skin had taken on a yellow hue. "You made good time getting here."

Lion ventured farther into the room with a cocked eyebrow. "Is everything okay?"

"Of course. Why wouldn't it be?"

"Have you fired the maids?" Lion asked carefully.

"Those spies! Good riddance. Always poking through my things." He flung a small suitcase onto his mattress. "Hand me that map, would you?"

Lion glanced at the partially unfolded paper Oz pointed at on the end table. Circles with symbols he didn't know how to read dotted the fae countries north of the Land of Oz. "Are you going to a diplomatic meeting?"

Oz snapped his fingers anxiously until Lion handed the map to him. "Just a trip. Nothing to worry about."

Lion shifted suspiciously. "Am I to come along?"

"What? No. I'm going on my own. Guards would only get in the way." Oz shot him a withering look. "Why would I bring you with me, of all people?"

"Why would you summon me?" Lion asked. Oz hadn't bothered him since Dorothy returned to Kansas. Lion was gifted a cozy cottage inside the city and a small stipend for his part in killing the Wicked Witch, Reva, but that was the last personal interaction they had. "It's been years since we've seen each other."

Oz's hands shook as he stared into his closet where his clothes were stuffed haphazardly. He murmured under his breath about foreign weather and something called *galoshes*. Lion scowled. How much fruit had he eaten today?

"Wizard," he said in a stern voice. "Why am I here?"

Oz blinked and looked at Lion as if he'd forgotten he had company. "Right. Yes. I have a quest for you, but the walls have ears."

Lion looked around at the glimmering green wallpaper with its swirling pattern of leaves. That was either another strange human saying—because there were no ears—or Oz's addiction to faerie fruit was worse than anyone feared.

"Go to Langwidere. Tell her I'll legitimize her rule of the West now that Reva's dead, if she..." Oz jerked into a crouch as if something had flown at his head. "I've written it all down. Names and locations. Everything you'll need, it's there ... in the top drawer."

Lion moved slowly as he tugged on the round knob and

picked up an envelope with his name on it. Part of him wanted to put it back and leave, but he couldn't help being curious. If the letter contained the ramblings of a madman, perhaps he could use it to blackmail the Wizard into taking him on the trip. An adventure would do him some good and Oz clearly needed someone to go with him for his own safety.

"It's vital you finish this before I return," Oz said.

Lion cracked the wax seal and scanned the letter with a pounding heart. "You're not serious?"

"Completely."

Lion licked his lips. Tin was the killer—not him. Not to mention that the people Tin assassinated were much less important than the name on this paper, and their deaths had earned the woodsman an iron scar. "You're not thinking clearly."

"I am!" Spittle rained from Oz's mouth. "Oz is changing. If we don't remold it to our advantage then our enemies will."

Our. Lion bristled. There was no *our.* Oz had no use for him before today, and now he wanted him to act as a hired gun. Lion hadn't worked so hard for his courage to waste it on a good for nothing addict. If he was going to kill an important figure, it would be because he got something out of it. Something he'd been searching for since Dorothy, Tin, and Crow left him alone in the Emerald City: a person to need him. And not only because he was convenient at the moment, but really and truly *needed* him. The only way for Lion to secure that kind of devotion was to give something no one else could give.

Lion smiled to himself as he slipped the envelope into the back pocket of his tan pants. "Consider it taken care of."

Chapter Two

Langwidere

Langwidere cherished her heads more than anything. Heads. Heads. *Heads.* She loved them blonde, loved them even more brunette, loved them red, loved them with perky noses, rosebud lips, arched eyebrows. She switched them out like she did her frilly white dresses. And when she grew tired and bored of them, Langwidere buried the heads beneath the dirt, burned them to ashes, or sank them to the bottom of the ocean.

The Wicked Witch of the West—Reva—was dead. The Wicked Witch of the East—Inora—was dead. Both had died at the hands of the same human girl—one melted by magic, the other crushed by the girl's house. The witches got what they'd deserved because neither one was ever fit to rule, just as Glinda—the Good Witch of the South—wasn't. She'd loathed Glinda and her insufferably deluded optimism for as long as she could remember.

Langwidere had made a visit to see Locasta, the "Good" Witch of the North, to make a deal to divide the territories between the two of them once she'd discovered the intruder—

Dorothy—had melted Reva. The truth was, Locasta was never good—she had secrets of her own locked and buried away. Locasta was just as bad as Langwidere, and if Langwidere didn't respect the witch for her secretly wicked ways, she would've swiped her head. But Locasta's head didn't have the sort of beauty that Langwidere yearned for.

Now, her fingers twitched at the thought of collecting even more faces. She craved the feel of cleaning them up, wiping the blood away from their delicate skin, twisting their features into an expression that she wanted them to hold as they sat in their boxes and waited their turn to be worn.

As Langwidere gazed at her blonde wavy hair and pouty lips in the golden full-length mirror, she imagined the crown that would be atop her different hairstyles each day. But there was one problem still to solve. A nuisance. Glinda. Langwidere would need to get rid of the dopey witch so she could take over the South territory. And to achieve this, what she needed was a helper... Someone who would follow her lead...

She tapped several times at her dimpled chin then ran her hands down the lace of her dress. Oz would've been a good tool, but his body had grown too old and frail over the years. Besides, who knew how much longer he had to live. His mind was growing too forgetful from his addiction to faerie fruit, along with age. But alas, he was human after all—they all died in the end. Oz had been the perfect lover for a time—brainless, a follower, one who would eat the faerie fruit right out of her hand, lapping up each speck of juice from her palm, as she moved her naked hips against his.

Dropping her fingers from the front button of her dress, Langwidere focused on what needed to be done, and she removed her head from atop her neck. Holding it in between her fingers, she could still see by maintaining skin contact. She gazed up at the row of silver and ivory cabinets with clear glass displaying her collection. Even without her head attached, she was still beautiful with a willowy body, luscious breasts, a narrow

236

waist, and soft pale skin. Every single inch of her was perfect in every single way—she knew this because she explored it with her hands each chance she got.

Opening an empty glass case in the middle, Langwidere placed her spent head inside, the world growing dark as she released her touch on it. She shut the glass and felt around for the case beside it, turning the bumpy knob. Langwidere pressed her palms inside and as soon as her fingertips brushed the fluffy curls of one of her beauties, sight came barreling back. Smiling, she brought the head toward her after shutting the case.

With a soft click, she adjusted the new head atop her neck. Each head contained a silver rounded disc at its base, as did her neck, so the attachment was flawless. She then wrapped a black ribbon around her throat to hide the thin line.

"There," she murmured as her new emerald eyes met her image. In the glass sat a beautiful heart-shaped face with freckles, a button of a nose, and thick obsidian curls, falling just past her shoulders.

A heavy knock came at her front door, making her jump a fraction, interrupting *her* moment. Letting out an irritated sigh, Langwidere sauntered out of the room and down the hall as the skirts of her dress swished. All she could think about was how several of her cases were empty, and how she needed more heads to fill them. Ones that she could watch with pleasure, that she wouldn't grow bored of. She would find the missing silver slippers, and she *would* take all the territories.

Her heels clicked across the hard-emerald floor before coming to a stop in front of the jewel-covered oval door. She pulled it open. To her astonishment, there stood a male—bare-chested, with long, wavy blond hair and wearing a fur-lined cloak resembling a lion's mane. She knew who this was right away—she knew what he did to help a little girl take care of Reva—she knew how gullible he could be. He would be the perfect specimen, the one she now didn't have to look for, the one who would do what she wanted in her bed as well as out of it.

"And what brings you to my home, Lion?"

CHAPTER THREE

LION

Lion's smile oozed charm and confidence. The Wizard had told him that Langwidere was a fae of many faces, but he neglected to mention how attractive the rest of her was. He didn't bother to hide his examination of her body before meeting her eyes again. The old Lion wouldn't have known what to do with himself.

"The tales of your beauty hold true, Lady Langwidere," Lion said with honesty.

She folded her arms. "Don't tell me something I know full well. I asked what brought you here."

"Oz ordered me to come and I owed him a favor." Lion stepped closer to the threshold and attempted to touch Langwidere's curls. She flicked his hand away. "Let me in so we can chat."

"Your newfound courage has made you foolish, Lion. Why would I let an enemy into my home?"

Lion looked up at her from beneath his lashes. "Are you so sure I'm your enemy?"

Langwidere's full lips turned into a frown. "You helped the mortal girl. It was very difficult to deal with Locasta after the human killed Reva, and it almost cost me the West."

"Sorry about that." Lion wasn't sorry. Not even a little bit. Lion was glad to leave his cowardly ways behind, no matter the cost, and he'd do the same to *keep* his valor. "Oz may have a solution to your territory problems, if it would please you to listen...?"

Langwidere scoffed but stepped aside. "This better be good."

Lion grinned and turned to maintain eye contact as he sauntered inside. "All of my ideas are good," he told her and licked his lower lip.

"I thought this was Oz's idea?" She glared at Lion, unamused, then stepped forward and picked up a lock of his hair. Her face softened. "Such a lovely color."

"I—"

"Shh." Langwidere's index finger landed on Lion's lips. It stayed only a moment before she traced each angle of his face with exaggerated slowness. Her eyes glazed over as she examined every inch of skin, from his neck up.

"Do you like what you see?" Lion inquired as she lightly skimmed his long eyelashes.

"Tsk." Langwidere dropped her hand to her side and her eyes cleared. "It's too bad I only wear female heads. Yours would do quite nicely."

Lion smirked at the compliment. "Then you'll just need to keep me around to appreciate my beauty."

Langwidere narrowed her eyes at his confidence and spun on her heel to lead the way into a large room with high ceilings. A plush white carpet was settled over emerald flooring and gold filigree coated the walls. Between the molded leaves, faces stared out. There were elves and fauns and centaurs—every kind of fae was represented at least once, with one thing in common: open-mouthed, wide-eyed terror. The hair on Lion's arms lifted and he tore his eyes away to take in the rest of the room.

The only piece of furniture was a gold high-backed chair with a white velvet cushion. With a snap of Langwidere's fingers, bright orange flames sparked to life in a pit set in the center of the room. The faces on the wall seemed to glow as the flames danced across the filigree, but Lion forced himself not to look.

"A throne," Lion commented.

Langwidere circled the fire once before sitting down. She crossed her legs and propped her elbows on the arms of the chair. "As any queen would have."

Lion approached the fire and held his hands out to warm himself after traveling from the Emerald City. Early spring had left him with a deep chill. "Queen of what, my lady? You may have taken control of the West after Dorothy killed Reva, but Glinda still rules the South. That's what you *really* want, isn't it? Without the South, how will you ever have enough power to take the rest of Oz from Locasta?"

Langwidere wrapped her fingers around the ends of the chair. "Is that what Oz told you?"

"No." Lion looked across the flames at her, sitting so regally with someone else's head on her shoulders. "I wasn't the fae without a brain, dearest Langwidere. It's easy enough to see your intentions and you can be sure that I'm not the only one. Which is why I think you should take the Wizard up on his proposal."

Her eyes narrowed. "You tread on thin ice."

"That's half the fun."

"Out with it before I toss you from my home," she warned.

Lion let his arms drop back to his sides. "Oz is succumbing to his love of faerie fruit—which I'm not to tell you but I'm sure you know as you're rumored to be the one who got him addicted to it. He's losing his grip on the capital right along with his mind. Without the Emerald City, he holds no sway over the territories or their leaders."

A small smirk graced her lips. "I fail to see the problem with this."

241

"Nor do I. We never should've allowed a mortal to rule over fae lands, which is why you should accept his offer."

"You make no sense, Lion."

He grinned widely, proud of his plan. "He wants you to acquire a new head. A specific *powerful* head that belongs to someone who won't fall in line. In exchange, he will legitimize your claim to the West."

"Will he?" Langwidere's laugh bounced off the walls. "It's already mine with or without his acceptance."

"Yes." Lion's wicked grin grew, showing his perfectly white teeth. "But if you appear to fail the job Oz gave you, with the simple change of a head, you could take a territory without anyone being the wiser."

Langwidere leaned forward. "And what would you get out of this?"

"You, obviously." When Langwidere opened her mouth, outrage written on her face, he held up a hand to stop her. "I want to be valued for my service. Use me, my lady. Make yourself a queen and me your knight."

The crackle of the fire was the only sound in the room. Lion knew this was a long shot. Langwidere's loyalties were largely unknown, other than to herself. There was an equal chance she'd tell Oz of his betrayal as there was of her accepting his help. He was banking on her seeing the genius of his plan. Fail in appearance only and gain both a territory and a new head.

With a sharp clap, Langwidere summoned a servant. A young female on all fours rolled into the room with wheels fused to her hands and feet. Her limbs were long and slender, her spine curved to accommodate her posture. A white ribbon, stained red with blood where it pierced her skin, sealed her mouth shut. How did she eat? Lion's stomach twisted as the female's pink irises focused on her master. She was no servant—she was a slave. And he'd just offered himself into Langwidere's control.

"Show Lion to a guest chamber. Make sure he feels at home until I decide what to do with him."

242

Lion tore his gaze away from the slave and gave Langwidere a playful smile. This would be a test of wills. He didn't want power for himself—that was too much responsibility—he simply wanted to be close to power. To be needed and important now that he had the courage to become someone of note. He only hoped it would be worth it.

CHAPTER FOUR

LANGWIDERE

So Lion wanted to be her knight... This was making everything so much easier. It was as though all the heads were falling into place.

Langwidere would not only have the West but the South as well. And one day, not soon, she planned to take Locasta's territories, too. But for now, she would need to build little by little, and take it slowly.

She gazed at the male before her, wondering if he could truly pass her test. Lion's beauty could spin tales, but she'd also heard of his cowardice. Had he truly gained the courage that would be required?

"I'm tired of wearing this," Langwidere said in a bored tone. *New day, new head.* "Come, Lion. We must prove your worth."

He nodded, shifting his stance, his golden eyes seeming to dance beneath the light. "Of course we must."

Pivoting on her heels, Langwidere walked down the hallway, her ivory dress swishing against her legs. Lion followed behind her, too close, almost predatory. He was lucky he wasn't female because his face was one of the most beautiful she'd ever seen. But there were plenty of other ways he'd be beneficial—instead of wearing him one way, she could wear him another. His skin pressed against hers.

The rows of curio cabinets slipped into view, all the heads at the same angle and position. Their expressions were all the same, frozen, lifeless, until their flesh connected with Langwidere's.

Langwidere whirled to face Lion, pressing her hand to his cheek. "Choose one you like." She was curious as to what his type was. Would he select one that had raven-colored hair like she originally used to have, or something the color of wheat? Perhaps one with a button nose or freckles? Did he prefer full or thin lips?

She thought about her original head, the one she'd burned to ash once she'd collected her first prize to replace the old. The kill had come from a fae before the female was to be married, already dressed in a white gown. On Langwidere's body, the head appeared much better—as did the white dress. After that, Langwidere no longer had to think about her disfigurements of her original face—the uneven eyes, the missing nose, the crooked mouth.

He cocked his head and scanned the cabinets. "I like them all."

"If you could have only one for a night, whose lips would you want yours pressed against." She tapped her fingers against her thigh, waiting for him to choose wrong.

Lion sauntered around the room, his tail swinging back and forth. He looked at each face before lifting his index finger and pointing to the glass to his left. "That one." It was a female with porcelain skin, ruby red lips, and thick black curls. Hair like she used to have. He'd made the right choice.

"If you are to be my knight," Langwidere said, inching toward the glass, "next time you answer me right away."

"I will."

"Zo!" Langwidere called as she opened the glass, then she

245

turned to Lion's confused face. "The Wheeler who was in here earlier. I took her and the others from the border near the Deadly Desert, and now they're mine."

"Such extravagant ... creatures."

Zo rolled to a stop, silent forever by the string in her mouth. The string was sewn in by Langwidere of course. But the Wheelers willingly volunteered.

"Zo, can you bring Lion a white robe?"

She nodded and pushed away on her oversized arms and legs.

Lion arched a perfect blond brow. "A robe?"

"You'll see." Langwidere opened the cabinet to her right and took off her head with a click. As she set it in its place, everything fell to darkness when her hands left the head. She felt her way back to the other open cabinet until her fingers brushed the thick curls.

Her sight came back to her as she cradled the head and set it in its proper place atop her neck. She blinked and blinked again as she focused on Lion who watched her in what looked to be awe. "How do I look?"

"Even more beautiful." And that was the sort of honesty that she yearned for.

The sound of Zo's wheels echoed down the hallway, growing closer and closer. She came to a halt in front of Lion, the robe draped across her back. As soon as he plucked it up, the Wheeler zoomed right off.

"Now"—Langwidere grinned—"I want you to get dressed ... or undressed, then meet me in the back of my home." Without another word, Langwidere turned on her heels and left the room. She wandered down the long winding hallway to the very back room where she'd left the door shut.

She didn't have to wait long before Lion sauntered down the hallway, as though there was something new in his step.

"Ready?" Langwidere asked.

"Yes."

With a smile, she opened the door and slipped inside. Emerald fire lit up the entirety of the room, making it appear as though flames were dancing atop the walls.

A rustling came from the corner and Lion's gaze moved in that direction, catching sight of what Langwidere wanted him to see.

"What is this?" He continued to study the trembling female dressed in a thin white gown.

"A female fae I took from the Emerald City." Langwidere shrugged. "I saw her dancing and spinning, such lithe movements, such a unique face. Her freckles are like their own constellation. I *need* her. Or rather, I need her head."

"For your collection?" Lion nodded. "I understand."

Langwidere remembered how she'd first heard about Lion— it was because he'd helped the human girl—Dorothy—on a quest. That girl had been the one to defeat two powerful witches of Oz.

"So you were friends with Dorothy, part of the party who defeated Reva?"

"More like acquaintances. We helped each other get what we needed and then said goodbye. Nothing more." He paused. "Besides, our world has gotten worse because of her."

"Perhaps if she ever returns, I shall wear her head."

"Perhaps. Dorothy did desert Oz, after all."

Langwidere would never do that. She would conquer and she would stay, for as long as her immortality allowed her to.

"When was the last time you were with another, my courageous Lion?" She brought her hand to his cheek and stroked his flawless skin with her thumb.

Straightening his spine, his eyes met hers and gleamed with pride. "Never."

Lion's answer surprised and intrigued her. She felt pity for him, because he'd been so cowardly that he couldn't even bring himself to lay with another. "Perhaps I'll give you a reward if you finish this task."

His brows drew closer together as he studied her face. "What task?"

"If you're to be my knight, then you're going to have to prove your loyalty." Langwidere grabbed the sword from against the wall and pressed it into Lion's strong hands, then turned him to face the fae. "Now, show me just how brave you are."

Chapter Five

Lion

Lion didn't need to be told twice. He'd been waiting for a chance to prove himself since Oz gave him courage. Sword gripped tightly in hand, his lips curled in disgust, Lion approached the cowering female fae. Death was inevitable—she should accept it with dignity.

"You'll look better on her body," he said with venom.

Then he swung.

The female's scream was cut short as the blade passed cleanly through her neck. Hot blood splattered onto Lion's chest. Red splashed across the corner of the room like a macabre painting, while the body slumped on the tiled floor.

Langwidere stepped around him and knelt beside the blood-slicked head. "It's a clean cut." She lifted the head by the hair and studied the wide nose and strong jawline. "Perhaps there's hope for you after all."

Lion's chest swelled with pride. "I'm happy to be of service."

Langwidere smiled wickedly at him before setting the head

into a waiting box with a wet thump. She took a moment to lovingly brush the hair off the dead fae's forehead then settled the top over it. When she turned, flicking blood from her fingertips, a wild look flashed in her eyes.

"Take off the robe," she told Lion.

He obeyed instantly and stood tall as she drank in his naked body from a few feet away. This time, he wouldn't shy away from a good fuck. "Am I pleasing enough for you?"

"Don't be cocky," she chided. Her gaze fell to his crotch at the last word.

Lion grinned, smug. "And your gown, my queen?"

"Not yet." She spoke slowly as she sauntered up to him. "You have to earn the sight of my body."

Lion stared at Langwidere's white dress as if he could see through it if he tried hard enough. His cock swelled as he caught the hint of her curves. His eyes traveled up to hers and held her lusty gaze, daring her to look lower with an arched brow.

Langwidere moved closer until there was only an inch between their bodies. Her hand, still covered in blood, landed on his chest. She dragged it slowly over Lion's firm muscles, exploring, and his tail twitched in anticipation. The lower her hand dipped, the more his body shook, but Langwidere was careful not to touch the one thing he now desperately needed her to.

Perhaps she was waiting for him to make a move. To take charge and show her that he could be brave in more than one arena. He gripped her wrist as her hand slid up his side, then back down. Just as he was about to place her fingers on his hard cock, she snatched her wrist away and swatted the back of his hand.

"Presumptuous, aren't we?" She looked down for the first time then back up through her lashes. "Sit down."

Lion tilted his head, caught between amusement, confusion, and growing need, but he would play along. Give her what she wanted. *Control.* He would let her command him as any good

250

knight would do.

So he sat down on top of his discarded robe, legs stretched out before him, and propped himself up with his palms. He stared up at Langwidere, waiting, as his cock throbbed in anticipation.

Langwidere moved slowly, purposely, showcasing her power without lifting a finger. Her hands gripped the front of her dress and gradually hitched the fabric up. Lion stared hungrily as, inch by agonizing inch, her smooth legs appeared, and he licked his lips.

When Langwidere's hem reached her knees, she stopped and stood over Lion's legs. It felt like ages to Lion before she lowered herself. Longer still until she took his length inside her. His head fell back with a moan as she rode him without touching him anywhere else. *Good fucking lord.* Nothing had *ever* felt as good as this.

Lion wanted to bury his hands in her hair, his tongue in her mouth, but somehow he knew she wouldn't allow it. And he couldn't risk her stopping. He needed this—needed *her.* His breath came faster and faster. His pulse thundered. His hips shifted up so she took him at a deeper angle.

"Look at me," Langwidere commanded.

Lion obeyed. The way she stared at him made him groan again, his breath increasingly uneven. He wasn't going to last much longer. His release was building, building, building, and he clenched his jaw to hold it back. A moment later Langwidere cried out, her movements slowing as she climaxed, and he let himself go, too.

They both sat there, chests heaving, for a long minute. Then Langwidere stood, threw her skirts back down, and stalked back to the closed box. "I have to prepare my new head before it gets too old."

Lion glared at her in disbelief. "And me?"

"What about you?" She lifted the box and cradled it in her arms. "You've served your purpose today."

"Does this mean—"

"I'm still considering your offer," she said.

"But…"

Langwidere stalked to the door and paused. "I'm pleased with you so far. Don't ruin it."

Lion laughed quietly. She was going to agree—he could sense it—but she had to make a show of it. Had to be the one in charge. That was fine with him, as long as he was needed and important. With his plan, that wouldn't be a problem. "Yes, my queen," he replied.

Chapter Six

Langwidere

Langwidere continued to teach Lion her lessons. Each day, she had him remove another's head. It was more than usual, but he needed to learn the proper technique to make sure her new heads remained undamaged. She'd have him discard the old ones she didn't feel the need to wear anymore—usually in the ocean or beneath the dirt. Then she'd reward him with another fuck.

For someone new to the art of pleasure, he excelled at it, more than she'd expected. Before him, Oz had been an exceptional lover, but that was because the faerie fruit enhanced the urge for humans to obey *her* better, but not Lion. He didn't need to be under influence, because she was naturally his drug, and he was a generous and obedient lover.

Langwidere straightened her dress as her eyes roamed Lion's glorious body drenched in sweat. This time she let him be behind her, plowing into her over and over until she couldn't control herself from shouting his name.

"Now, get dressed." She ran the tip of her finger slowly from his clavicle bone to right under his belly button, his cock already hardening again. "We'll be leaving after you and the others place everything into the carriage." Leaning forward, she purred at his ear, "Be extra careful loading the new case. It's large enough to hold a head with a crown."

Langwidere was tempted to take him for another round, or this time have his head between her legs again, but they could do that while traveling in the carriage. She had more important things to do right then.

Lion pulled on his trousers and boots, leaving his shirt off as she liked. His golden eyes met hers and she touched the side of his cheek. "You've pleased me more than I could've wished for. Now, gather the trunks into the carriage. Then we'll load the heads." All the trunks were filled with her ivory dresses. Langwidere wouldn't dare to leave them behind unless she grew tired of her need for them individually. Ivory brought out her complexion better than any other one, and the color represented perfection.

As Lion obeyed and lifted the trunks near the front door, Langwidere wandered to her now-empty cabinets of heads. It was strange seeing them this way. They had never *not* had anything inside, except for when she'd first started.

A squeak of wheels came barreling up behind her. Zo picked up her wheels, softly batting them at the floor, wanting to know if Langwidere needed her for anything. "You will gather the others and follow us to the new place. There, you will be first guard and in charge of the rest of the Wheelers. I'm going to put you and the others to good use."

Zo nodded, her nostrils flaring, eyes wide. She was silently thanking her. Zo and the others appreciated what Langwidere had done to them—they had to, or she would've thrown them all into the Deadly Desert, then watched them turn to sand.

As Zo wheeled out of the room, Lion turned the corner and came to a halt in front of Langwidere, his muscular chest glistening under the light.

Damn him, she couldn't help herself. "Take it out."

In answer, he slid his cock from his pants, already hard. His golden eyes appeared thrilled by what was to come next.

"Pump it for me," she demanded.

"As you wish." He obeyed thoroughly, stroking slowly at first.

"Now"—she stepped closer—"have you told me all your secrets?"

"Every last one."

"Since Oz only wanted me as a tool, is there anything about that bastard you're leaving out?" Did Oz truly believe that he could pick someone to use her? Langwidere was the master at control, and he just so happened to pick someone who would fit perfectly with her. Oz was nothing but a halfwit.

Lion's hand increased its pace as he remained watching her. "Before I left, there was a map."

"What kind of map?" What was the imbecile planning now? He was fine with giving up his hold on the Emerald City for some reason. And perhaps this map had to do with it.

"I don't know," he groaned. "It was a drawing of the Land of Oz, all the deserts surrounding it, and the outer layers of Oz. But there were several strange markings on the outer layers, and the territory of Ev was circled in red."

Langwidere tapped at her chin and noticed there was crimson staining her gown from the head she'd collected earlier. "That old dolt is up to something."

"I'll kill him for you," Lion gasped.

"Perhaps one day." She watched Lion's hand move faster. "Now stop."

His hand immediately halted, and he didn't even beg for release. He truly was learning well.

"You'll come when I say you can." Since he'd played all the cards right, it was time for her to reward him. The blood staining her dress couldn't have come at a better time. She pressed her hand near the first button at her clavicle bone and unclasped. Lion licked his lips. Then she did the next and the next, exposing her plump breasts, her nipples pebbling. Finally, she let her dress drift to the floor. It would need to be buried since the blood would never come out.

"Say it," she said as she sauntered toward him, swaying her naked hips, knowing she was as beautiful as he. Lion was permanent, she could already tell. Her executioner and her lover.

"Please," he begged, voice rough, desperate.

She lowered herself to her knees, something she never did for anyone. But he was unlike anyone she'd ever had control of. Gripping his firmness tightly in her hand, she could feel the throb against her palm.

"I love you," he rasped.

"Of course you do. I can be what, and whoever, anyone wants." Langwidere then slipped his length inside her mouth to provide him the pleasure that would satisfy them both before they started their journey. Together, they would take over the South, and one day, she would be queen of *all* of Oz.

Also From Amber R. Duell

The Dark Dreamer Trilogy
Dream Keeper
Dark Consort
Night Warden

Forgotten Gods
The Last Goodbye (Short Story Prequel)
Fragile Chaos

Faeries of Oz Series
Lion (Short Story Prequel)
Tin
Crow
Ozma
Tik-Tok

Darkness Series: Temptation
Darkness Whispered

When Stars Are Bright
The Prince's Wing

Vampires in Wonderland
Rav (Short Story Prequel)
Maddie

Also From Candace Robinson

Wicked Souls Duology
Vault of Glass
Bride of Glass

Cruel Curses Trilogy
Clouded By Envy
Veiled By Desire
Shadowed By Despair

Faeries of Oz Series
Lion (Short Story Prequel)
Tin
Crow
Ozma
Tik-Tok

Cursed Hearts Duology
Lyrics & Curses
Music & Mirrors

Letters Duology
Dearest Clementine: Dark and Romantic Monstrous Tales
Dearest Dorin: A Romantic Ghostly Tale

Campfire Fantasy Tales Series
Lullaby of Flames
A Layer Hidden
The Celebration Game

Merciless Stars
The Bone Valley
Between the Quiet
Hearts Are Like Balloons
Bacon Pie
Avocado Bliss

Acknowledgments

Thank you, dear readers, for sticking with us through the series! We'd like to thank our families and friends for supporting us. To Amber H. and Elle, thank you two for everything you do! And to the amazing people who helped us with this story—Tracy, Vic, Jenny, Jerica, Lindsay, Ann, and Gladys.

I hoped you enjoyed our fae version or Oz. These characters will remain with us forever. And if you have a favorite character, we'd love to know who it is!

About the Authors

Amber R. Duell was born and raised in a small town in Central New York. While it will always be home, she's constantly moving with her husband and two sons as a military wife. She does her best writing in the middle of the night, surviving the daylight hours with massive amounts of caffeine. When not reading or writing, she enjoys snowboarding, embroidering, and snuggling with her cats.

Candace Robinson spends her days consumed by words and hoping to one day find her own DeLorean time machine. Her life consists of avoiding migraines, admiring Bonsai trees, watching classic movies, and living with her husband and daughter in Texas—where it can be forty degrees one day and eighty the next.

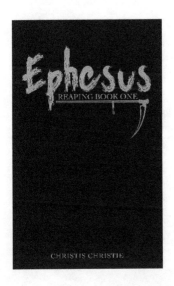

Ephesus by Christis Christie

As a soul lost before it could live, Ephesus was gifted a special role—he must collect the dead.

Ephesus has known no other existence than reaping souls, experiencing life only from the shadows. Remaining separate was easy, until the day he meets a unique little girl with an ability she should not possess.

But can friendships be nurtured when life and death aren't meant to mingle beyond the point of passing? Ephesus must navigate the world fulfilling his purpose while also balancing his newfound curiosity of the girl's life. However, when a threat arises, will it mean their ruin?

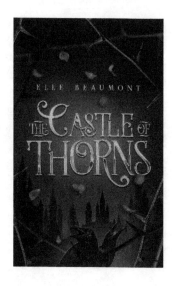

The Caste of Thorns by Elle Beaumont

After surviving years with a debilitating illness that leaves her weak, Princess Gisela must prove that she is more than her ailment. She discovers her father, King Werner, has been growing desperate for the herbs that have been her survival. So much so, that he's willing to cross paths with a deadly legend of Todesfall Forest to retrieve her remedy.

Knorren is the demon of the forest, one who slaughters anyone who trespasses into his land. When King Werner steps into his territory, desperately pleading for the herbs that control his beloved daughter's illness, Knorren toys with the idea. However, not without a cost. King Werner must deliver his beloved Gisela to Knorren or suffer dire consequences.

With unrest spreading through the kingdom, and its people growing tired of a king who won't put an end to the demon of Todesfall Forest, Gisela must make a choice. To become Knorren's prisoner forever, or risk the lives of her beloved people.

CPSIA information can be obtained
at www.ICGtesting.com
Printed in the USA
LVHW051412021121
702213LV00004B/420